Marion Eames was born in ~~...~~
Dolgellau, Gwynedd, wher~~...~~
music at the Guildhall Sch~~...~~, and is now working
with the BBC in Cardiff, as a radio producer. She is married
to Griffith Williams, who is a journalist.

Her first novel, *Y Stafell Ddirgel*, appeared in 1969, and was
enthusiastically received by critics. A translation, *The Secret
Room*, followed in 1975. *Fair Wilderness*, her second novel,
originally appeared as *Y Rhandir Mwyn* in 1972, and both
novels have been televised by Welsh television. She is
currently working on her third novel, which is based on the
Welsh speaking community in Liverpool during the last
century.

Also by Marion Eames
THE SECRET ROOM
and published by Corgi Books

Fair Wilderness

Marion Eames

*Translated by Elin Garlick
in conjunction with the author*

CORGI BOOKS

FAIR WILDERNESS

A CORGI BOOK   0 552 13004 4

Originally published in Great Britain by Christopher Davies (Publishers) Ltd.

PRINTING HISTORY

Christopher Davies edition published 1976
Christopher Davies edition reprinted 1986
Corgi edition published 1987

This book is set in 10/11pt Times.

Corgi Books are published by Transworld Publishers Ltd., 61-63 Uxbridge Road, Ealing, London W5 5SA, in Australia by Transworld Publishers (Australia) Pty. Ltd., 15-23 Helles Avenue, Moorebank, NSW 2170, and in New Zealand by Transworld Publishers (N.Z.) Ltd., Cnr. Moselle and Waipareira Avenues, Henderson, Auckland.

Reproduced, printed and bound in Great Britain by Hazell Watson & Viney Limited, Member of the BPCC Group, Aylesbury, Bucks

Fair Wilderness

CHAPTER ONE

The only sound in the autumn stillness of the forest was the regular chop of the axe. She watched her husband's muscular arms rise and fall, rise and and fall, cleaving the air like a hawk. She shifted the child and gave him the other breast. With a little moan, he began to suck greedily once more. She leant back against the old chestnut tree and let the peace of autumn wash over her.

Around her she could see tree stumps, like giant white mushrooms pushing through the red leaves. No need to cut more, Tomos had said. There were more than sufficient trees felled for their first cabin. It would be good to be able to go inside her own home and lock the door against . . . against what? Certainly not their gentle neighbours. Five months of camping with them on the bank of a strange river had taught her that kindness came into its own in adversity.

Her own door . . . There were no doors to the caves along the banks of the river Schuylkill; only three walls and a ceiling dug from the soil and supported by interwoven green twigs. The fourth wall open to the world and Tomos and she would lie on their straw beds at night and gaze out over the expanse of river. Cosy enough in the hot summer, and even in the gentle autumn, but winter was at hand and Sion Ifan had warned them about the rigours of winter in that part of the country. Hence the rush to build a cabin against snow, wolf and bear. She had tried to help Tomos saw wood, but, still weak from the birth of Rhys, she had been forced to give in. They had been grateful for old Johan's help but when the leaves started to fall, his breath had become shorter. Sion Ifan was the one who had been their strength and shield. He knew how to build a cabin,

7

knew how to live through the winter, knew how to live on nothing.

Sion Ifan was quite a character. He did not belong to the Quakers. According to him, he had been told of Pennsylvania at St. Peter's Fair in Bala after hearing that Price Rhiwlas was out for his blood for shooting pheasant in Rhiwlas Woods. Not being enamoured of Bala Jail, he had legged it to London and waited there for a ship. He had hung about the docks for three months watching the ships come and go, sails billowing in the wind. In an inside pocket of his jerkin, safe from thieves, he had carefully saved his earnings from the odd job here and there, scrubbing the decks of ships at anchor, or minding the horses of the gentry. Sion found himself in company of Edward the Doctor, with the first band of Welshmen to set foot on the new land. And an extraordinary sight amongst those ultra-respectable men and women he must have looked. Small wonder he had chosen to strike out on his own and head for the forests of the North. He had wandered without food or shelter looking for means of subsistence and longing for the rich, thick buttermilk of his home at Llanycil.

Lisa could appreciate that. When a man is homesick, he will grasp at the one thing that sums up his whole sadness. To Sion Ifan, that one thing was the buttermilk of Llanycil, and she herself could remember the full churn in the buttery at Bryn Mawr with the small blocks of butter floating on top. Yes, she, too, had been homesick in spite of having told Rowland Ellis so long ago: 'I could not go far enough away from this place!' But then she had not even remotely realised how far was far.

Sion had been lucky to hit upon Johan Svenson when he had, even though the Swede was roaring drunk at the time. He had been given shelter by Johan and his wife Gunilla, and to his great surprise found that, after a month of wandering, he had arrived back at virually the same spot as he had started from on the banks of the Schuylkill.

Sion was a born storyteller, and every time he came to that part of his tale, he would throw his head back and laugh until everyone had to join in, especially Lisa.

Tomos could also enjoy Sion's stories, but more discreetly.

He would smile and nod his head slowly without a word, but his eyes would be riveted on Sion's face, watching for more. Then Sion would jump to his feet and start mimicking people; mimic Johan in his cups, mimic the ship's captain scolding Edward Jones and refusing to sail further than Uwchlan; mimic the Indians coming to their camp to sell stag meat for sixpence a quarter. But above all he would mimic that pompous whippersnapper, Charles Ashcombe, waving his hand, pursing his lips and shaking his head importantly.

'No gentlemen, I have nothing to add to what I said yesterday. I am but His Excellency's undersurveyor. I have no authority to define the boundaries of your lands without the prior seal of His Excellency.' And, in uttering 'His Excellency,' Sion's voice would drop reverently as if referring to The Almighty himself.

Everyone would laugh at Sion Ifan and his hilarious mimicry, but in fact, all the Welsh settlers had long since tired of brother Ashcombe. There was neither sense nor reason to be had from him and it was due to him that they had been forced to live so long in the caves. He had utterly refused to tell Edward Jones and the others where the land they had bought was situated. All they knew was that the first batch of settlers had been allocated five hundred acres on the Eastern side of the Schuylkill, but its exact whereabouts and subdivision remained a mystery. Huw Roberts had exactly the same experience when he arrived with the second batch; then Tomos and the others got fed up with waiting and began the preparation for building their cabins. If Ashcombe wasn't prepared to help, they had no alternative but to choose their own land. 'O no, you can't do that,' Ashcombe protested, 'What would His Excellency . . .?'

By now, the Welsh cared very little for His Excellency. They had bought their land, had paid in full and had received assurance from the Founder himself that they would stay together in one region. The winter would soon be upon them and everyone was hurriedly trying to get the cabins finished.

Tomos and Lisa had chosen a spot by a stream that ran with the main river; a flat spot on a rise where the bubbling stream reminded Lisa of the river Aran by Pandy Woods except that in this country even a stream was three times the size of a river at home. The logs were by now heaped into neat piles, ready for building. Tomorrow Tomos and Sion would set to, and, with luck, she, Tomos and the baby would be cosily under roof by tomorrow night. She already had a name for the cabin, *Red Pass,* after Tomos's home in Wales.

She looked down on a now sleeping Rhys, his cheeks crimson and satisfied. Placing him down on a red woollen shawl, she started to do up her bodice. Suddenly, she stiffened like a rabbit about to be caught. There was nothing to be seen but she sensed that she was being watched. She turned her head slowly and a scream leapt to her throat.

Standing right behind her, straight as a pine tree, was an incredibly tall Indian. He was wearing a spendid multicoloured feathered head-dress and his legs were clad in very tight trousers edged with fringes. Notwithstanding the first chills of autumn, he was naked to the waist. But what frightened Lisa were the vivid blue stripes on his forehead and cheeks. Picking up Rhys, she got up and ran as fast as her legs could carry her, shouting for Tomos. She turned her head once and saw that the Indian still stood, immobile as a statue. This quietened her a bit but she was still shaking when Tomos ran to meet her.

'Tomos, what does he want?'

Tomos looked over her head towards the forest. The Indian's dress and colour so melted into the background that Tomos could hardly see him.

'He's not doing any harm, just standing there. There are hundreds of them living about here as thou knowst,' he murmured sympathetically.

'Yes, I know. But those stripes, Tomos. Dost 'ee see those blue stripes on his face? They look so fierce.'

Tomos shook his head slowly. Like all immigrants, he had become accustomed to seeing Indians wandering hither and thither on the river banks, their wives following silently, carrying their young strapped to their backs. But he had been too shy to start speaking to them, although Sion Ifan had told him, that the Leni Lenape Indians were quite friendly, provided they were given the odd toy or buckle or piece of cloth every

10

now and then to keep them happy. Tomos did not know what the blue stripes meant.

He suddenly realised that the Indian was no longer there, but seemed to have disappeared, melting into the forest. At the same time, he heard a familiar voice.

'Ho, Tomos! Lisa!'

Huw Roberts stepped towards them through the tree stumps, looking with satisfaction upon the log piles.

'Ready to start tomorrow — eh, Tomos? But — what's the matter?'

Lisa raised her head.

'Oh, we are glad to see thee, Huw Robert. Look over there. Can 'ee see that Indian over there?'

'He's gone, Lisa,' said Tomos.

'Indian? What Indian?'

'He was standing directly opposite me over there,' said Lisa, 'Between the trees, with those horrible blue stripes on his forehead and cheeks.'

'Blue stripes?' Huw frowned and peered into the woods. 'He must be annoyed at something. I've never seen them like that before.'

'But what did I do to him?' cried Lisa.

Nobody knew.

'Perhaps something else has upset him. Something which has nothing to do with us.'

Perhaps. The three of them tried to forget the incident. Tomos asked Huw how it had fared with him on his first visit to the town. Huw sat down on a stump with a deep sigh of weariness.

'It's quite incredible. I never heard anyone talk so much and say so little.'

He was a man approaching forty, and spoke firmly and rather abruptly.

'Did 'ee stay there long, Huw Roberts?' asked Lisa.

'Doctor Edward was there before me, and then Robert David and William ab Edmund joined us. I should say that the four of us were there today for about seven hours all in all, and for eight hours yesterday!

'Who was there this time?' asked Tomos. 'Ashcomb again?'

11

'No indeed. He carefully kept out of the way. Some other little minion. Jennings or something.'

'What about Thomas Holme the Surveyor?'

'No sign of him anywhere.'

'So we're none the wiser?'

Huw shook his head.

'No, not as far as the boundaries are concerned anyway. I told this Jennings that we were going to go on building our cabins, that we were claiming the acres we'd already paid for, and that no officer under the sun was going to force us to pull our cabins down once they were built.'

'And what did he say to that?'

'He made a fuss about the fact that we had come out here before the Founder, saying that he, Jennings, didn't have the right to decide on the boundaries without the consent of the Founder.'

'What nonsense,' exclaimed Lisa. 'Thomas Holme has been given his instructions. What's making him delay so long, the old fox?'

'Doctor Edward told him bluntly that we had to have a meeting with Thomas Holme and that we weren't going to move an inch from the place until we'd been given a definite time and place for the meeting.'

'Is that what kept thee there so long today?'

'Yes. And after waiting three hours longer, we were given one very important piece of information. Jennings admitted — very reluctantly — that they were expecting the *Welcome* to dock any day now. And William Penn will be aboard.'

'Well indeed,' said Tomos slowly. 'It was certainly worth waiting to hear that. The Founder will not take long to decide on the boundaries. There will probably be enough time to clear the land for ploughing ready for the spring!'

Lisa looked at the two men, reflecting how good men were always willing to look on the bright side. Somehow she suspected they had too much faith in William Penn.

She remembered Marged Ellis's words doubting the inducements put forward by the Founder. He had been so generous in his promises: all the Welsh were to be allowed to stay together in one area, with their lands side by side. The

Welsh were not to be asked to pay quit rent like the others. Part of their lands were to be freehold plots in the city itself. The laws and administration of the Welsh region were to be in the old British tongue. And had not Penn himself suggested that the whole colony should be called 'New Wales?'

But she had already heard from Sion Ifan that Germans, Swedes and Englishmen were claiming land in the region — having bought it from Penn, so they said. No wonder the minor officials in the Surveyor's Office were not prepared to take the responsibility of making final decisions.

Night was beginning to fall, and it was time to return to the cave. Lisa wrapped the red blanket tightly around her child, and having said goodbye to Huw, she and Tomos walked along the bank of the little river until it opened out into the Schuylkill where they had their home. Lying awake beside her husband that night, she began counting the hours until she could turn her back for ever on this place. Most of the first immigrants had already left and it was rumoured that the comfort of the empty caves was attracting sailors and their whores. It was true that she and Tomos had heard screams in the night, screams they had not heard before.

She stretched out her arm to touch Rhys, and felt his soft warmth through the layers of clothes enveloping him. Tomos turned in his sleep and Lisa threw her arms around him, trying to thrust the picture of the Indian out of her mind.

Robin Wynn felt someone shake him roughly by the shoulder and reluctantly he woke up from a deep sleep. Who but his uncle would have disturbed his dreams like this?

'Hurry, Robin. We must go on deck.'

A great change had come over the ship. Instead of the noise of the sea and the familiar lurching, there was now peace . . . The *Welcome* was moving along smoothly and steadily. Robin put one foot slowly out of his hammock.

'Hurry up,' shouted the voice again. 'The Founder wishes us all to share the first sight of our new land with him.'

'Is land in sight then?' asked Robin, yawning. Both his feet were now on the floor.

13

'Land!' snorted the Doctor, pulling his hat down firmly on his head. 'Land! We're already halfway up the Delaware river. Come along!'

Robin made an attempt to dress himself more quickly than usual. His uncle had followed all the others out of the cabin and he was the only one left. He was glad to have the place to himself for once, in spite of his desire to see dry land again. Only the sounds of pigs, cows and sheep remained below. Really he preferred their noise and their smell to the endless chatting and unpleasant smells of human company. The *Welcome* was a three hundred tonner, but with a hundred immigrants aboard it was almost impossible to escape from the filth and ceaseless noise. And to think that smaller ships than this had carried larger numbers of immigrants before now! Robin tied his belt, and shook out the frills at his wrist that always annoyed his uncle.

'The friends will chastise thee, thou silly peacock. Whilst thou be in my care, thy clothes and appearance must be decent and modest.'

Robin was truly fond of his uncle, but he insisted on clinging to his frills. He did not bother to argue, but he was ready to draw attention if necessary to the dress of the Founder himself. While William Penn was able to wear embroidered gloves and jewels in his hat, he, Robin Wynn, was going to stick to his frills. When necessary, he too could roll up his sleeves just as Penn could. Robin had been with him and his uncle looking after the sick when a terrible epidemic of smallpox had swept through the ship.

He stroked his cheek, feeling the prickles of his overnight beard: under that beard the skin was smooth — not pockmarked like that of William ap Sion and that girl from Gloucester. And they had been two of the lucky ones. Thirty-one bodies had been lowered over the side and conveyed with prayer to the depths of the Atlantic. A nightmarish fear had crept through the *Welcome* during those weeks, and things would have been much worse if it had not been for his uncle's unending care and devotion. The fussy mannerisms, the fastidiousness had disappeared, and Robin had seen the true doctor at work —

14

quiet, quick and sympathetic.

And William Penn too. He had moved fearlessly among the striken, his courage allaying the terror that could otherwise have spread like wildfire through crew and passengers alike. Above all, Robin carried in his mind a picture of the Founder on his knees on the deck imploring the Lord to save them all.

Even so, it was whispered that behind that door with the heavy lock, beautiful furniture was stored, along with valuable china, and wines from Madeira. Robin had himself seen sailors carrying an enormous finely carved portico into this storehouse — for the Founder's new home they said. How many emigrants could have been accommodated behind that door in comfort, instead of having to lie half-awake every night elbow to elbow?

'Robin Wynn, I'm ashamed of thee!'

His uncle was standing on the bottom step of the companionway leaning down, his face bright red.

'Everyone else has been up on the deck for hours.'

Robin smiled and raised his hand in salute, then slowly climbed up the companion-way to join the others standing around William Penn, the Quaker.

And here they were, on the 24th of October, in the twenty-second year of King Charles's reign — a hundred sober men and women looking, for the first time, at the grey flat shores of Delaware Bay. The land grew more expansive and distinct as the ship drew nearer the shore. The wide river stretched away northwards, dark forests lining its banks. Here and there, they could see huts and cabins, and people pausing in the middle of their work to watch the dignified approach of the ship with its spreading sails. Most of the watchers were wearing the same plain dark clothes of the people on the *Welcome*. They strained their eyes to look at the distant ship, searching for a familiar face. And here and there, stood tall, still men, red-skinned, looking like carved idols.

Robin Wynn stared at them with interest. So these were the natives, the Red Indians, the Algonquins described by Edward Jones the doctor in his detailed accounts to his uncle.

'. . . they have been living here from time immemorial

15

apparently. They can give no account of themselves, not knowing where or whence they came here. But they have extraordinary natural endowments, and they are very observant in their ancient customs. Their main food is whey, boiled and mixed with beans, and different sorts of fish. They cover their bodies with grasses, and sometimes paint blue stripes on their faces, enough to frighten anyone. But these natives, who are called the Leni Lenape, are peace-loving men, only too ready and willing to sell their lands in exchange for a few colourful toys and small articles offered to them by the white man . . .'

And the white man clearly getting the best of the bargain, thought Robin Wynn. There were more cabins to be seen now, and here and there a stone-built house. Large crowds had gathered along the river banks. The *Welcome* turned her bow towards the long landing-stage of the port. Robin's eyes moved quickly from one face to another, until at last he saw one he was looking for. Slipping quietly from where he was standing, taking care not to disturb the others, he made his way over to Dorti Llwyd. As he stood beside her he secretly tried to squeeze her hand. She did not move a muscle, although Robin noticed the blush deepening on her cheeks. He waited for a return pressure, but in vain. He bent to whisper something in her ear, but she frowned, and pulled her hand away.

William Penn was speaking now. Robin turned his attention to the broad bulky figure. Heavens he thought, how long-winded he is. Penn never missed a chance of making a speech, and always got lost in the forest of his own words. And what a sense of humour! Robin winced, remembering the heavy humour they had all had to pretend to enjoy. Like that awful time when they had just sailed out of London Dock and Penn had observed a goat chewing the top of a brush handle. He had called Huw Dafydd to him saying: 'Huw, dost 'ee see that goat? That's how tough the Welsh are! They can live on brush handles!' He paused, waiting for his audience to laugh, and indeed the English among them had done so. Too late, Penn had noticed the look on the faces of the Welsh, and had added quickly: 'But there it is, Huw, I'm a Welshman myself . . .' going on to explain that his grandfather was a man called John Tudor of Penmynydd,

16

that he had come to Wales from Ireland, and was known thereafter as John Pen. This had made the English laugh more. Had Penn been telling the truth, he wondered, or just joking? Clearly the English had not believed him. Was there really a connection between Penn and the Tudors of Penmynydd?

He was raising his arms now, thanking the Lord for His generosity in leading them safely to the end of their journey, and asking His blessing on the Holy Experiment. They were all standing around him, a dark company, the only flash of colour being the wide, blue ribbon worn by the Founder across his left shoulder and tied in a knot on his right side. He was walking slowly down off the ship now, and along the landing stage, followed by his subjects. Just like a bishop parading out of church, thought Robin, remembering how George Fox had thundered against the *steeplehouse*, as he had called it, and its priests.

Waiting for him on shore was the most remarkable group of people. At their head stood two men, one wearing magnificent Cavalier dress, with a wig of black curls falling to his shoulders, and an emerald green feather curling over the brim of his hat. The other man too was wearing feathers on his head, dozens of feathers, sticking wildly out of a skin band on his forehead. Over his shoulders, he was wearing a scarlet mantle and around his waist a belt of bright shells. His eyes flashed fire in his dark brown face.

William Penn went up to the Cavalier, holding out his hand in greeting.

'William Markham, cousin! God's blessing on thee!'

'Greetings, your Excellency,' replied Markham. 'King Taminent has come here to bid you welcome.'

The Indian held out his right hand to indicate that there were no arms in it, and Penn did likewise. Then King Taminent turned to one of his servants who was standing behind him holding a wooden tray. From it he took first of all a piece of turf and gave it to the Founder, and then a twig, and finally a cup of water.

'These are tokens that you are now the owner of this land,' said Markham.

Suppose the Indian had refused to present the tokens, thought Robin rather frivolously. Would the ship have had to turn round and sail back across the Atlantic? After all the Indians were the natives. But Penn was pretty sure of himself, and Markham, his representative, had taken good care beforehand that the Indian would obey his requests, and had given him some sort of payment. But why all the pomp and ceremony, the sort of behaviour that Quakers ought to despise? Respect for other peoples' customs, he supposed.

William Penn spoke in a quiet unassuming voice as he greeted the Indian.

'We are met on the broad pathway of good faith and good will. My desire is that all shall be openness, brotherhood and love . . .

'There is one great God and power that hath created the earth and all that is in it, the God to whom you and I and all the peoples of the world owe their being, and to whom we must one day give account, for all that we do in this world. Now this great God hath been please to make me concerned in your parts of the world, where I come. I desire to enjoy it with your love and consent that we may live as neighbours and friends here.'

The Indian answered in his own language. Markham turned to Penn:

'He is saying: so let it be, while the waters flow and while the sun and the moon and the stars endure.'

Then King Taminent removed the belt he was wearing and tied it ceremoniously around the waist of the Founder.

'Wampum,' he said. 'Brother!'

Every eye was fixed on the two men as if they were actors in some great drama — as indeed they were. Robin noticed tears on Dorti Llwyd's face and in spite of himself felt a tightness in his throat.

Dorti's hair was hanging down her back as far as her waist. This was the first time he had seen her like this. Usually she wore it tied up neatly out of sight under her cap. She looked very young today. He tried to think of a way of getting to speak to her on her own — and that would not be easy. She never

18

moved away from the side of Lowri Llwyd, her sister-in-law.
Throughout the voyage, this woman had suffered severely
from sea-sickness, and she appeared to be as weak and ill
as Dorti was strong and healthy, and Dorti cared for her like
a mother. Robin had been told that Lowri was the widow of
Thomas Llwyd from Penmaen near Bala, and that Dorti was
Thomas's sister.

> 'You have heard tell in the Vale of Clwyd
> Of Tomos Llwyd of Penmaen . . .'

Robin remembered Sion Dafydd Las's jingle, but Thomas
Llwyd himself had been as good a poet as the Nannau family
bard. Hadn't Dorti said so? It was no doubt jealousy which
had caused Sion to write so cruelly about him after hearing
that he had joined the Quakers.

Robin was surprised at the extraordinary interest he felt in
this quiet girl. He had never experienced anything like it before.
Usually it was the other way round. He put his hand inside
his shirt and felt the tightness of his flesh, recalling briefly
the inn-keeper's wife in Oxford who had first taught him the
secrets of love making. And there were plenty of others later
who had been more then anxious to educate him further. But
Dorti had about her a distant, don't-touch-me quality that was
more than just a young girl's modesty.

William Penn had said goodbye to King Taminent, but only
temporarily, for he had promised to meet him the next day in
a place called Shackamaxon further up the river, so that they
could smoke the pipe of peace together according to Indian
tradition. They all followed Penn obediently as he went back
on board, although Robin was anxious to pick up his belongings
at once and find a place to sleep alone in the quiet of the forest.
His uncle bustled up to him with an air of importance.

'We have been invited to stay in Friend William's house until
our own is ready,' he said.

Well, Uncle Thomas certainly deserved this favour after all
he had done for the sick, and a wave of pleasure flooded
through Robin at the thought of a soft bed and sheets and room

to move. But what about Dorti and Lowri? Was there a place for them? 'We'll be all right,' was Dorti's answer. 'We can stay with Huw Roberts, and his mother and sister. They're expecting us.'

Robin was glad. He was looking forward so much to staying in the Founder's house that he was not prepared to allow his conscience to spoil his pleasure. Penn had told them that his new home was in a place called Coaquannock, but that barbaric name would have to be changed. During the next few days he enjoyed himself changing several names.

The first place they reached after leaving Newcastle was the second harbour, the one called Upland by the Swedes, and Uwchlan by the Welsh. As he looked up the cove full of small boats, towards the place where a smaller river broke through into the Delaware, William Penn turned to a Friend called Pearson who was standing beside him.

'Providence has brought us safely thus far, Ned. Thou hast been my constant companion during all the dangers of the journey. What name wouldst thou like to give this place?'

Pearson was a simple man, and could not reply in a similarly dignified tone. He blushed furiously and said the first thing that came into his head:

'Ch—Chester . . . .?'

And since Penn was still smiling at him expectantly he added in explanation:

'That's where I come from.'

His Excellency nodded his head graciously and prepared to leave the ship to go and tell the inhabitants the new name of their village.

It was obvious that William Penn had studied in great detail the maps prepared for him by the surveyor, Thomas Holme. As they approached Coaquannock his enthusiasm became contagious. Most of the trees had already been cleared away, but straight avenues of elms had been left standing there, like soldiers on guard. There were ropes and posts all over the place marking out the houses and squares that were to be built there.

"This will be a green city,' he said proudly, 'with square of grass in the centre. The residences will be havens of rest and comfort and thanksgiving. We shall be able to praise God in our own city, perfectly free to worship as we wish. And its name shall be — Philadelphia, city of brotherly love.'

'Thou didst work on the plans before ever seeing the place!' exclaimed Thomas Wynn in surprise.

'There is more yet, Friend Thomas,' said Penn. 'Wait until thou seeest the Governor's House!'

And indeed the house was a remarkably fine one, one of the most beautiful that Robin had ever seen — much more beautiful than Maes-y-coed or Bronfadog in Caerwys. Pennsbury was not large compared with some of the mansions in Wales, and it was built of brick and stone. But it was situated on rich, fertile land, and surrounded by a fine guard of trees. In front of the house a deep river flowed quietly, and between the river banks and the great oak door of the house lay well-cut green meadows. The estate stretched for two miles along the bank, and lying at anchor on the river, was a large, beautiful, six-oared boat, its sails ready to be hoisted.

Weapons hung on the walls in the hall of the house, and a suit of armour stood in one corner. There were no carpets, but the floors were made of smooth waxed wood.

The Founder explained that the house was not yet finished, and for the next hour Robin and his uncle along with a dozen or so of the chosen few had to hear details of his plans — not only for the house itself but also for the new city.

The guests were longing to see their bedrooms, but there seemed no end to their host's energy and volubility. But at least the servants had been instructed to prepare food, and when at long last it came, it was certainly worth every minute of the waiting.

Some of the Quakers stared suspiciously at the silver candlesticks, the Delft china, the venison and the whole roasted piglet, the Italian sauce and the fruit. How much of this had travelled with Penn on the long sea journey? Or had Markham, his faithful servant, succeeded in inducing the Indians to give their finest meats? And what did Friend William want with all this luxury, they wondered, noticing the glittering Madeira in the glasses in front of them.

But Robin was not one of those who found luxury unacceptable. Nor was his uncle either, to his nephew's great surprise. He was now speaking to his host with great enthusiasm, and gobbling his food as if he had been fasting for months. Chewing vigorously, he urged Penn to tell them about his plans for the region.

'But I shall be presenting my plans for the Frame of Government to the settlers in the Meeting tomorrow, Friend Thomas,' said the Founder, his quick smile removing the rebuke from his voice, and his personality. 'But why should I not tell you about it now?'

A silence fell over the company. The Madeira made Robin feel pleasantly sleepy, but his interest was awakened. He sat upright to listen with the others.

'Let me speak first about the basic principles. This city is to be a city set upon rock. Every soul will be subject to the Higher Power, for there is no power but of God. The powers that be are ordained of God, for rulers are not a terror to good works but to evil . . .'

Penn uttered these words like a lesson learnt long since. This is the speech he has prepared for tomorrow, Robin realised. He was practising it now in front of his first audience. But were these not strange words? Robin's eyes darted from one face to another. In the light of the candles each face appeared to be wearing a mask. Perhaps he himself was too tired to understand the meaning . . .

'Government seems to me a part of religion itself, a thing sacred in its institution and end . . .'

Robin was wide awake now. Was Penn really trying to say that all authority was derived from God? Let Kings and politicians be as tyrannical as they wished, they still represented a divine authority? Is that what he was saying? A strange agitation started to stir in Robin's breast. Why doesn't anyone contradict him? Do they understand what he is saying? Again he searched for some sign of reaction in the faces around the table. His uncle was nodding wisely, but Robin saw that his eyes were almost closed and that his mouth was hanging open sleepily. Christopher, the farmer from Leicester; Caleb Pusey, the miller; Markham in his military uniform; shy Ned Pearson; John Pennock, the architect, whose father had been one of

Cromwell's best soldiers: was he totally unaware of the great principle for which his father had fought and died?

Robin had a sudden desire to laugh. These people were Quakers, some of them had been in prison for their beliefs, his Uncle Thomas among them. And yet, here they were listening quietly — no, *avidly* — to one of the leading Quakers of the world uttering words which were in complete contradiction of their predecessors' beliefs. And the only one who appeared to feel uncomfortable was Robin himself — and he was not a Quaker.

No, not the *only* one after all, he now noticed. At the far end of the table, Doctor Edward Jones was glaring furiously at the peach stone on his plate, and turning the thin stem of his glass impatiently in his fingers. He gave a sudden lift of the head like a horse curbed too hastily, and appeared to be going to say something. But good manners prevailed. Having finished his introduction, Penn was now outlining the administration of the new government.

A council of seventy-two would be elected by the free holders of the province. The Governor himself, or a deputy appointed by him, was to be President of the Council. The Governor would have three votes and everyone else one. Under the Council there was to be a second chamber, the Assembly, with up to two hundred members in it.

'That is fair,' murmured John Pennock. But from the bottom of the table came a deep voice:

'And it is the Assembly, of course, that will be appointing the officers of the law, the sheriffs, and the justices?'

Penn hesitated a moment before replying.

'Yes in time, Friend, in time. But at first, in order to save time, I myself shall be responsible for these appointments.'

He went on quickly to indicate who would be allowed to vote — landowners only.

'I'm sure that all of us here realise our responsibility in this matter. A vote is a privilege, and to be able to use it worthily, one needs education and intelligence. Tenants are usually simple uneducated people, people who have not had our opportunities to realise the obligations involved in administering a government.'

23

'Thou art quite right, Friend William,' said Christopher Banks. 'If we were to allow every tenant a free vote, we would have to give a vote to slaves before long.'

'What about women?' barked out Doctor Edward Jones. Penn gave him a look full of gentleness and lifted his eyebrows.

'Women, Friend?' he asked quietly.

'Yes. Many of them own land. So I presume they will be entitled to vote in the same way as men?'

Penn took out a silk handkerchief and swept some crumbs away from his sleeve.

'Come, Friend! Thou art joking surely?'

'The Friends thank God for their services as ministers. why cannot women be allowed to serve in wordly matters as well?'

'But what do they know of serious matters such as law and property? Thou, Friend, like Thomas here, art a distinguished physician. Everyone around this table has had the advantage of a good education, even young Robin here. Our women have been gifted with great spiritual resources, but their duties in the home make enormous demands upon their strength and energy and time. How can they be expected to have worldly wisdom too?'

The subject was closed. Edward Jones could not presume to argue further with the Founder on his own hearth. But it was as if Penn realised that he had strayed away somewhat from Quakers beliefs by stressing the importance of worldly matters, and he hurried on to talk about the basic rules of the new community.

There was to be no entertainment of any sort, neither games nor play acting. Anyone found playing dice or cards would be punished; there would be no revelling, and no bull or bear-baiting, and no cock-fighting. Penn was in his element talking about his own dreams. But not a word about how the ordinary people were going to keep themselves amused, thought Robin. Life would be dreary indeed for those who did not have the deep convictions of the Quakers. He ventured to open his mouth and ask:

'What sort of punishment will be meted out to criminals?'

Ah! That was where Penn's dream rose to its apex. His eyes shone.

'There will be no imprisonment as in the old country. Our prisons shall be homes — institutions run on humanitarian lines and common sense; homes where the poor sinners can work and so make good their debt to society, to the persons injured by them.'

Everyone applauded this statement, even Edward Jones.

'*Galanas*,' he said.

'What?'

'Compensation. It is an old Welsh law.'

A cloud came over Penn's kind face for a moment. Was it not he who had pioneered this new legal system? He had prayed for guidance for long hours in his study, and had written and rewritten it, putting every detail in place. This was *his* plan, and no one else's. Robin saw the cloud, but no one else noticed. His uncle's head had sunk onto his breast and the others were now overcome with a comfortable drowsiness. That was why Doctor Edward Jones's next words sounded so much the sharper. He started to speak on a quiet enough note:

'And since we are discussing the customs of the Welsh,' he said, 'may I say how glad we, the Welsh, are that thou hast been able to join us here at last. We came here because of our faith, our hope, and our love, never doubting but that the Lord himself was showing his strong hand in putting this land under thy care. But thou shouldst know about our difficulties here. Things are not as easy as thou dost think.'

He turned towards Captain Markham who was looking rather uncomfortable now.

'Thou hast told thy cousin of these troubles, no doubt.'

'Troubles? What troubles?' asked Penn.

'He has only just arrived,' replied Markham, annoyed with the doctor. 'How could I be expected to have told him yet?'

'If there is any kind of trouble I should have been told at once, William,' said Penn reprovingly.

'Tis naught that cannot be settled after . . .'

'Tis naught to thee perhaps, Friend Markham, with thy comfortable home,' said the doctor, cutting in. 'But the Welsh are used to having their land worked in proper seasons. They are anxious to start straight away. But they cannot — because of the unwillingness of thyself and thy servants, the surveyors, to determine the boundaries.'

While he spoke the Doctor waved his hands about, emphasising his words.

'Thou art perfectly well aware that I and others have spent day after day in the Surveyor's office trying to get someone to say something definite on the subject. That's why it's such a relief for us to see thee here at last, William Penn – to set things in order once and for all.'

His words were courteous in spite of his impatient tone. He kept reminding himself that Markham, like himself, was also a guest in the Founder's house, but it was difficult for him to keep the peevishness out of his voice.

'Dost thou know that our people are sleeping out in the caves on the banks of the river?' he asked.

'They are free to build cabins where they will,' snapped Markham.

'But of what use would it be for them to build cabins before they know for sure where their plots are?'

Penn got up, pushed his chair back and walked over to Edward Jones, and put his hand on his shoulder:

'It shall be done tomorrow, Friend. Don't blame my cousin. He is an obedient soldier, waiting for orders from his superior officer before taking action.' He smiled at the two men. 'Be reconciled. This is a Holy Experiment, remember. Will, tell Thomas Holme to bring his maps here tomorrow morning. Does that satisfy thee for the moment, Edward Jones?'

The doctor thanked Penn, a warm smile appearing on his face for the first time that evening. Penn too glowed under the influence of his own munificence. He was born to bring about understanding between men. After this he did not say much. Before long he rose to his feet remarking that it was time for bed. Markham and Edward Jones departed for their own houses, leaving behind only those who had travelled together across the Atlantic.

Robin opened the window of his bedroom and breathed in the sweet night air. The moon was shining above the chestnut tree in the garden, and the branches were moving gently across

26

its face. The river shone at the bottom of the meadow like a band of silver. The Founder had certainly chosen a magnificent piece of land on which to build his house. He climbed into bed and stretched out sensuously. It was pleasant to feel the sweet, clean, cold sheets warming up to the heat of his body. Was Dorti Llwyd's bed as comfortable as his, he wondered? Was she thinking of him at this moment? He smiled in the dark. A fine young pony, that was what she reminded him of — although she would hardly like to hear herself called that! A bridled pony, though. Nevertheless, a pony that could gallop like lightning given the opportunity. She had a strong walk, like that of a young boy. But although she was taller than average there was nothing of the boy in the soft curves of her body. He could see her now, her hands folded quietly as she sat there, but Robin suspected that this was a quietness imposed upon her by the demands of her religion.

It had not been easy to get into conversation with her. Even the most imaginative of men would only have been able to utter generalities, or to joke and tease all the time, under the constraint of the constant presence of someone else. Dorti had been amazingly faithful to her sister-in-law, staying beside her all the time, although the older woman was often very prickly.

One day he had happened to come across the two of them, Dorti and Lowri, sitting in a dark corner of the ship, Dorti engrossed in a bundle of papers on her lap. As he approached, Robin could see that the pages were covered with fine handwriting, and his interest was aroused, especially when he realised that it was poetry. So immersed was Dorti in what she was reading that she had not noticed his shadow falling on the page, and Lowri's eyes were shut.

Robin ventured to read some of the words aloud quietly over her shoulder:

> *Moli gwaed mil o gedyrn*
> *Twysogion, marchogion chwyrn.*

> *Praising the line and birthright*
> *Of warriors, princes and knights.*

27

She had raised her head slowly, as if dragging herself back into the present.

'Yes. They are lines from Sion Tudur.' She was looking at him now with a heightened interest.

'Art thou familiar with his work then?'

Not caring to admit his ignorance, Robin said: 'What a handsome script! Whose is it?'

'It is the hand of Thomas, my brother.'

She spoke softly, but on hearing the name Lowri opened her eyes, and a strange look flashed between the two women. Robin could have sworn that he saw the vestige of a mocking smile on the lips of the elder. But she shut her eyes again almost immediately.

'Thy brother must have been fond of Sion Tudur's work.'

'O yes indeed! Very fond.' Dorti spoke eagerly now, but still very quietly so as not to disturb Lowri. 'Sion Tudur understood things, didn't he? It was a strange period — all that fawning and currying favours from arrogant nobleman, people who had sold their birthright . . .'

'I don't remember . . .'

But Dorti didn't hear his murmured apology. She was too busy turning over the pages looking for something.

'Here it is!' She lifted up one sheet of paper in order to see it better in the semi-darkness. 'Thomas always loved this one . . .

> *'Ninnau'r beirdd a wnawn, rai bas,*
> *O'r arddwyr wyr o wrddas,*
> *A rhoi achau rhy wychion*
> *A mawl i Siac mal i Sion.*
> *Pop chwit chwat yn lladrata*
> *Penillion prydyddion da . . .'*

> *'We poets, lowest of men,*
> *Make princes of the ploughmen,*
> *And give every common Jack*
> *An undeserving lineage.*
> *With every fool demanding*
> *The poets' stately art . . .'*

Robin did not bother to listen to the meaning of the words. His attention was riveted by the way Dorti had come to life while reading the poem. Instead of the over-prudent girl, here was a new Dorti, eyes sparkling, head held high, and in her voice all the scorn of Sion Tudur's words. The shining eyes turned on him were blue-green jewels. But although she was speaking to him — passion and enthusiasm in every sinew, he felt she was completely unaware of him, Robin Wynn, except as a listener. This was a new, rather intriguing experience for him, and he tried hard to bring a personal element into the talk, to force her to notice him.

'Is your brother a poet too?'

It was as if someone had turned a light out. The new life had disappeared from her face, and the old Dorti had come back.

'My brother *was* a poet . . . He died in February.'

There was a moment of uncomfortable silence, then not wanting to let go, Robin asked:

'What was his name?'

'Thomas Llwyd of Penmaen.'

Instinctively Robin threw a glance at Lowri, but her eyes remained shut this time, although her eyelids moved slightly. This was when he had remembered Sion Dafydd Las's couplet. There was something else, too, lurking in the depths of his memory, but it remained vague and disappeared again almost at once.

'Was he a good poet?'

'Yes.'

Her voice contained not a shred of doubt, and the abruptness of her answer curbed the host of questions he had in his mind. Lowri stirred uneasily, and started rubbing her eyes and opening her mouth rather affectedly. It was difficult to tell how long she had been listening. There remained one question, however, to which Robin was determined to have an answer, and now was the time to ask it.

'Why did you two come on this ship?'

Everyone on board had a different answer to this question. It was obvious to him that these two women were very different from each other, and it was only fair to suppose therefore that

29

their reasons for coming were very different. In spite of the undoubted care that Thomas Llwyd's sister took of his widow, Robin felt it was highly unlikely that the two were companions from choice.

Dorti answered for herself:

'Thomas was converted to the Quakers after hearing John ap John preaching in the Shrove Fair, and he taught me to understand the nature of my sins and the Inner Light, and Christ's merciful love.'

'And he taught his wife too?'

'Yes. Both of them had agreed to come over here. So when he died everything had already been sold.'

'But why did you come, Dorti Llwyd?'

Dorti started to gather the papers together, rolling them up tightly. She gave the impression that she felt she had already revealed too much of herself to him.

'*I had to,* after Thomas's death.'

An answer that was no answer at all.

Robin turned over luxuriously in his bed, almost too comfortable to sleep. He must try and see Dorti at the first opportunity tomorrow – after attending to his uncle first, of course. There were a number of questions churning around in his mind. But, strangely enough, it was of Lowri Llwyd that he dreamt that night.

CHAPTER TWO

'I was very distressed to hear of your troubles,' wrote Rowland Ellis, 'and hope very much that you are both in your own cabin by now, and that order has come out of chaos. Creating a new country is an enormous task, and I implore you to be patient and brave and sympathetic. May the Lord help you both. Take Huw Robert's advice before doing anything. As soon as the opportunity arises, I shall bring my son, Rowland, over to join you. But my children are still very young, as you know; Rowland is but three, Beth two and Robert one. I cannot leave Marged Ellis to care for them on her own, and look after Ann and Sian as well, and the youngest is too small to face the dangers of the sea at present . . .'

As Huw Roberts read out the letter to them, the thought came to Lisa that their master felt guilty at having sent them on ahead of him. But she was quite happy here now. Here she was mistress of her own hearth with no one above her to order her around. Much as she wanted to see the Bryn Mawr family again, she feared that things would be very difficult after their arrival. Tomos worked hard from morning to night in spite of the uncertainty about their land. He had taken Huw Roberts's advice to forget the dispute about the boundaries for the time being and had tilled the piece of ground around their cabin as best he could. He had to help with the building of the Meeting House too, because that had to be finished before the winter set in. In the meantime the Meetings were held in the open air.

Sion Ifan did not attend the Quaker Meetings. He was too great a sinner, so he said, but Lisa knew that he preferred to wander through the forests, his gun at the ready, while the

31

others were at worship. He had learnt a great deal about hunting from the Indians. Of all the colonists, he was the one who had had most success in dealing with the natives. Although he did not speak their language, apart from a word or two, there existed some instinctive understanding between him and the Indians. Several weeks had gone by since Lisa had been frightened by the Indian with the blue stripes on his face, and he had never reappeared. And yet she had a strange feeling that he was still around.

She was delighted with her new house, the first real home that she and Tomos had ever had. It had two rooms, shuttered windows which locked safely at night. One day she would have a garden in front with bluebells, violets and columbines growing in it. Tomos had laughed when she had talked to him about it, saying that time and land were too precious and too hard won for such frivolities. Sion had told her that sunflowers grew wild here right into the winter. She hoped that they would be able to stay where they were and not have to pack their bags and leave once the boundary question was settled.

Tomos had cut his way through briars and thorns, ripped away the bushes with an axe, and discovered that the soil underneath was black and moist. If he could only finish turning the soil in time, divide it up into fields and put up fences before the snow and ice came, he would be able to buy enough cows and sheep by the springtime to send from field to field to fertilise the soil. And then he would be able to plant Indian corn.

Tomos had always been rather a taciturn person, and after hours of working against time out of doors he would come home to the cabin at night too tired to say anything at all, almost too tired to eat. He would fall wearily onto the bed, and for days at a time Lisa and he would hardly exchange a word. In his letter Rowland Ellis had asked them to make preparations for the building of a house for him and his family, but up to now they had not started on it.

While Tomos was out working in the fields Lisa would sometimes take Rhys with her to Huw Robert's house to help the other women with the spinning and sewing. He had a fine house, built of stone hewn out of enormous rocks from the nearby river. Since he had brought with him a host of servants and their wives, it had not taken him long to build his house. He had ventured to do this in spite of the fact he was no more sure than anyone else about the boundaries — even after Penn had discussed the matter with Thomas Holme as he had promised. They had been given to understand by Thomas Holme that the Welsh Tract would be divided into three townships, and the land bought by the different Welsh people would be divided up again — some acres were to be in the wild country away to the north-west and some in the more southerly countries on the lower banks of the Delaware. But what annoyed him was that none of the Welsh was to have any land in the city of Philadelphia itself.

'And I heard William Penn with my own ears say that everyone who had bought more than five thousand acres was to have up to a hundred and ten acres each of freehold land in the city,' Edward Jones complained to Huw Roberts.

'There is no reason therefore why we cannot get them. In all, we Welsh have bought forty thousand acres.'

'The surveyor seems to have a strange way of reasoning — he reasons to suit himself every time. Holme says that what Penn really meant was five thousand acres allotted to one person, not five thousand divided between a number of small colonists as we have supposed. And that's not all. His latest excuse for not determining the boundaries is this — that not all the Welsh have come over yet to take possession of their lands, and that that is a bad thing for the colony, that hundreds of other people are waiting to buy these lands if the Welsh don't want them.'

The two men had to admit an element of truth in this. Dozens of settlers had not yet arrived, some through fears of debt because they had not yet saved enough money to be able to keep themselves after paying for the land; others, like Rowland Ellis, stayed away because of family demands; and some because they were beginning to ask themselves if it were wise after all to leave their homes in Wales.

The women sat quietly at their work listening to the two men talking. Although these troubles worried them too, they were a happy company around the fire. Gainor, Huw's sister, and Catrin, his mother, were mending a sheet, one at each end. Lisa sat at the spinning wheel. The two new women, Lowri and Dorti Llwyd were sewing the cloth. Lisa had not yet had enough time to size up these two, but she had been watching them quietly. They both looked very different from each other, she thought. Lowri was very thin, with small bones, rather like a kitten with her short upper lip. Her hair grew in fair ringlets on either side of her face. She looked very unwell at first after leaving the ship but now that she was on dry land she had colour in her cheeks and her walk was much more lively. Every now and again she gave a quiet sigh, and Lisa remembered that she was a widow.

Dorti on the other hand was tall and her skin was sunbronzed like Lisa's own. Her hair was probably dark too, but it was hidden under her cap. She kept her eyes fixed on her work, but Lisa knew that she was listening attentively to the men's conversation and had almost interrupted once, but had changed her mind. This was when Huw Roberts said: 'Griffith Jones says that we are claiming too much from William Penn, that he has enough problems without having to worry about petty quarrels in the Welsh camp.'

After a moment's silence he went on hesitantly:

'I'm sure we should think of his words. He has a right to his opinion.'

That was when Dorti had lifted her head as if to say something, but the doctor spoke before she could.

'We were given a promise,' he said abruptly. 'And I for one do not like to think that we are being cheated. If some of the land is sold to other nationalities that will be the end of a Welsh Tract. It would be better for Penn if he kept to his word. We Welsh could keep our own community in order, given the responsibility. He wouldn't have to bother about us at all then.'

'Yes. That's exactly what John Eckley was saying yesterday,' agreed Huw.

'But at the same time we must be careful not to fix our thoughts overmuch on the material affairs of the colony, especially if by doing so we impair the loving and reconciliatory spirit of the Society of Friends. Satan lurks in hidden places. William Penn has his dream, his great plan, and I shouldn't like the Welsh to be responsible for shattering it.'

'Thou hast been listening too long to Griffith Jones, Friend. I'll tell thee one thing for sure. I wouldn't have come over at all if I hadn't been certain that the Welsh would be able to stay together, administering their own laws and speaking their own tongue. That is how we shall be able to make a worthwhile contribution to the success of the colony. Otherwise, we are nothing.'

When Lisa walked home that evening the first snow of the winter was beginning to fall. She wrapped her arms more tightly around Rhys, and quickened her step. Tomos had not come home yet, so the cabin was empty. Putting Rhys down in his cradle, she hardly heard the knocking on the door, so loud was the roaring of the wind. She jumped with fright on hearing someone lift the latch. It was Sion Ifan.

'Anybody in?' he called.

'Come on in and shut the door this minute!' screamed Lisa, for the snow was blowing in unceremoniously on to her clean floor. 'Take off thy cloak and come and get warm.'

'Tomos not in yet?' asked Sion, obeying her.

'He'll be here before long. What weather!'

'And this is only the beginning,' laughed Sion. 'Wait until the rivers are frozen hard and the snow piles up higher than the cabin, and the wild ducks are all flown away, and the cold shrivels everyone's bones . . .'

'Oh be quiet, Sion Ifan. Th'art frightening me!'

'Well, you will not starve here anyway. Look!'

And Sion opened the door again and pulled in half a carcass of a huge animal.

'What on earth . . .?'

'Bison. Wild ox. My first one,' he announced with pride.

'But merciful heavens, that's much too much for Tomos and me.'

'You'll see, you will be glad of it yet. I've given some to Johan and Gunilla, and kept the rest for myself. It should last until the spring. Let me get it in through the door.'

But Lisa was not listening. Sion saw her lift her hand to her mouth, as if to stop herself screaming. Her eyes were fixed on something behind him. He turned round, and saw the tall figure, snow flakes whirling around the feathers of his head-dress. Instinctively Sion reached for his gun, but changed his mind suddenly, and shouted:

'Holo!'

There was no answer. He tried again:

'Meda! Meda!'

He whispered to Lisa: 'Stay behind the door.'

'Meshinauwa!'

The Indian did not move.

'Hell!' Sion snarled under his breath. 'I don't know any more of the language. What do you want, man? Here, Lisa, take the gun. Don't let him see thee, and whatever happens don't shoot unless thou hast to!'

'What are 'ee going to do, Sion?'

'I'm going out to him. We shan't find out what's bothering him unless I do.'

Lisa was too frightened to try and stop him. She took the gun although she had no idea how to use it. She watched, terrified. Sion Ifan was standing in the porch. He lifted his right hand slowly:

'Friend!' he called.

No answer came from the still figure. Holding out his hand, Sion stepped out into the twilight:

'The blessing of Maniton on thee!' he shouted, his deep voice carried away on the wind.

Was the man moving now? Or was it only the feathers on his head blowing in the wind? Sion took a couple more steps in his direction. Yes, the other was coming towards him very slowly. He searched his mind in panic for the words he had learnt from some of his Indian friends. What on earth was the word for 'friend'?

Lisa felt as if she were on the point of fainting. Where was Tomos? Was the Indian carrying any weapons? What would she do if Sion Ifan were killed and the Indian came

36

in and killed her too, and Rhys?

They said that if the Indians were angry, they burnt people's houses, tied you up and set fire to you alive. It's very quiet outside now, she thought. What's happening? It's stopped snowing. Stay behind the door out of sight, Sion had said. But what if he's lying dead in the snow? How long do I have to stay here? I must go and take a look.

Slowly and carefully she put her head round the door. The land looked so strange in its white blanket of snow.

'Sion!'

No sign of anybody. Oh God! A cold fear crept through her body and there was an emptiness in her stomach. The trembling hands holding the gun were damp with sweat, and her voice shook with fear.

'Sion!' she whispered again. 'Tomos!'

Rhys started to cry, his voice shattering the silence. Lisa almost joined in − anything to break that menacing silence. She dared not turn her head to comfort him. Her eyes were staring into the forest. Then she almost screamed with relief − and surprise.

Three men were walking towards the cabin: Sion Ifan, Tomos − and the Indian. They appeared to be friendly, Lisa noticed, and a great wave of gratitude washed over her. Putting the gun out of sight, she waited for the three expectantly.

She stood quietly at the door while Tomos led the Indian past her and into the house. No one said a word, but Lisa felt reassured when Sion winked at her as he passed. Tomos walked straight up to the bed and, to Lisa's great surprise, pulled the red blanket off, folded it carefully and then gave it to the Indian. the latter accepted it silently, staring without expression at Tomos, who looked momentarily confused, then crossed over to the clothes chest and, after some deliberation, took out an old hat and emptied the button box. He reached down again into the chest and dragged out the best pewter dishes. Sion lifted his finger at Lisa warning her not to make any objection. Tomos handed everything to the Indian who now looked very contented. At last, when the Indian had as much as he could carry, the silent trio moved towards the door, and there the

Indian took his leave of the other two ceremoniously.

'And what was the meaning of all that?' asked Lisa, her eyes flashing.

Sion fell into a chair and started to laugh uproariously. But Tomos was looking uncomfortable.

'My goodness!' laughed Sion. 'What a good bargain, upon my soul!'

'Bargain? What bargain?' asked Lisa, beginning to lose her temper.

'I don't know what to think,' said Tomos. 'I don't feel very happy about giving him all that old rubbish.'

'Rubbish? My best dishes! Tomos, will 'ee tell me at once what's going on.'

'The Indian was insisting that he was the owner of this land that I've started to till. He and his family apparently have lived here for centuries.'

'But William Penn owned the land, and Rowland Ellis bought it from him.'

'Yes, but the Indian didn't know anything about that,' Sion broke in. 'And he's been waiting for compensation for a long time.'

'And the bargain was — my best pewter dishes,' said Lisa drily.

But Tomos misunderstood her: 'Yes,' he said. 'That's what's worrying me. Pewter dishes and buttons are a poor exchange for good land.'

'Don't be so silly,' said Sion, stretching out on the settle. 'You know perfectly well that Penn sent a message to say that the Indians were happy enough to accept any trinkets of odds and ends from the old country in exchange for the land.'

'Well, I don't know . . .' said Tomos again unhappily.

'Honour is satisfied anyway,' said Sion, 'Lisa won't be frightened again by the blue-striped Indian as she calls him.' And he started to laugh again.

Doctor Edward Jones had been thinking a great deal about William Penn's words on the night of the big supper at Pennsbury. But everyone was so busy working on the land that there had been no opportunity of calling a meeting to discuss administrative matters. The Meetings for Worship were pleasant oases in the midst of hard, physical labour, and no one wanted to spoil them by talking too much about worldly matters. But the Founder's words continued to rankle. '. . . each man will be subject to the Higher Power.'

Well, yes, of course they were all God's subjects. But somehow the doctor was unable to believe that it was of God alone that Penn was thinking. Was it possible that he was preparing the way for his own dictatorship?

'. . . government is a part of religion, a sacred institution . . .'

But whose government? Was it the *people's* government, a government based on society's united conscience, or was it the government of one man? And what about the Welsh? Not one word had been said that evening about the fine promises that had been made; there was no mention in the Frame of Government of any special arrangements for independent units within the colony.

Most of the Welsh Quakers continued to believe in the sincerity of Penn's promise although Edward had mentioned his doubts to people like Huw Roberts. The only one who felt the same degree of misgiving was the young John Eckley from Herefordshire, who had gone so far as to air his doubts in one of the Meetings for Worship, and had brought down the wrath of some of the older members of the congregation on his head.

'God's hand has led us, the old Brythons, down the centuries, like the Israelites of old. Our goal is the Promised Land, the new Jerusalem. And on our journey, we have swerved to the left, and have swerved to the right. Our nation was deprived of her natural leaders, men of highest birth. We are abandoned by our bishops and the great men of the church. But the Lord left the seed of his Word in our care, in the care of the Welsh, and we have been led here to worship him in our own language, according to our own traditions. Let not God permit our indifference to destroy this vineyard.'

He turned an unusually fierce look upon his listeners:

'We have been careless, Friends. Oh, I know that Friend

William's whole history, his courage and his devotion are a dyke which will not allow us to lose faith in him. But there are limits sometimes to the understanding of even the best of men. And I do not believe that our Friend has any conception of our aspirations as a nation, I believe that he made us these promises without realising the seriousness of our intentions.'

Griffith Jones interrupted:

'He has a huge colony to administer. Who art thou to criticise the Founder?'

John Eckley's answer was conciliatory.

'Perhaps thou art right, Griffith Jones, and the Founder only needs more time. Perhaps it is his officers who are to blame. It could be that they have not understood his instructions properly. But what I am saying is this: let us be on our guard. We must make sure of our identity as a people before the Frame becomes constitutionally irrevocable.'

Edward Jones began to feel that he should get up and support John Eckley, but Huw Roberts was already on his feet.

'I cannot believe in my heart that William Penn will have any objection to our remaining together in one Barony.' he said. 'In the spring Doctor Griffith Owen and Thomas Lloyd himself will be here. They have both been to London — they were the ones to whom the promises were made in the first place. Would it not be better to wait until then and forget about administrative details for the time being? We have more than enough to do as it is.'

And they did have enough to do, it was true. They had to cut roads through the forests, build mills, and arrange for a good ferry across the river to be able to take their produce to market in Philadelphia.

On his way out of the Meeting John Eckley felt someone pull gently at his sleeve.

'My brother thought that way, too,' said Dorti Llwyd. 'He believed that the Welsh had some special mission to fulfil; that every nation had a different mission, and that to disregard it would be to do harm to our very existence.'

The young man looked at her with gratitude, for he had begun to feel that everyone was against him.

'That's why I came over here,' he said, 'to start again from the beginning using our old laws and our own language.'

'And I too,' said Dorti.

When they had first made their plans, the Welsh Quakers had forgotten about the winter. In Wales the snow can stay on the mountains for the whole of the winter, but it is only very rarely that it remains for any length of time in the valleys — for a week or two at the most. In 1683, in this huge, strange new land, the snow was like an unwelcome guest that outstays his visit. For the immigrants who had succeeded in building their cabins in time and had taken care to fill their store-houses and have enough firewood laid by, the main discomfort was in finding themselves prisoners for weeks at a time, and having to listen to the grey wolf howling in the nearby forest. But for the poor people caught in their caves it meant starvation and fever. Some of them died trying to struggle through the storms for help. Others slipped on the ice by the river bank, and had the Schuylkill not been frozen hard from one end to the other they would have fallen in and drowned.

In the city itself things were better. Anybody who wanted shelter could get it — and a fire, beer and good company too — in the Blue Anchor, near the landing stage. There were now almost twenty large houses facing each other across the flat park. The townspeople could get to Aaron Trimble's shop fairly easily when provisions ran short, and Thomas Coats too had succeeded in putting the last pane of glass to the window of his draper's shop before the blizzards struck.

Robin Wynn and his uncle were still living as grateful guests in William Penn's house, Pennsbury. Thomas tried hard to be allowed to pay his host for his hospitality but the Founder refused to accept a single penny. Robin passed the time pleasantly, reading, writing endless letters for his uncle, listening to Penn going over his plans, and eating and drinking abundantly and well. He had to admit to himself that Penn was not merely an inactive dreamer: his plans were realistic and showed the vision of a true architect. Since Philadelphia was situated between two large rivers, the Delaware and its tributary, the Schuylkill, Penn's idea was to build a number of parallel streets running from one river to the other, with other streets crossing them from north to south. Then there were to be two main streets, one along the bank of the Delaware and the other along the Schuylkill. In the centre of the city there was to be a huge square, ten acres in all, and all four quarters of the city were to have their own squares too, eight acres each. Neat, wide, stiff and Puritanical, thought Robin, especially the idea of giving the streets numbers rather than names. But a few of the streets were to have names, all the same, the names of trees since this land of Penn is a Sylva," explained the Founder.

Throughout the winter smoke rose from the brickworks, for Penn did not want to lose any time once the spring came. His inttention was to build nearly a hundred houses that first year, to build more landing stages and market places for exchanging goods. He went to Philadelphia every day in his carriage, for there was a good road from Pennsbury to the city and plenty of slaves to clear the snow away.

The only time Robin ventured outside the house was when he went with his uncle to visit the sick. Although he liked nothing better than to sit lazily in front of the fire, sometimes shame forced him to accompany his uncle — shame and the knowledge that it was his uncle who held the purse-strings.

He still thought a great deal about Dorti Llwyd, but while the weather continued to be so bad she might as well have been a hundred miles away instead of only twenty-seven. He did not know for certain what his uncle's intentions were, but it was unlikely that they would be able to stay indefinitely at Pennsbury. Yet he never spoke now of building his own house in the Welsh area. The truth was that Penn liked to have a Doctor near at hand. Knowing that so much depended on him personally he greatly feared falling ill. The arrangement also suited the doctor very well; and since it was with Quakers that he was living he did not feel a traitor to his fellow Welshmen. As for Robin, he silenced his conscience by claiming that he was his uncle's servant.

Spring came at last, and the settlers started to emerge from their cabins like butterflies out of their chrysalises. They began to go down to the city to meet their fellow men once more. Violets and anemones pushed their way up through the moss, the green of the arbutus tree was decorated with white flowers, and in the city the avenues of poplar and sycamore were coming to life again.

Neither Lisa nor Dorti nor Lowri had been into the city as yet, and Huw Roberts offered to take them there one day to buy provisions. The journey, by horse and trap, was very uncomfortable, for the road was little more than a path made by the Indians. But so great was their pleasure at being able to move from their winter cage that they hardly noticed the discomfort. Even Lowri looked lively today, thought Lisa, trying to hold Rhys still on her lap.

High above their heads the clouds were changing shape every minute, and when the sun came out, as it frequently did, the women had to shade their eyes with their hands. They were travelling now through the forest again, the forest of tall, thick trees, that looked as if no man's hand had ventured to touch them. The interior of the forest was so dark that the green leaves lost their outlines in the dark mass, and the whole area looked like a fairy cavern decorated with fine misty lace.

Dorti murmured the words of a couplet describing perhaps an even lovelier forest, now a long way away.

> *Fflwrens mewn pwrffil arian,*
> *Ffristial o wydd fforest lan . . .*

> *A silver train of riches,*
> *Chessmen carved out of fine trees . . .*

'Th'art very fond of poetry, art thou not Dorti?' remarked Lisa with a smile.

She enjoyed hearing Dorti talking although she never said much. Lisa did not understand everything that Dorti said for Dorti knew her letters and the bardic rules of poetry and could recite the works of the old poets. Lisa liked poetry too, but all she knew were some funny jingles and harp verses and things like that. She would never have dared admit to Dorti

43

that she knew some of those. Tomos had told her that she must try to forget the bawdy songs she had learnt in the old country, for this new colony was a new and pure land, without sin and without uncleanness of mind, and if she, Lisa, sang these immodest songs here, she would be guilty of contaminating the godly society in which she now lived.

She prided herself on the fact that Dorti spoke more readily to her than to anyone else. She did not know exactly why, for she could not answer her in the same manner. Their talks occurred only on those rare occasions when Lowri was absent. It was a very different Dorti who spoke to her then about the poets, Grufydd Hiraethog and Tudur Aled and Guto'r Glyn. From her she heard how Welsh noblemen had gone to the courts of Elizabeth and Elizabeth's father Henry, and how they had quarrelled among themselves.

'Dorti, what was that poem by Tudur Aled from Llansannan? The one about the Welshmen going to the English court?'

Dorti turned towards her with a warm smile on her face, like a teacher taking pride in a responsive pupil, and her voice was soft,

> *Afraid i'n penaethiaid ni*
> *Eu treigl oedd at arglwyddi.*
> *Er rhoi iddun' aur heddyw,*
> *Ni wnewch chwi ben yn eich byw.*
> *O bu lid rhwng blodau Rhos,*
> *Edrychwch ai da'r achos . . .*
> *Cymru'n waeth, caem, o'r noethi,*
> *Lloegr yn well o'n llygru ni . . .*

> *Futile for our leaders*
> *To pay homage to other lords,*
> *Although they bow to the purse*
> *They will never be leaders.*
> *In your strife, warriors of Rhos,*
> *Ask if the cause is worthy . . .*
> *Wales the poorer, denuded,*
> *England the richer instead . . .*

44

Lisa liked to see Dorti's eyes flashing. She told another story about a harpist called Sion Eos who had killed a man by accident. He was found guilty and was hanged according to the rules of English law. This had happened two centuries earlier. But one of the poets had written an elegy about him, asking why he had not been tried according to the law of Hywel, for Hywel's Laws did not allow the taking of anyone's life.

But Lowri preferred to talk about other things.

'I don't like all this harping on murder and hanging,' she murmured 'Dorti, thou shouldst have learnt poems about flowers and little children, and things like that.'

Dorti became silent again. The river was now in sight. Here it was smooth and almost completely still — very different from the wild rushing torrents higher up, where their homes were. The waves lapped lazily against the little landing stage where a boat lay at anchor. On top of the bank was a wooden cabin surrounded by a number of posts. A man came out of the cabin, followed by a woman and several children. They were Swedish, explained Huw Roberts, and it was here that the horses and traps were left before the crossing to the city.

It took only a moment to descend from the trap and hurry down to the landing-stage. While Huw Roberts went to pay the Swedes for looking after his horse, the women started chatting with Amos Howel, whom the Welsh had just appointed ferryman to row them across the river to Philadelphia in his flat-bottomed boat.

Amos looked unusually troubled.

'What's that bruise on thy forehead?' asked Dorti.

'Oh, that man's been causing trouble again,' he said.

'What man?'

'That giant who runs the other ferry lower down the river.' By now, Huw Roberts had joined them and was listening closely.

'This isn't the first time either. His partner came with him last time, and they nearly tore a hole in the bottom of my boat. Fortunately I caught them just in time. But last night . . .'

He put his hand to his forehead and rubbed the bruise slowly. 'Last night, when I had just anchored and was tying the rope around the capstan, he came up from behind and kicked me in the backside. I knocked my head against the post as I fell and then the rascal stood there with his foot on my back shouting: "I'll teach you to try and snatch the food from my mouth, you cowardly devil!" '

'Who is he, Amos Howel?'

'A man called Philip England, and he claims that he, and he alone, has the right to run a ferry.'

'But that's nothing to do with us Welsh people. We have the right to run our own ferries.'

'Not according to Philip England, we haven't,' said Amos, looking rather reproachful.

Huw Roberts stood there uncertainly for a moment, and then, as if making up his mind suddenly, he stepped into the boat and helped the women over the side.

'Never mind, Amos Howel. I'll go and speak to William Penn himself this afternoon. Thou'lt be left in peace then.'

Rhys loved the boat and Lisa had difficulty in holding him still. He insisted on crawling around the bottom, and when he felt the water splashing on his face from over the sides he screamed with pleasure. Lowri sat there sedately, her shawl wrapped tightly around her against the breeze. Dorti had moved to sit in the bow on her own and was gazing dreamily at the little waves dancing on the surface of the water. Before long she turned her head and called to Huw Roberts:

'William Penn lives about twenty miles the other side of the city. How wilt thou go to see him, Huw Roberts?'

Huw shouted back: 'He called a meeting of the Council for today in Philadelphia. I shall insist on seeing him there.'

The boat was drawing close to the landing stage now and the three women had their first glimpse of Philadelphia. The quayside was bustling for the *Morning Star* was expected to dock that day with more immigrants aboard, and the *Amity* was getting ready to sail. Some people were strolling along the path leading to The Blue Anchor, laughing and joking with the whores who depended on the sailors for their livelihood.

The tavern itself was built of neat rows of bricks set between beams in Tudor fashion. It was here that letters and parcels were collected and distributed; here that all sorts of food, from corn to oysters, were on sale; and here too that slaves could be bought.

On the way to The Blue Anchor stood the shops of Thomas Coats and Aaron Trimble, and the three women looked in wonder at the silk gowns, gloves, hats, fine linen from Ireland, silver-topped walking sticks, riding whips, guns, gingham materials of all colours, bonnets and shawls and embroidered waistcoats. They had never seen such an array of finery before, even in the Fairs at home. Lisa and Lowri fingered the materials eagerly, but Dorti looked rather coolly at them.

'Which will you have — a beaver hat or a white bonnet?' murmured a voice in her ear.

Dorti turned to see Robin Wynn smiling at her. How splendid he looked in his dark velvet suit, his waistcoat and his yellow stockings! This was not the Robin she had known on board ship, and she felt very shy and uncomfortable with him. Her reply was confused.

'One hat is good enough for me. I'm not very interested in fashionable clothes.'

She realised at once how tactless she had been, and blushed. Good gracious, he thought, disappointed, has she no wit at all?

'But Dorti, you mustn't dress like an old maid who has given up all hope!'

He knew at once that he had gone too far. This was no way to speak to Dorti Llwyd. It was all right to joke about hats and bonnets with the women who came to call at Pennsbury. The Founder, of course frowned upon any sign of moral looseness, and expected a high standard of behaviour from those around him. Yet he tended to invite soldiers and embassy officials into his family circle, friends of his youth, whose wives enjoyed being teased by a good-looking young man, and were only too ready to return the compliment.

But Dorti knew nothing of such cleverness, and even had she known of it, would have treated it with disdain.

'Art thou comfortable in William Penn's house, Robin Wynn?'

Somehow he felt that there was a touch of disapproval in her question. The gap between them now seemed wider than ever, and Robin did not like this, for he wanted people to like him.

'Comfortable? Yes of course. But it's very far from my old companions.'

Dorti almost said that the distance was more than one of miles, but kept quiet.

'My uncle naturally is essential to the Founder's comfort, and the two are inseparable,' said Robin rather apologetically. 'And I am essential to my uncle, so' — feigning sadness, 'I have to put aside my own personal preferences.'

He smiled at her, and she was forced to return the smile.

'What would Sion Tudur think of us all here today, I wonder?'

He waved his hand in the direction of The Blue Anchor. The afternoon's business was at its height with the merchants and buyers shouting noisily at each other. Sacks of flour were stacked high, flour to be sold to the new immigrants and to those others who had not been able to sow their crop and harvest it in time to send their wheat to the mill. Next to these stacks was a platform where six or seven Negroes were standing, one of them a woman. Farmers were walking about in front of this platform, weighing and measuring the slaves with their eye, and asking their owners questions about them. Dorti stood still, stunned into silence.

'They're never *selling* those people?'

'Yes, of course,' answered Robin, unconcerned.

'But — those people who are looking them over are Quakers!'

'Well, yes they are, and that means that the slaves will be fairly treated — which is not always the case.'

Robin saw that she was shaking.

'Here, you're cold. The wind is too keen for us to stand around here.'

And he held out his hand to her, inviting her to come into the warmth of the shop, but she continued to gaze at the Negroes.

'I shouldn't like to be in their place.'

Robin laughed.

'Of course not. But you are you and they are they. That's life, you know! They're like children; they know no better. And remember, William Penn guarantees them a fair deal, and he cares for their morals, and arranges their marriages for them. They're able to live almost like us.'

'But they're not *free*.'

Lisa was calling to them, and Lowri waving.

'Lowri's bought a straw hat,' shouted Lisa. 'A straw hat with roses like cabbages on it.'

By the time Dorti and Robin had come up to them, Lowri was wearing the hat, and tying it under her chin with ribbons.

'Isn't she a picture?' appealed Lisa, tidying Lowri's hair from behind like a maid.

She does look a picture too, thought Robin, looking at her as if he were seeing her for the first time. She was like a china shepherdess. Lowri was enjoying the attention she was getting, her cheeks blooming now, and her eyes brilliant.

'Madam,' said Robin, bowing low. 'Princess!'

Lowri giggled, and turned full circle for Robin to admire her the more.

She held out her hand to him and took two little steps backwards as in a dance.

'Oh!' sighed Lisa, 'I'd love to have a hat like that!'

'Buy one then, little one!' Robin called over his shoulder.

Lisa's mouth tightened, as if determined not to yield to temptation.

'No. Tomos hasn't got the money to spare at the moment.'

'What about you, Dorti?' asked Robin.

There was no reply. Dorti had disappeared into the crowd.

Huw Roberts was waiting in the entrance hall of the building where the council was being held. He had been there two hours already, and was beginning to think of all the work the Welsh people there could have been doing in the time they had been waiting to see the Founder or his officials.

He was on the point of giving up and leaving when the door opened and the members of the council started to pour out. Among them was Doctor Thomas Wynn.

'Huw Roberts, my friend!' The doctor greeted him warmly.

'We haven't seen thee for a long time, Thomas.'

'Well, no.' The doctor looked uncomfortable. 'I'm staying with the Founder.' He couldn't keep the pride out of his voice. 'And there's more than enough to keep me busy . . . But, how is everybody?'

'Come and see us sometime. And Robin too. Everyone would be glad to see thee. We are trying to keep together in the Welsh Tract.'

The rebuke was intentional. the Doctor hastily changed the subject.

'Art thou waiting to see the founder? It could be a long wait . . come with me!'

There was no doubting the Doctor's influence. In less than no time Huw Roberts was standing in front of William Penn. He recited his message without wasting words.

'A ferryman by the name of Philip England is claiming that he owns all the rights to the ferry over the River Schuylkill. He had been threatening our ferryman, Amos Howel, more than once. Wilt thou send a message to stop him, William Penn?'

Penn looked thoughtfully at the strong short-legged, Welshman standing there.

'Come into the other room, Huw Roberts,' he said, 'We can speak more comfortably there.'

The other room was behind the Council chamber, a private room furnished with easy chairs, oak tables and thick red velvet curtains. So this was where William Penn did his work. Huw Roberts looked around him with great interest. Through the big window he could see the river, with a large ship sailing towards harbour. At that moment came the sound of a gun being fired, and Huw Roberts saw smoke rise from the ship.

'Ah!' said Penn, crossing to the window. 'The *Morning Star* has arrived. Isn't she magnificent? Didst thou hear the salute?'

'Yes,' said Huw drily. There were times when he did not understand Friend William at all, with his childish delight in guns and soldiers and things like that, things which were so repugnant to most Quakers.

'Dost thou not agree, my friend,' Penn continued, turning away from one window and walking across to another, 'that

50

this city is most beautiful? Look at that square — how dignified the houses surrounding it look, with those trees sheltering them. And look further, over there, at the smoke issuing from the brick-works. Those works are producing hundreds of bricks every day. By the summer there will be eighty houses in Philadelphia.'

Huw Roberts said nothing. The Founder's enthusiasm was obvious, but they had more important things to discuss.

'This sacred city, and the whole state, represent the realisation of my life's dream.'

He turned away from the window and walked away slowly and thoughtfully up to the spendid fireplace.

'But, Huw Roberts, the realisation of a dream has to be paid for. This venture has cost me more than I could afford, and I've received very little repayment up till now.'

Huw thought at once of the money handed over by the Welsh to Penn's officials in exchange for lands not yet defined.

'And the landing stage, and the new roads . . . they all have to be paid for.'

'We are ready to pay our taxes for what we use,' said Huw Roberts.

'Taxes, yes. But the taxes go to the Council, and rightly so. Much money has been spent, and has yet to be spent. Should not I too get back the money spent by me? Thou knowest, Huw, that I am anxious to spread religious freedom, but I must have some payment for my trouble. No one has paid me one penny quit rent as yet.'

Huw Roberts answered him quietly:

'I'm sorry if thou hast suffered a financial loss. No one would wish that. But there was no mention of paying quit rent in thy first promises to the Welsh. We are not used to paying for leases as well as for our own lands. Even if we were willing to do so, I can assure thee that no one is going to pay anything until the land-surveying has been completed, for it is not yet possible to make proper use of the land.'

Penn insisted that the surveying had already been done — by Thomas Holme, but Huw Roberts held his ground, saying that in that case it was a highly unsatisfactory piece of work.

51

'I am sure that the incompetence of thy officials is not thy fault, William Penn,' he said seriously. 'But there is another question that has yet to be settled: the question of the remaining plots.'

'Plots?' asked Penn, mystified.

'Yes, the freeholds. Every buyer of five thousand acres was to receive an additional parcel of land in the city area. But your officials are refusing to let us have any.'

'But, Friend — every *individual* buyer of five thousand acres . . . How can I give freeholds to every one of the small land-owners?'

So the surveyor had been active on Penn's own authority.

'Land patents worth more than five thousand acres were taken out by individuals in Wales.'

'Yes, Friend,' said Penn patiently. 'But the lands were then resold in small plots to several different farmers. And not all the individual buyers came over themselves. I had not forseen that. Think of the number of people who could claim a vote. No, I have arranged matters in such a way as to ensure the success of this venture. If I deviated one way or the other now we should be faced with failure. And then what would happen to everyone?'

'The Welsh feel that they have been misled by false promises.'

'The Welsh should realise that circumstances can change, and that plans sometimes have to change with them, no matter how sincere the promises given in the first place.'

Huw Roberts could see there was no point in going on arguing. After all, the Founder had spoken the truth when he said that the Holy Experiment was a huge venture. His verdict had to be accepted in a spirit of love and tolerance. If individuals had to suffer because they felt that they had been misled, what was that compared with the great suffering now behind them? Everything would come right in the end, Huw consoled himself.

'I'm sure thou art right, Friend,' he said, preparing to take his leave. 'And what about Amos Howel?'

'Yes, I was coming to that,' said Penn, sitting down at his desk, 'Philip England is paying me seven pounds a year for the right to carry people and horses and goods across the river. No wonder he feels angry about your ferryman. Philip England owns the rights.

'And since thou art here now, there is something else I should like to discuss. Caleb Pusey is my miller — my official miller. I have been given to understand that the Friends from Merion are building their own mill and intend to send their wheat there.'

'Well yes, of course,' said Huw, rather sharply, 'or the harvest will be upon us. We are hoping to build more than one mill, to tell the truth.'

The Founder lifted his head and looked the Welshman squarely in the eye.

'I'm sorry, Huw Roberts,' he said. 'It is obvious I didn't make the position clear enough. I must forbid you to build your own mills. I am the King's deputy here, as thou knowest, and the dignity of that office must be upheld in order to keep authority. Upholding dignity costs money and this state of Pennsylvania is a poor enough investment for me at the moment.'

'Investment!' exclaimed Huw.

'Yes,' said Penn emphatically, still looking Huw in the eye. 'There's nothing wrong with investing if the conditions are legal and good. I based my investment on Christian principles. The state was founded at a rather fortunate time for those good Welshmen who had suffered so severely. I have been a means of saving them from persecution. But there will be no help, no refuge, for them if their Governor becomes bankrupt. Huw, Huw, thou canst see that what I say is reasonable.'

Huw Roberts was a fair man, and a simple one. He now searched his heart and sensed the justness of Penn's words. But then he remembered with some irritation His Excellency's fine boat on the river, the costly food and drink which had been transported to Pennsbury, and he said:

'Caleb Pusey's mill is rather far away for us, William Penn. We shall have to carry our wheat a long way.'

Penn shrugged his shoulders, implying that that was their business. And the interview was at an end.

Dorti had wandered through the crowd until she found herself by instinct back watching the slaves. She noted the expression-less faces of people who had accepted slavery as part of God's design on earth. But the Lord had not intended that men should be bought and sold at will, no matter now kind their master might be. Freedom was a pearl beyond price, the Friends knew that very well. How therefore were they able to reconcile slavery with freedom?

'What would Sion Tudur have said?' Robin Wynn had asked. But she, Dorti Llwyd, preferred to ask what her brother, Thomas Llwyd, would have said. The brother who had taught her to love freedom and independence, and who was now himself captive in his grave. Things would not have been so if—

But Dorti pushed the hidden thoughts back into the secret recess of her mind. She loved Lowri, she told herself. Loved her. She had to compensate her, care for her as long as she lived, or at least until there was someone else to do that. In her mind's eye she saw again the straw hat decorated with roses as large as cabbages, and the lively interest in Robin Wynn's eyes. The angry tears threatened to run down her cheeks. Not again, she breathed.

Oh God, not again!

54

CHAPTER THREE

It was only very slowly that the other Quakers came over from Wales. The English poured off the boats which arrived regularly in the port of Philadelphia but there was never more than a handful of Welshmen among them. The leader of the third group to arrive was John Bevan of Llantrisant. This group was nearly all from Glamorgan, and no one else had arrived since April although it was now nearly June. Huw Roberts and Doctor Edward Jones were very worried. As leaders of the first groups, it was only natural that they should have expressed their disappointment in their letters home. But they were already beginning to be afraid that they had said too much and had depressed the others. After all, it is not easy for a man to turn his back on his old home and venture out into the unknown — and if the unknown be also unsettled, so much the more difficult. By writing as they had done, their only intention had been to warn their fellow Welshmen not to expect Pennsylvania to be a land flowing with milk and honey.

But perhaps they had complained too much. Penn's officials were now quite definite: no finalising the boundaries until all those who had bought land had come over.

The Welsh hated giving the officials any excuse for further delay. They began to regret their too honest descriptions. That was why they were so glad to see Thomas Lloyd arrive.

In fact they were all rather surprised that Thomas Lloyd had remained behind for so long. Had he but realized how important these first few months were . . . but who in Wales had dreamed that such troubles lay ahead?

It was not only the Welsh who welcomed his arrival. William Penn had been deeply hurt for some time at the apparent inability of the 'fiery Welshmen' as he called them, to appreciate his difficulties. He complained to Doctor Thomas Wynn about the continual grumbling of his fellow countrymen. The Doctor sided absolutely with his patron, and he felt ashamed of their pettiness. But Penn knew perfectly well that the Doctor had no influence with the others. He hardly ever saw them, and when he did, they made no bones of the fact that they looked upon him as a traitor.

It would be quite a different matter now to have a man of Thomas Lloyd of Dolobran's standing here to act as mediator. The Welsh respected him as an intelligent and able leader. William Penn respected him as a man of noble descent who had been educated at Oxford, and who knew Latin and English as well as, if not better than, Welsh. The story of his meeting with the German, Francis Pastorius, on board ship had become one of the legends of the new state. Although Lloyd could not speak German, and Francis Pastorius could not speak English, they had become warm friends by communicating with each other in Latin. He was a truly cultured man, one who would doubtless be able to understand not only the spiritual but also the practical way Penn ran the state.

Thomas Lloyd went to his first Meeting of Worship in Pennsylvania on the 18th of June, 1683. He gazed with admiration at the new Meeting House built by the Friends from Meirion. It had been built of wood for there had not been time to fashion stones. Later on they would be able to collect plenty of these from the Schuylkill waterfall, but at the moment it was all being done in a great hurry.

Rows of benches faced each other, with one row set on a small platform where all the elders sat. There was nothing else in the building, neither picture nor pulpit nor altar. The wooden walls were simple and unadorned and the floor was earthen. But here there was peace. Thomas Lloyd marvelled at the joy of being able to worship without fear — the fear of a sudden knock at the door and a rush of constables. He stood up and thanked the Lord for this precious freedom, and for inspiring their dear Friend, William Penn, in his great venture.

The Welsh Quakers betrayed no sign that they had any

reservations about this last observation. They had decided to leave their troubles in the hands of the Lord, and of Thomas Lloyd. Let him judge for himself. They were not going to rush to him with their complaints.

Lisa and Tomos had arrived late for Tomos had insisted on carrying one last load of hay before leaving. They were sitting near the door, and this seat suited Lisa very well, for she sometimes felt the heat stifling her. Here she could feel a breeze, and look out at the trees. The quiet of the forest has a kind of noise, she thought. The more carefully she listened the greater number of new sounds she could hear — the murmur of thousands of bees, and occasional screech of a bird in the distance. She couldn't remember hearing anything like this in the woods around Bryn Mawr, but of course she had never sat still there for long enough. Presently she could distinguish the murmuring and bubbling of the river. The sound came and went, disappearing and returning again, and sometimes it was completely shut out by the coughing of one of the congregation, or the deep sigh of another, repenting his sins.

The ferns were young and green. While one of the more long-winded Friends was speaking, Lisa passed the time pleasantly counting the number of different types of ferns she could see from where she was sitting. Sion Ifan had counted thirty-two, but she could only see six from here.

She admired those Friends who were able to close their minds to everything but thoughts of Jesus Christ and brotherly love and the sins of the world and such like. Tomos's mind was fixed on these things now, she felt sure, as he sat there beside her. And Huw Roberts and Doctor Edwards and John Bevan and John Eckley and Catrin and Lowri and Dorti too. But her own mind kept on wandering in its unfettered way through the forests, her ears listening for the sound of the wind and the cry of an animal, her eyes seeing the trout in the stream, and hemlock bushes and hickory trees. She was a gypsy, Tomos always said, half laughing and half reproving. But Sion Ifan understood.

She almost jumped out of her seat with joy: she had seen a humming-bird fly down towards some wild flowers, its flight so quick that she had hardly been able to see the wings move, but she had recognised the most perfect blue and gold and red of its feathers. He had a long beak, like a needle, and little beady eyes, bright as diamonds. She must remember to tell Sion Ifan. Her husband gave her a little nudge, and she was reminded of where she was; she turned her eyes down obediently.

The meeting for Worship came to an end, but there were matters to be discussed, to do with the running of the state and its moral welfare. Huw Roberts stood up and spoke deliberately and slowly:

'Friends, there are two matters to be discussed today. First of all the disagreement between two of our Friends, Rhys ab Owen and John Lewis of Pencoed, concerning money Rhys claims John Lewis owes him.'

He looked at the men who were sitting as far away from each other as possible.

'I am going to ask first: have you settled the argument yet, Friends?'

The two men stood up and without looking at each other replied together: 'No.'

They sat down again, and a thoughtful silence fell over the meeting. Then John Bevan got up:

'I am of the opinion that we should establish a tribunal at the next Monthly Meeting to listen to the case of both these Friends, and any other instance of a personal disagreement among us.'

Huw Roberts rose again, this time to ask the opinion of the congregation on this point, and having obtained everyone's consent, turned again to address the two men involved.

'Would you, Friends, be ready to accept the verdict of such a tribunal, when they have considered your case?'

'Yes,' they both answered.

Huw Roberts now moved on to the other matter. This had to do with a Friend of the name of Dafydd Lawrence, known as Dai the Skinner. This man's weakness was rum, and the previous week he had been caught for the third time drunk and disorderly on the streets of Philadelphia. Huw Roberts asked for permission for the offence to be written down on paper and nailed to the porch of the Meeting House for everyone to see. This he got.

Thomas Lloyd listened and nodded his head approvingly. It was obvious to him that the Welsh had lost no time in bringing order to their new life. Doctor Edward Jones was on his feet now:

'Since Friend Thomas Lloyd has now joined us, it is time for us to go ahead and start thinking seriously about the work of deciding on and collecting taxes, so that we can begin improving our roads and draining the bogs and raising the river banks. I believe those are the most pressing needs.'

He looked at Thomas Lloyd from the corner of his eye to gauge what effect his next words would have on him:

'Since we are an independent Barony, we must accept the full responsibility of that honour. Friend William, through his generous promises, has shown his faith in us, and we are grateful to him. We must show that gratitude now by moving at once to make the Tract a working concern. We must appoint justices and jurymen so that we can administer our own law in our own language; we must appoint councillors and send representatives to the State Assembly in Philadelphia.'

Most of them knew what lay behind Edward Jones's words and Thomas Lloyd's response came as a great relief. He was taking the administrative independence of the Tract for granted. It was clear that it had never occurred to him that there could ever be any question of anything else, and this consoled the others greatly.

So they had not misunderstood William Penn's original promises. Huw Roberts felt that he might as well strike again while the iron was hot. With a new confidence he ventured to raise the issues that had been bothering him since the day he had had his talk with William Penn, namely the ferry and the mill.

'I wonder whether William has considered seriously what this will mean to us in the Welsh Tract?' he asked, directing his question at Thomas Lloyd, for the others were long familiar with his doubts and arguments.

'How are we going to organise our marketing if we have to

compete with everybody else for room on Philip England's ferry? Having to pay this man will add considerably to the cost of our produce. Then the mills. I wonder if William realises how difficult it will be for us if we have to carry all our wheat to Philadelphia. Are there not plenty of waterfalls and wells in the upper reaches of the Schuylkill, so near here, which could become power for turning the wheels? Why therefore waste time and money sending our crops all that way?'

'Of course,' explained Edward Jones, 'had the Founder kept his promise and given us freehold plots in the city itself, sending our wheat to Caleb Pusey would be a much simpler matter.

'No freehold plots?' asked Thomas Lloyd. This was news to him. For the first time he began to sense what the Welsh Quakers were trying to tell him: that there was something seriously wrong with the plans, but that they were afraid to say too much. He looked surprised, but kept quiet until after the Meeting was over.

'You are disappointed,' he said to Huw Roberts and Edward Jones. 'Things are not as you expected them to be.'

'Not by a long way,' answered Edward Jones bluntly.

'Perhaps the officials are to blame,' suggested Thomas Lloyd. 'It's clear there is a misunderstanding somewhere. I shall go and see William Penn tomorrow. I am sure that once he realises that the Barony has started to work as an administration he will see how responsible our requests are.'

The two other men remained silent. Maybe indeed Thomas Lloyd would have more influence with the Founder than they had.

'Lowri wants us to go with her to Philadelphia,' said Lisa to Tomos.

'Again?'

This annoyed Lisa. 'It's more than a month since we last went there,' she said. 'And I didn't spend a thing.'

She knew perfectly well that that was what was worrying him. She knew too that he was feeling guilty at not having given her any money, for he had heard all about Lowri's straw hat, and about the attractive goods at Aaron Trimble's and Thomas Coats.

60

Tomos had told her dozens of times that he had to save every single penny if he was to buy his own land. Having seen how easy it was to please the Indians, and how simple it was to persuade them to part with their lands in exchange for trinkets, he had decided that it was his duty to himself and to his family to become a landowner himself. He did not intend to forget his duty to his master, of course, and did not spare himself in working on Rowland Ellis's land. But he had recently bought his own first strip of land in the Gosen area and this meant that he was having to work hard from morning till night. Work doesn't kill anyone, he would say.

Lisa sighed. The only subject Tomos discussed with her now was how much wheat or Indian corn should be sown in such and such a field, how to improve the quality of the grazing, and that five pounds was far too much to give for a cow which could be bought in Wales for only forty shillings. Lisa worried about his having to work so hard. She was certain that Rowland Ellis would not want him to do so much, and yet, their master's letters were full of plans and instructions. Was there not more to life than endless toil?

Recently Tomos had been too busy even to go to Meeting, and certainly too tired to take her in his arms as he used to. She saw her life stretching out in front of her in an endless monotony, the same tasks to be done day after day until eternity. And yet, perhaps, she was being unfair; this was only a temporary period. Some day perhaps Tomos would once more need her as a wife and she would stop being plagued by these urges and un-named longings.

'Wilt thou take Rhys with thee?'

So she was being allowed to go after all. Her face brightened, and she turned to touch him, but he was already walking towards the door.

'No. Dorti's going to look after him.'

'And Huw Roberts is taking you both, I suppose.'

This was not a question, so she did not think it necessary to reply that it was in fact Sion Ifan who was taking them this time. She did not know exactly why she had chosen to hide the fact. Lowri and Lisa had had quite a lot of trouble persuading Sion. 'I like to feel moss and leaves under my feet, not hard city pavements,' he had said. But he knew that Lisa was longing to go, and that Tomos had thought and energy only for the farm.

It was silk gloves that Lowri wanted to buy, she had told Lisa, climbing before her into the back seat of the trap. Oh well, she would enjoy helping Lowri choose. She told herself how glad she was of the peace and quiet here after all the trouble they had had in the old country. No, life was very different here, although she had heard about some strange things happening in one of the Northern states where the Puritans had settled. But this was Quaker land, the land of freedom, the land of promise, the New Jerusalem. What on earth then still made her long sometimes for the old, exciting, dangerous times?

Sion Ifan was going to go back to Wales at the first opportunity, so he said. That was where his roots were. Lake Tegid and the Arenig Mountain . . . and no doubt Price Rhiwlas would have forgotten all about that partridge by now. A man divorced from his roots, he once told Lisa, was like a torn up tree; you could transplant it if you took the trouble, but it would never do as well as in its first home.

She looked now at his straight back, his arms under the rolled-up sleeves burnt brown by the sun, and the surprisingly slim hands holding the reins. He turned round for a moment, and laughed at them, and she saw the scar on his chin where an Indian arrow had scraped it in the early days. Why hadn't Sion married? she wondered. Plenty of girls would have been more than glad of the opportunity of waking up in the morning and seeing that black curly head on the pillow beside them. Lowri, for instance, she thought suddenly and resentfully.

Lowri was laughing at some remark of Sion's. She was leaning forward and touching his back as if to steady herself — Lisa noticed how reluctant she was to let go, even when she no longer had any need to hold on. This was something new. Lowri was usually too tired and too weak to do any more than smile wanly. But come to think of it, a great change had come over her recently, ever since she had bought that straw hat in the market, the straw hat with roses like cabbages on it, the one she was wearing now. Not at all the sort of hat a widow should be wearing, in Lisa's opinion. Lowri wouldn't suit Sion Ifan at all, Lisa was quite sure of that. She could not imagine her following him through ferns and strubs, getting her hair wet in the rain and spoiling the carefully arranged curls. How would she look taking off her shoes and stockings and tying her petticoats up round her waist to cross the stream looking for trout? For that was the sort of life Sion Ifan's wife would have to lead.

They had reached the ferry now. Lisa jumped down from the cart like a young goat. Lowri was slower, and Sion had to go and help her. Lowri screamed that she had hurt her ankle as she jumped down, and Sion had to bend down and rub it. Lisa turned away impatiently, and that was when she saw a very strange sight.

Amos Howel's boat was tied to the capstan on the landing stage, but the ferryman himself was standing on the bank arguing fiercely with three uniformed men. He was flaying his arms about like a windmill, to emphasize his words, whatever they might be. Suddenly one of the men had taken hold of him by one arm, while a second one took the other, and they both started to pull him towards a horse and cart standing nearby.

'Sion Ifan!' shouted Lisa. 'Look down there!'

No sooner had Sion seen what was happening than he had run as quickly as his feet could carry him towards the men.

'Leave him alone at once, you rascals!' he shouted.

The men turned round in surprise. Sion's fist launched out and struck the jaw of the man standing nearest him. The second man then came to his companion's aid, and punched Sion in the face. To do this he had to let go of Amos, but the latter was too taken aback to take advantage of the situation and was immediately held by the third man. Sion fought like a dog with the other two, but they were strong, and since they were constables, they were well used to dealing with muscular men. Sion was soon lying on the ground, and Amos was still a prisoner.

'What's the matter with thee, man, interfering with officers of the law?' one of them asked in a reasonable enough voice.

'What do you want with this man?' demanded Sion in reply, gasping for breath.

'We have a warrant for his arrest, if that's any of your business.'

'I've done nothing wrong,' Amos said tearfully.

'You have disregarded the instructions of His Excellency,' replied the constable. 'That's enough, I should think.'

By now Sion was beginning to feel rather concerned. Perhaps Amos had really done something he should not have, after all, and the punishment for attacking officers of the law was heavy.

'What has he done?'

The senior constable allowed Sion to get up. 'He has ignored His Excellency's instructions,' he said once more.

'*They* asked me to do it,' wept Amos. 'My employers.'

'If it's not your fault, you have nothing to fear,' said the constable consolingly. 'You will be allowed to go home immediately. But we have to do our duty, and you must accompany us now.'

Turning to Sion, and frowning at him he said: 'As for you, young man, I'm going to let you go this time, but before you rush at anyone again with your fists raised, wait and think for a moment or you'll find yourself in prison next time.'

Sion Ifan had no idea what Amos was supposed to have done, but Lisa and Lowri knew very well, for there had been a great deal of talk among the Quakers about Philip England's behaviour, and the way Penn had taken his part in the dispute.

'Come on, Sion Ifan,' whispered Lisa, for on seeing Amos being led away, Sion looked as if he were going to start fighting again. 'It's no use.'

'May we borrow thy boat?' Sion shouted after Amos Howel.

But before Amos could reply the senior constable had sent one of the others down to fetch the boat to take it with them to the city and so prevent other Welsh Quakers from getting their hands on it.

Neither Sion nor Lisa wanted to take Philip England's ferry, but Lowri insisted that she still wanted to go to Philadelphia, and that a little fuss like that wasn't going to stop her. So rather unwillingly, they started to walk with her towards the other ferryman's landing stage. An hour later they were in the market on the other side of the river.

Even after she had bought her gloves Lowri did not appear to be in any hurry to return home.

'We don't often get the chance,' she said. 'Let's go and see the new houses.'

Beautiful houses, surrounded by trees, had been built around the squares. The three walked past them eyeing them appreciatively. They were all two-storied houses, built of a mixture of brick and wood. Each one had a wide entrance porch, and roofs rising like caps above all the bedroom windows. Every house was different, but they all formed a pleasant whole.

'The people living in these houses must be very rich,' remarked Lisa.

'That's the sort of house Thomas Llwyd and I had,' said Lowri.

Lisa could not be certain that she was telling the truth. Lowri always like to stress the fact that her status in the past had been considerably higher than it was now. What sort of man had Thomas been? wondered Lisa.

'What sort of man was thy husband, Lowri?' she asked, regretting the question almost immediately. She knew it was unkind of her to remind Lowri of the fact that she was a widow but she could not help it. The way this widow was making eyes at such an innocent creature as Sion Ifan was enough to shock anybody.

But if Lisa expected Lowri to show any grief, she was mistaken. Lowri continued to smile at Sion Ifan, while answering Lisa — and it was a very light hearted answer that she gave.

'Well indeed, if thou really wishest to know,' she said, 'Why not listen to Dorti? She talks about him frequently enough, goodness only knows . . . Oh! There's Robin Wynn.'

Robin's appearance saved the others from feeling uncomfortable at these words. He was coming out of one of the nearby houses. Lowri called to him, and walked towards him gaily. Since the other two were not acquainted with him they stayed where they were, and Lowri was in no hurry to introduce them.

'Robin Wynn — it's been ages!'

He greeted her pleasantly enough, and then asked:

'Where's Dorti?'

'Oh — Dorti! Dorti!' she said reprovingly, but smiling. 'How polite of thee, sir! *I* am here now.'

He blushed slightly. 'Yes of course you are — and I'm extremely pleased to see you.'

'If thou wert really glad to see me why not visit me oftener!'

Good Heavens, thought Lisa. She's ready to flirt with all the men. Shame on her. But yet, in her heart, she was glad that Lowri's attention had moved on to someone else. She wouldn't do for Sion Ifan at all.

'Come and sit on that stone over there to wait for her,' she whispered to him.

Robin Wynn felt out of humour. He had been trying to console one of his uncle's patients who had been complaining that she did not get enough attention from the Doctor. The Doctor was busier than ever now. The hot weather was threatening to spread the fever beyond control, and so he had very little patience with those who were only playing at being ill. In such cases Robin was very useful to him. With his ready smile and his jokes he could charm the most bad-tempered of people and save a great deal of his uncle's time. But this woman had been more fretful than usual today. The heat was oppressive, and after trying to soothe one widow, he had little patience left for another — although the first was sixty, and this one only twenty five.

'Thou art worn out,' remarked Lowri, her voice full of sympathy. 'Come and sit with me out of the heat for a moment.'

Robin looked inquiringly in the direction of Lisa and Sion, but Lowri only laughed.

'Oh, never mind them. They'll be glad of a rest. Come under the shade of that tree.'

Lowri was determined, and since it was against Robin's nature to be discourteous he had to agree to go with her.

'Tell me — what sort of place is Pennsbury, Robin Wynn?' she asked, curling one finger through her ringlets. 'They say the house is like a palace inside, with the most marvellous furniture. No wonder thou art reluctant to come and live with plain, ignorant people like us!'

But she was looking at Lisa and Sion, and in spite of her words, she was obvious that she did not include herself among the plain and the ignorant.

'Is it true that William Penn's boat is sixty feet long, and that twenty Negroes guard it day and night?'

Robin had to laugh.

'Someone has been using his imagination! Penn doesn't have all that many Negroes.'

'But he has *some*, doesn't he? I heard Huw Roberts criticising . . . . Oh, I'd love to have my own maids again. I had three in Penmaen.'

'Did you really?'

'And one of them used to brush my hair and curl it in the most beautiful ringlets. Oh, those were happy days.'

Lowri took a silk handkerchief out of her sleeve and touched her eyes.

'I'm sorry . . . but I am not over my grief at losing Thomas. It's barely nine months . . .'

She swallowed, as if making a heroic attempt to control her feelings.

'The trouble is, Robin Wynn, I was born delicate. My mother was related to the Fychan family and my delicacy has been bred in the bone. It's harder for me than for the others to get used to the dull life of the small holder, for that is the status of most people here.'

Robin said nothing, but he felt the first prick of impatience.

'But thou art different. I could close my eyes now, and imagine thee in Pennsbury sitting straight-backed at a long full-laden table, the silver shining in the candle-light, servants walking backwards and forwards with the dishes, with conversation over the wine, and women in their silks and satins. And no one handsomer than Robin Wynn . . .'

'You paint a very happy picture, mistress.' But Robin was feeling very uncomfortable, for the picture came very close to reality. Was this how Dorti saw him?

'I see it so clearly because I feel I belong there,' sighed Lowri gently, rubbing her cheek playfully with the ribbons of her hat.

'Why did you come over here then?'

That question again. Perhaps he would get a more satisfactory reply from Lowri than he had had from Dorti. Neither woman fitted his picture of the devoted Quaker: Lowri with her silk gloves and her obvious invitation to him with her eyes; Dorti with her delight in poetry. Come to think of it, he had only once heard Dorti mention her religious faith, and that was only when she was repeating her brother's words. It seemed the two women had come to Pennsylvania in the wake of Thomas Llwyd's conversion.

Lowri was sighing again. 'There was nothing else we could do. Everything was already arranged for me to come — the stock, the land, and the house had already been sold when Thomas fell prey to the mortal fever. We had no choice at all.'

'Nor Dorti either?' Robin ventured to ask.

Lowri wrinkled her forehead. She bent down to pick a blade of grass, bit it thoughtfully between her teeth, and then said: 'Poor Dorti.'

Robin held his breath, hoping to hear more. The sweet childish voice continued.

'Thou art a friend, a friend who can understand . . . but there are some things that I would not dare tell . . .'

A hundred yards away Sion and Lisa were beginning to move restlessly. Why on earth don't they come over here, thought Robin, then I would not have to listen to any more. And yet he wanted to hear more.

Lowri had noticed the others too, and began to speak more quickly.

'I should like it so much if she could meet an eligible man and marry him. That would be such a blessing for her. She is so clever — she knows all about poetry and history, and she's always reading books. Too clever for most men's liking, I'm sure. But . . .' Lowri threw the blade of grass away. 'No . . . I have to tell someone. But only thee, of course . . . thou must understand that. The secret has been weighing on me so much, sometimes, it has made me sick . . .'

Well, tell me then, he thought. No, don't tell me. But Robin remained silent, his nerves taut. Lowri's eyelashes hid her eyes now.

'When I married Thomas Llwyd, his sister's life was shattered. Dost thou understand what I'm trying to say Robin? There has been no other man in the life of Dorti Llwyd!'

He closed his eyes now, wishing he had put his fingers in his ears to close out the odious insinuation. But Lowri's voice went on relentlessly. "Thou canst imagine what life was like for me knowing that my husband's heart was bleeding for his sister. We had to be careful not to feed her malice and her jealousy, knowing that she resented my presence in her brother's bed.'

Robin managed to stand up at last, although he felt that someone had tied his feet down with chains. In the heat of the summer afternoon he felt cold.

'No, Lowri, you should not have told me that . . .' he said.

Looking at him from the corner of her eye, Lowri saw that the shaft had gone home. But her voice was shaking with sudden regret.

'Thou art right. I should not have told thee. And I implore thee now to forget everything I said.'

She had told him too little. And yet too much. Robin could not control the quivering in his stomach. I must think carefully and sanely later on some time, he told himself, for she is probably lying, the minx. But I must have time to calm down first. He bade farewell politely, but not before she had noticed now pale his face was.

The Elders came to the Meeting House to discuss Amos Howel's trouble. Apart from Thomas Lloyd no one was surprised to hear that Penn's officials had taken action so quickly, and so thoroughly. To the man from Dolobran, the behaviour of the Founder was incredible, and contrary to everything he had believed about him. Even now he was searching his heart for excuses. The officials were to blame for the disorder; they were responsible for Penn being short of money. This overbearing attitude was surely something temporary, something which would disappear when the state was properly established on a sound footing.

The others sympathized with his inner conflicts. They all had experienced the same doubts, and fears of disloyalty, and this was one of the Founder's closest friends.

'Let me read our Friend's words,' he said. 'And you shall judge for yourselves if this was written by an unjust man.'

He opened one of William Penn's many pamphlets and started reading:

'Every government is free when the people are given a voice in its formation and administration. Without that, every government is tyrannical and violent.'

Thomas lifted his head and looked around the congregation silently for some seconds before proceeding.

'Governments depend more on men than do men on governments. If the men are good, then the governments cannot be bad. But if the men are bad, laws, however good, can be bent by them to further their own aims.'

Thomas Lloyd closed the pamphlet, and raised his white head in a dignified manner.

'Dear Friends, it is only right that we should trust a man of such vision. If difficulties and petty troubles arise on the way, it is we who have failed to understand properly, and we must pray in a spirit of humility and love to the Lord of Life for enlightenment.'

The Quakers felt Thomas Lloyd's words sink down into their hearts, comforting them. But some of them, especially Doctor Edward Jones and John Eckley, could not help remembering how different were the words read out now, from the ideas proposed by the Founder in his Frame of Government. The former were the words of a young man, the latter the ideas of a man approaching middle age.

But John Eckley was the only one to give voice of his doubts openly.

'I am only a young man, Thomas Lloyd,' he said, 'and perhaps it is presumptuous of me to speak out like this. But it seems to me that there are dangers involved in trusting people. Trust in God, yes; that is our duty and our privilege. But man is human and liable to change his views. We should be very cautious about accepting any man's word, be he Quaker or liar, unless it has the seal of legal obligation.

'Friend William Penn has written many wise and inspiring words in his day. Why I myself heard him preach outside Hereford Cathedral, and my heart was gladdened. But man is an inconstant creature. He can change — oh, not in his basic beliefs perhaps, but his earthly progress towards his spiritual goal can be confused by compromise.'

It was only very slowly that John Eckley had gained enough confidence to stand up and express his own ideas before men of older experience. Because of his youth, and because he came from Hereford, he had felt separted from the close communities of Friends from Meirionnydd and Glamorgan, though this had never been their intention.

Maybe it was this inner loneliness that enabled him to see the problems of the Tract with a clearer eye, but his youth made him less ready to accept that a man's motives were not necessarily black or white, but more often degrees of grey. His intense feeling gave his voice a new richness, and everyone listened intently.

'I am a Quaker, like all of you, but I am also a Welshman, and I am ready to admit that what brought me over here was my ardent desire to serve God in an independent Welsh community, since all hope of that had disappeared in Wales. You say we were given this assurance by the Founder. But if he or his officials now want to deny us the right, you shall see, Friends, that the trust you speak of has been your undoing. Since promises were given verbally that day in London, have you any proof on paper that those promises were ever made? I am afraid that the blind faith of the Friends who went to London made them careless.

'Our Friend Thomas quoted from one of Penn's pamphlets. I have another quotation, words written much later than those. Here it is: "Let the people think they govern and they will be governed." There you have the new William Penn, Friends. *That* is his political philosophy.'

The young man sat down, breathing audibly, his face red. Doctor Edward Jones smiled at him and nodded, but Thomas

Lloyd was looking rather worried. There could be another explanation, he said. They did not know all the facts. He *knew* Penn, knew him personally, but he was afraid to emphasise this in case the Welsh began to think that he was siding with Penn against them — and against the evidence.

'I still think we should give him time,' he said.

Robin Wynn had convinced himself by the end of the week that malice alone had prompted Lowri to make her disclosure, and that he should take no notice of her. He blamed himself for having been so foolish as to give the impression that Dorti was so much more important to him than she, Lowri was. He was not used to making such elementary mistakes with women. He promised himself that he would go and see Dorti at the first opportunity thereby showing Lowri that her words had made no impression on him.

In the meantime he had other things to think about. On the previous evening he had heard a conversation that had rather troubled him.

Proof that Penn considered Robin and his uncle belonged to 'us' rather than 'them' was his readiness to discuss the troublesome Welsh quite openly in front of them. Having listened to his conversations with Markham, Thomas Holme, and some of the other officials, Robin began to sympathise with Penn. We Welsh are eternal whiners, he thought, always quarrelling about our petty rights, while so many great, important plans are being made here on our behalf. If our continual shouting about independence and language is listened to, could not the Swedes and the Germans also make the same claim, and where would we be then? He admitted that he himself had cherished certain disloyal ideas about Penn when he had first come over, but living in the same house as the great Governor, far away from the sound of Welsh complaints, had raised his sights and broadened his vision. The overwhelming need was for an effective administration and order, and the Founder and his plans must be given every support.

Penn knew very well how Robin felt by now, knew it was not necessary in front of him.

It was after supper, and the company in Pennsbury were relaxing pleasantly having eaten their fill of ham, roast potatoes, carrots and beans, cherry tart and cream, cheeses, cider and the red wine of France. There was an easy chair for everyone and a silk cushion on each one. From where Robin was sitting he could see through the vast window, out over the gardens of flowers on the terrace. Beyond the lowest terrace a copse of beautiful trees had been planned for the owner by an architect from Scotland. There were carefully placed avenues of poplars, and wild flowers brought from the forests and transplanted here. Stone steps led from one part to another, the whole making an attractive composite pattern.

In the corner of the panelled room, a grandfather clock was ticking the minutes away sleepily, and on the wall immediately in front of Robin's eyes, on either side of the white silk curtains, hung six maps. The whole place was so civilised and so pleasant. Robin felt his eyelids droop and Penn's voice receding into the distance.

'Truly, if everywhere else was as peaceful as this I should be the most contented man on earth.'

'There is a spirit of reconciliation about,' said Thomas Wynn. 'I heard good news today. Rhys ab Owen and John Lewis Pencoed have settled their argument. They've been quarrelling with each other for about a year.'

That was the sort of thing Penn liked to hear. It was a sign that his basic ideas were working. His kind face beamed with pleasure, as he asked for details.

'Apparently the Elders of the Meeting House in Meirion had decided to institute a Tribunal with the idea of bringing the case of the two men before it in the next monthly meeting. But, on hearing this the two men were so shaken that they got together at once and settled their differences.'

But Penn's reply was not exactly what the Doctor had expected. He shook his head anxiously.

'They are really taking too much on themselves,' he said. 'It is a dangerous precedent to institute a Tribunal without the consent of the rest of us. This sort of thing could lead to anarchy and inconsistency. It could be in contravention of the basic plan. We must warn our Friends in the Tract that it is not proper for them to undertake such things . . . Once again!' he added with a sigh.

Thomas Wynn looked surprised, but Thomas Holme broke in excitedly.

'And that's not all by a long way,' he said. 'I was going to tell thee William Penn. I heard that they'd started to fix taxes in the Welsh Tract and moreover, that Thomas Lloyd had given all this his blessing.'

Penn closed his eyes as if he were reaching the end of his tether.

'Thomas Lloyd is one of my closest friends,' he said sadly. 'He must be told what the situation is. Here am I, becoming poorer every day because poor Thomas Holme is having such trouble getting the money for the quit rent, and here you have these people now planning to collect their own taxes without consulting me or anyone else about it. We must put an end to all this foolishness once and for all!'

Since it was he who was responsible for the turn the conversation had taken, Thomas Wynn felt very uncomfortable, and in his heart he was tired of the perpetual running-down of his fellow countrymen. When the opportunity came he got up and excused himself from the company. Before long, having added fuel to the fire, Thomas Holme did the same.

Night was beginning to fall, and the other two did not notice Robin Wynn asleep in his chair. Actually, he was awake now but still too sleepy to move. He heard Penn talking, his voice quiet and secretive.

'To tell thee the truth, Cousin, I have a host of worries. Giulielma is still unwell. Her health has been very poor for some time past, and she is longing for me to return to Worminghurst. I had hoped to have her here with me by now, of course.'

He lowered his voice again. 'And as for my financial worries, things are getting worse every day. Today I had a letter from London from Philip Ford . . . He was saying that he had sold several parcels of land in this state for eight thousand pounds, and that he was keeping the money to defray the debt he claims I owe him.'

Markham was not as careful to lower his voice.

'What authority has a bailiff for doing such a thing?'

The silence became oppressive. When Penn next spoke Robin had difficulty in recognising his voice, so indistinct had it become.

'A few days before I set sail for Pennsylvania, Philip Ford handed me a memorandum claiming that I owed him almost three thousand pounds in salary and costs, and for a loan he had made me. I had no time to look it over in detail, and so I signed it — fool that I was. Dost'ee know, the knave had forced me to sign a promissory note for three hundred acres of land here in Pennsylvania if I did not pay him the three thousand pounds within two days. Of course, by the time I had realised what I had done, I was far on the Atlantic. Ford has used the memorandum with my signature on it to sell land to all and sundry in London, and I haven't seen — nor ever shall — one ha'penny of all that money.'

It was now a very wide awake Robin who listened in wonder. Such a careful planner, such an orderly man, as William Penn — what on earth had caused him to be so stupid as to sign a document without first examining it properly? He knew about this Philip Ford. He was Penn's estate manager in Worminghurst, and had been in Penn's service for many years. Penn must have trusted him absolutely — but the wisest of men can sometimes make errors of judgement, thought Robin.

'Thou seest then, Cousin, why I must get every possible ha'penny out of this venture. We must be more diligent in the collection of quit rent — and the Welsh will have to agree to start paying too, and not continue to expect special favours. Moreover they must be made to forget this nonsense about collecting their own taxes!'

The Captain made an affirmative sound.

'But I shall have to leave all this in thy hands, I have decided that I must return to London for a period. My affairs are so confused — only my presence there can possibly straighten things out. And Giulielma will be glad to see me.'

'I would take over with pleasure, Cousin,' said Markham. 'But only yesterday I received my instructions from London

75

informing me that I must go to New York with the Guards. I am afraid I shall have to set off next week.'

'But what will become of the state? I had expected to make thee my Deputy in my absence.'

It was clear that the Founder was feeling extremely worried. He had not considered the possibility of his cousin having to rejoin the regiment. His plans were now completely spoiled. Markham's careful, sharp voice answered:

'I thank you for your trust in me. I am sorry to have disappointed you. But this may prove to be a blessing in the end.'

'A blessing?'

Markham chose his words carefully:

'I am a soldier, and one who believes absolutely in strategy, whether in the treatment of an enemy or of a friend. In battle, one has first to guess what the next move of the enemy will be. And there is no better way of knowing that than by studying the enemy's past history. For his weak point and his failings remain the same; his reactions are invariably the same.'

'I too was a soldier,' Penn reminded him. 'But I am not at war with the Welsh or with anyone else.'

Markham was not listening to him. He continued, lost in his strategy.

'A century and a half ago, the Welsh were still causing trouble. Small dissident bands were rising up all over the country, in a spirit of independence, insisting that they must rule themselves. But a stop was put to that very effectively.'

'How?'

'Very simply — by inviting one of them to become King of England. Don't you see? The stupid Welsh thought that the privilege and the victory were theirs. But the plain truth was that their natural leader had been moved to England, taking his noblemen with him. The best way of conquering a nation is not by imprisoning her people. Under tyranny they unite. But give their leader honours and authority, and the rest fall like a pack of cards.'

Markham laughed, but there came no immediate response from Penn.

'Well,' continued the soldier. 'Human nature doesn't change

76

in a hundred and fifty years. Who, do you think, is the leader of the Welshmen here?'

Penn was beginning to understand what Markham had in mind.

'Thomas Lloyd?'

'Good. There's your deputy.'

Penn thought for a long time before answering. Then, at last, he said:

'Thy reasoning is faultless, although I should reprove thee for thy cynicism. But I have a different way of looking at this. My appointing Thomas Lloyd to deputise for me would be an act of faith and trust in the goodness of the Lord.'

'And in Thomas Lloyd,' said Markham rather drily.

But Penn's answer was sincere. 'And in the goodness of Thomas Lloyd, yes. I shall do it, and perhaps then unity will come to the Colony.'

And the remarkable thing was, Robin told himself, William Penn really believed, from the bottom of his heart, that the unity of the state was more important than anything else. He was prepared to sacrifice everything for this ideal. It could be that his present financial difficulties were clouding his vision, but he obviously believed that he was fulfilling the Lord's will, and that the plaintive claims of the Welsh were hindering this work. What matter if he agreed to the original requests of the Welsh Quakers? Circumstances had changed. In his mind Robin was building up the arguments in Penn's favour. But he would have preferred not to have heard this conversation.

CHAPTER FOUR

Thomas Lloyd returned from his meeting with the Founder to his friends in Meirion full of jubilation.

'Did I not tell you?' he said. 'William Penn is a magnanimous man ready to put all his trust in us. Our troubles are over, Friends.'

'No conditions?' asked Doctor Edward Jones doubtfully.

'None at all,' replied Thomas Lloyd. 'He will be sending regular letters from London to keep touch with us. Oh, he did stipulate two things — but no one could call those conditions. One was that his name, and that of the King, be mentioned in the public documents of the state, and the other that the dignity of the office of Governor should be upheld in every thing.'

Although one or two of them still felt doubtful, the appointment of Thomas Lloyd was generally welcomed although it meant his having to move out of the Welsh Tract to live in Philadelphia. The only one to voice any definite opposition was Dorti Llwyd.

She rarely spoke at Meetings, although women had exactly the same right as men to do so. But she found it difficult to speak of spiritual matters preferring to leave others to express experiences which for her were beyond words. When anything threatened the unity of their community, however, an unusual fluency came to her. 'I fear the Greeks even when they offer gifts,' she quoted. 'This is a devious attempt to divide us. There are those who are jealous of our unity as Welsh people. History has always shown this. Oh, not William Penn himself perhaps, but the men around him. Neither Thomas Holme, nor Charles Ashcombe nor George Keith, no, nor Griffith Jones either — for there are traitors in every camp — not one of these men will be content until the Welsh speak English with each other, hold their Meetings in English, and submit to English law. It was certainly not for that we came here. If Thomas Lloyd leaves the Tract, others will follow.'

Everyone was surprised at this outburst, but John Eckley supported her. All the others were prepared to give the scheme a chance. A hundred times better, they claimed, to see Thomas Lloyd at the helm than one of William Penn's military cronies.

On her way home a preoccupied Dorti did not notice Robin Wynn standing beside his horse under the walnut tree opposite the Meeting House. He had been standing there a long time waiting for her to come out. He had not wanted to go into the Meeting House to her, for his secret knowledge about the conversation between Penn and Markham was still worrying him. And yet the wish to see Dorti had grown fiercely within him, as if seeing her could cleanse his conscience.

He kept out of sight until the others had gone. At first he felt disappointed that Lowri was not with her to see for herself how little impression her words had made on him. But come to think of it, perhaps it was a good thing after all. He now had an unrivalled opportunity of getting to know the real Dorti.

Since she was not looking in his direction he started to walk after her, leading his horse. Hearing the clip clop behind her, Dorti turned round and saw him, but at once her eyes became cold.

'Going home?' he asked. 'May I accompany you?'

'I'm sure thou hast better things to do.'

'I came here especially to see you. Dorti, what's the matter?'

She was too honest to deny that there was something wrong . . . but not so naive as to tell him the whole truth. There were several moments of silence before she replied.

'The Friends find thee a stranger.'

'Only the Friends?'

'I am one of them,' she answered seriously.

'Yes, I know.'

There were so many questions he wanted to ask her. But first of all he had to break through to her. He sensed what was worrying her, and decided that attack was the better form of defence. 'Some of them are creating something of a problem for William Penn.'

A sharp light came into Dorti's eyes, as she asked carefully: 'A problem?'

'Yes,' he said. 'He says that the Friends in Meirion are among the most stubborn he has ever met.'

'And he says that in front of thee?' exclaimed Dorti in surprise, reproval in her voice.

'Oh, I'm nobody. I listen and say nothing. Penn doesn't associate me with anyone in particular.'

Dorti looked at him for a long time, all sorts of feelings showing in her face.

'No, I know he does not,' she said.

'Well, I'm not either.' Robin felt impatient with himself for feeling compelled to explain himself to Dorti, and he went on. 'I'm very different from you. I have not been converted to the Quakers.'

'Why didst thou come here then?' Dorti flung his own question back at him.

'My uncle wanted company to come over before bringing his wife and family.

'I'm fond of him — and dependent on him too. The venture appealed to me, but that does not mean I have to accept his beliefs.'

'Does it mean nothing to thee that thy uncle and William Penn are breaking their promises to us, one by one?'

'What nonsense!' laughed Robin, uneasily. 'People like Edward Jones and Huw Roberts have not begun to understand the situation. It may be because they do not understand English all that well; it could be that they have not been able to explain themselves clearly enough. William Penn never intended that they should be allowed to run things all their own way. They have nothing to show on paper, after all. Think seriously — if he were to grant all that to the Welsh, would not every small sect thereafter demand their own rules. And then what a mess we should be in.'

He has swallowed everything he has heard in that big house, thought Dorti.

'A Quaker's word is better than any mere paper,' she said. 'Or it ought to be. Thomas Lloyd is one of Penn's closest friend's and no one can deny that he knows English even better than he knows Welsh. What has he misunderstood?'

But Robin preferred not to talk about Thomas Lloyd. He wanted to discuss more personal matters.

'Well, that's how it is,' he said. 'Penn is the Founder, and Penn is the Governor . . . and everything else you care to call him. He's a fellow who likes his pomp and ceremony, I give you that, but he has to find a way of keeping order. It is time the people of the Tract realised that.'

Dorti was looking out over the river. On the other side they could see the tall trees, black against the horizon. Seagulls were crying above their heads, the sky was turning green as if heralding a storm. The wind started to blow on their faces.

'Thou hast told me why thou camest over,' said Dorti. 'So, thou seest that people have many different reasons for coming. Thou didst ask me once why I came.'

This was exactly what Robin wanted to know. He came closer to her, but there was no response from Dorti.

'Let me guess,' he said. 'You were running away from . . .'

It was on the tip of his tongue to say 'from a lover.' That is how he would have teased nine out of ten girls, but he stopped himself in time. Lowri's words came back to him. Her lover was dead . . . no, that was not true! He went on, a bitter note in his voice.

'You believe that you are one of the Children of Light; you think everyone should be allowed to worship as he wishes; you are going to fight the War of the Lamb to the bitter end. Perhaps none of those reasons is true. Perhaps you are only a kind and gentle sister-in-law, taking care of her brother's widow, accompanying her everywhere, and keeping everyone else away.'

He had touched some deep wound somewhere and knew it. He saw her flush. She spoke quickly and intensely:

'It's all true, but not the whole truth. My brother was a great poet, Robin Wynn, and perhaps poets have a special preception that other men lack.'

Her brother. Robin Wynn was shaking inwardly, yet he

was afraid to move in case she stopped talking.

'He taught me this.' She took a deep breath. 'Family and nation and language are created by God. In the fullness of time men shall be one in the house of the Heavenly Father. But while man is here on earth, it is his privilege and his duty to cherish the land given to him by God and preserve its traditions. These are his roots, here is his world, his memory, his person. If he is not conscious that he stretches back along the paths of history, he is nothing.'

'And where do we — you and I — stretch back to?'

'Back to our fathers and grandfathers, back to the essence of our civilisation, back to the days of independence, to Glendower, Prince Llewelyn, to Hywel the Good and Aneirin, to everyone and everything that can tell us who we are.'

She was standing there, the wind rising now, and blowing through her hair, looking like some Boadicea in the New Land. Her small teeth were shining through her half open mouth. She was as vivid and passionate as the wines of France.

'Dost thou believe that Glendower's spirit died with him? The spirit is stronger than death, and this spirit has been given by God to the poets of our country. They were its only custodians when our leaders had sold their country in exchange for honours. The words of a poet have great strength which can last longer than the power of the sword. The common people of Wales lost their memory — just as thou didst — but the poets did not; our language was threatened . . . dost thou remember Rhisiart Phylip's words? "Now thou art cold and thin, a language ignored without a rich granary . . ." But these men cherished their language.'

Robin was beginning to feel uncomfortable. Dorti was speaking like someone who had some kind of mystic revelation.

'Who were these poets?' he was curious to know.

'A group of good men, of undefiled descent, and pure of vision,' she said, quoting again. 'When they heard of this state they decided to come over here so that they could continue to speak their own language and follow their own customs according to their ancient laws.'

82

'And what of the Quakers and the New Jerusalem?' Robin asked soberly.

'This is our New Jerusalem,' replied Dorti. 'Because we are true to ourselves, and to our own past, we are able also to be true to Christ and to his Heavenly Father. Did not Morgan Llwyd say: "The portals of thy forests, O present land of the Britons, are open to the devouring flames. If you do not bear fruit at this hour, you will be cut down and will no longer exist as a people." That is what happened in Wales. It can be different here. Dost thou not remember that Penn himself wanted to call this place New Wales at one time? That is why I came.'

But Robin still felt confused.

'What happened to the rest of the poets? Where are they?'

Her face clouded.

'William Penn says that circumstances change things so thou wilt understand this. After Thomas died the others changed their minds. They had heard rumours that the dreams lacked substance, that there was some doubt about the freedom that had been promised us. They began to think that it was their duty to stay in Wales. In any case, they had never been as enthusiastic as my brother about coming here. Perhaps they were right.'

'But *you* came just the same.'

They had reached the gate of Ciltalgarth now. Dorti opened it quickly.

'Yes,' she said. 'Thank you for escorting me home, Robin Wynn.'

Robin stood there, the rain beginning to fall on him. Dorti walked up the path, further and further away from him. It was with very mixed feelings that he turned to go back to Pennsbury.

Bryn Mawr was finished only in the nick of time. Tomos and Lisa received a letter from their master saying that the *Amity* would be calling at Milford Haven on her way from Bristol to Pennsylvannia, sailing from there on the sixteenth day of the eighth month, and that Ellis Puw, Sinai and the children, and he himself with his son, would be among the hundred emigrants aboard.

Tomos looked with pride at the handsome wooden house. He had followed his master's instructions to the last detail. It was a two-storied house, but the bedrooms in the attic, really made it three-storied. The great door opened into the front hall, with a wide staircase leading to a small landing, and then another staircase leading up from the right side of the hall to a narrow passage with the bedroom doors opening out on to it. His master should be pleased with this house, for, especially from the outside, it greatly resembled the old Bryn Mawr.

The glaziers had just left, and the multi-coloured panes were now shining in their oak frames. Yesterday the carpenter had put the last small touches to the settle, the dresser, the long rectangular table, the straight-backed chairs and the chests. There were no carpets on the floors or pictures on the walls, and that was how it was going to remain. But there was a fire in the huge fireplace, and the house was sheltered from the north wind by a gentle hill and by trees. The southern sun smiled on the other side and on the little clear stream at the bottom of the meadow.

Tomos was glad that the work of building the house was finished. He could turn his energies to his farm work once again, and it was good to know Rowland Ellis would soon be here, for he was longing to have more time to spend on his own land. If he had good crops next year he could probably sell enough Indian Corn to buy more land.

'Dost thou *have* to work so hard?'

Lisa was tired of asking the question. She received the same answer every time: it was for her and Rhys that he was doing this, so that they could have their share of the country's wealth. She was tired of telling him that she preferred things as they had been before. Servants they might have been, but they had time to do other things, to think of other things, instead of pinching and scraping and working their fingers to the bone. She herself was very busy, in the house, caring for Rhys, and in the Meeting House taking her turn with the other women to distribute corn among those less fortunate than themselves, or to collect money to send to those Friends who were suffering under the Puritans in Boston. Although he did not venture to say much, Lisa knew that Tomos begrudged the time and the money given to this work.

But Lisa insisted on having some time to herself. Rhys was old enough now to run around on his own tough little legs. Sometimes she would take him for a walk in the woods around their home, to look for flowers and ferns. They would wander along the river bank, and sometimes she would lie down on the grass and gaze up at the clouds. She would have liked to have walked further into the heart of the forest, but Sion Ifan had warned her not to.

'Not without me, anyway. There are all sorts of dangers lurking there that you know nothing about,' he said.

Rhys was remarkably like his father in appearance. He had very light blue eyes, a long strong nose, rather a thin mouth, and he was already showing signs of developing a neck like a bull. He ought to have a brother or a sister, Lowri said for she thought he was indulged far too much. Lisa, too, would have liked another baby, and sudden tears clouded her eyes.

Lowri called fairly frequently, and in a way Lisa was glad of her company. But she realised only too well that a visit to their cabin brought Lowri nearer to Sion Ifan's — only five hundred yards away; and he was a regular visitor too. What surprised Lisa was that Dorti encouraged Lowri to come on her own, making excuses not to come with her. And Dorti kept on asking questions about Sion Ifan. Was he kind? Was he hard-working? Had he anything suspicious in his past? Could he afford to keep a wife? Why wasn't he married? Why wasn't he a Quaker? It was easy to see in which direction her mind was working. But why all these enquiries on *Lowri's* behalf? Why not on her *own* behalf? If she, Lisa, were unmarried like Dorti, it would be on her own account she would be enquiring about Sion Ifan's eligibility. Anyway, why enquire? Were his qualities not there for all to see? Lisa turned over on her side on the grass, putting out her hand to fondle the warm pasture.

During the week which followed Robin Wynn got to know more about why William Penn had decided to return to England so suddenly. It is surprising how much a man can learn by just standing around quietly, not saying anything himself but just keeping his ears open. He had already heard at least three reasons for the sudden departure, each one true no doubt, but which was the most pressing he could not guess. Giulielma, Penn's wife, was ill and her condition had deteriorated. In addition Penn had heard that some of the Quakers in England were beginning to suffer persecution again, and that his friend, the King, was in ill-health and unable, or unwilling, to intervene on their behalf. Penn wondered whether he himself would be able to intercede for them with the King, as in the past.

But what worried Penn most was the news that Lord Baltimore was on his way to London to issue a complaint in person before the Land Commission claiming that Penn had interfered with his brothers in Maryland in the South. Robin knew about the trouble with Philip Ford, but this Penn had not mentioned. Then there was the question of his votes in the Council. He had been shocked to discover that the members of the Council were unwilling for the Governor to have three votes. Clearly there was some unrest beginning to stir under the surface.

So, thought Robin, it was not only the Welsh who were beginning to tire of the dictatorship; there were signs of disquiet among the English Quakers as well.

Apart from the matter of the note to Philip Ford, Penn did not attempt to hide his worries from his companions. Uncle Thomas lent him an extremely sympathetic ear.

'Robin,' he said one morning, 'I want to talk to thee on a very important matter.'

The doctor had got very fat of late, his mouth seemed squeezed in by his cheeks, and his stomach curved outwards. It was hardly due to laziness, for he was kept very busy working as physician and barber to the Founder's family and their immediate neighbours. But meals at Pennsbury were enormous. It was only because Robin had a small, though appreciative, appetite, that he, also avoided developing a big stomach and red face.

'Thou art twenty-one, Robin, time to accept some responsibilities,' said the Doctor, taking off his wig because of the heat, and wiping the sweat from his brow. Wearing a wig was a new experience for him, and his head itched.

'William Penn has asked me to return to England with him. The *Endeavour* will be sailing about the fourth of next month. The problem is, I have just bought two hundred acres of land in the Welsh Tract. To be fair to William, the Welsh are very slow in taking possession, and he needs money. It is excellent land and I am going to leave thee here to look after it until I return.'

'But Uncle Thomas,' protested Robin, 'I know nothing at all about farming.'

'Well, now is the time to learn. Engage one or two servants. Plenty of lads are arriving in Philadelphia from the old country who will be glad of work. Germans too. It is possible to get a strong Negro boy for only twenty pounds. Black cooks are very expensive — they're charging forty pounds for them at the public blocks. Thou wilt soon find someone to build thee a house on the land, and the sooner one takes possession the better.'

'Why can't I stay here until you come back?'

Robin was filled with apprehension. How on earth was he going to manage when he had never before had to take any decisions for himself?

'We have trespassed long enough on the Governor's kindness,' said his uncle, rather unfairly Robin thought, seeing there was no need for his uncle to 'trespass' here any more. But there was no moving him. Penn had asked him to accompany him, and he was going to do so, come what may. Well, it's his fault if things go wrong, thought Robin.

'Ask Huw Roberts for advice. He's a good farmer.'

And that was the only instruction he got.

Penn spent many hours in Thomas Lloyd's company, telling him, among other things, that copies of every law passed in the State were to be sent on to the Privy Council in London. It seemed that Parliament was very suspicious of the way things were being run in the colony. Not one of the colonists realised, as they said goodbye to their Founder and watched the *Endeavour* sail away down the Delaware, that they would not see him again in Pennsylvania for another fifteen years.

Robin felt he had to tell someone about his new responsibilities and his worries about the future. There was no one in the Pennsbury family to whom he felt close enough, and in any case, he must accept the fact that the care-free days spent in the pleasant manor house were now over. Would Dorti listen? He was not used to talking about himself. Much easier to question others for he was very curious about other people's activities and it amused him to listen.

But of everyone he knew Dorti was the one to listen to him. He could ask Huw Robert's advice at the same time about employing servants, and setting the land in order. He still wondered at his uncle's leaving him like this. Had he intended to do so from the beginning, he wondered, in the belief that Robin would never have come here of his own accord? The old devil — if that were really the case.

And yet, Robin felt something stir within him, some strange new feeling that he was now a land-owner himself. He looked at the soil around him with new eyes, trying to gauge its quality. He gazed with interest at the fields of wheat belonging to the different farmers, noting the convenient position of the streams. Some primitive feeling of pride swelled within him, but all this was still mixed with apprehension. He decided to set off towards Meirion the very next day.

He found Huw Robert's family at their evening devotions. Huw called 'Come in' in answer to the knock at the door, but no one moved when he entered. Huw's mother and sister were sitting on either side of him, with the maids and menservants around them. Behind Huw Roberts sat Dorti Llwyd. There was no sign of Lowri anywhere, for which he was secretly grateful. He felt uncomfortable, breaking into their prayers in this way, but Huw Roberts invited him to take his place with the others.

He did not dare look at Dorti until the blood had quietened in his veins. She was sitting as still as a cat, her blue-green eyes hidden under their lids, her hands folded on her knees. There was no sound other than the ticking of the clock. Robin listened until the sound began to deafen his ears. The silence became almost unbearable. As if sensing a restless spirit in the company, Huw Roberts opened his eyes and said simply:

'May the Lord bless everyone in this room.' Then he got up, and everyone else followed. The Meeting was over.

The farmer's welcome was warm and sincere. The fact that some of the Welsh had turned their backs on their old friends and had gone to live with the 'nobility' — as he called them, — had been a source of concern to him. But he sighed with relief now. Here was the young man, Robin Wynn, returned to them, the court at Pennsbury temporarily dispersed, and Thomas Lloyd in a position of authority. Truly, the Lord was answering their prayers.

The success of the wheat crop that year was yet another reason for gratitude; cattle were growing fat, and barns were being filled. He was not surprised at this. The farmers of Meirion were used to much less fertile land. This was not the case with all of them in the colony. Outside the Welsh Tract, many of the farmers had not been so successful — especially those who had come over with no knowledge of husbandry. Huw Roberts had been one of the first to send a generous proportion of his wheat to help those people and this was now being arranged regularly by the Monthly Meeting in Meirion.

Huw was glad to be able to give Robin the advice he asked for. The young man listened attentively but he did not betray any of his doubts. He kept those until he had a chance to talk to Dorti on her own.

'I can't sleep a night for thinking about my responsibilities,' he told her half-seriously, half-jokingly. 'I've never had to think before of the difference between a swede and a carrot.'

'Thy questions to Huw Roberts were quite sensible,' she said.

A thrill of pleasure went through him.

'Do you think so? Easier to ask than act!'

She turned to face him, and he was pleased to see the friendliness in her eyes. 'This has made a difference to thee already.'

'A difference? How so?'

She laughed so rarely, come to think of it.

'Well, thy back is straighter, and there is dirt on thy shoes.'

Robin had not noticed the dirt. He bent down at once to try and clean it away, but Dorti took hold of him by the arm.

'No, don't. It's good that there is something but thyself on thy mind.'

Robin held her hand.

'My mind has been on something else for sometime now.' But the familiar veil came down over her face, and she freed herself.

'Dorti, Dorti. Why don't you let me speak to you?'

The blue-green eyes were sad.

'Because I cannot. Don't ask any more.'

Robin felt the disappointment in the pit of his stomach. A moment ago she was so close to him, and now she was as far away as ever. She had started to move away, but he must keep her with him. With a great effort he managed to speak lightly:

'Very well, mistress, not another word. But don't leave me now.'

The smile returned to her face for a moment, but there was no chance to say more for Huw Roberts and Doctor Edward Jones had come in.

'I hope the *Endeavour* is having fair weather,' said Huw. 'They should be half way by now.'

'I cannot understand it.'

The Doctor had a deep voice, something of a singer he had been, they said, although no one had heard this Quaker sing since the day of his conversion.

'Cannot understand what, Edward Jones?'

'Why he had to go back now of all times.'

'Does it matter? This is the best thing that could have happened to the Welsh. It's giving Thomas Lloyd a chance to look after our interests.'

'Yes, of course. But all the same, I don't understand. He was like a King here, with his own little court.'

'The more credit to him for listening to the voice of duty.'

But what duty, exactly, none of them knew. Robin was longing to repeat the conversation he had heard, but he was afraid of being reprimanded for listening to a conversation not meant for his ears. What's more, he still did not know to which side he really belonged. If I stay here any longer,

I shall pour it all out, he thought, and he got up to go.

Sion Ifan was washing himself in the wooden tub standing on a slate slab behind the cabin. He had been helping Tomos all day with one of the dirtiest jobs on the farm, and now he was trying to get rid of the dirt and the smell. Lisa had given him some of her precious soap, unbeknown to Tomos, and she lingered now over the washing watching the white foam splashing over him.

It had been raining heavily for some days and the trees were dripping, but the sun had just come out to transform the water into jewels on the branches as it warmed the land. Vapour rose up from the pine trees. By the time she had finished washing the clothes it would be warm enough to dry them properly. She began to hum.

The soapy water shone on Sion's back like whipping cream. Lisa stared at the hand moving rhythmically and strongly over the body, over the hairs on his chest, over his slim flanks, and down over the knees. He looked so natural in his nakedness – she could have been his mother looking at him.

'What's that you are singing?'

He lifted the tub and poured the water over his whole body, the words came out in gasps.

'Oh, only some song I always sing when I'm at the washing.'

'Let me hear it properly.'

She was not going to refuse Sion anything, so she began to sing:

> *Fal yr oeddwn yn golchi*
> *Dan ben pont Aberteifi*
> *A golchffon aur yn fy llaw*
> *A chrys fy nghariad danaw*
> *Fe ddoeth ata' wr ar farch*
> *Ysgwydd lydan, buan balch,*
> *A gofynnodd im a werthwn*
> *Grys y mab mwya' a garwn.*

> *As I was washing*
> *By Cardigan bridge*

Holding my clap-staff in my hand
And under it my lover's shirt,
It chanced a rider passed me by,
Broad of shoulder, proud and smart,
And he asked me if I'd sell
The shirt of the lad I loved so well.

Come to me she thought. Let me feel those strong arms around me. Let me touch that black curly hair, and know that strange excitement again. Come and let me feel thy kisses over my whole body. Warm me, love me.

Lisa finished her song with a quiet groan in her throat, but Sion noticed nothing. He was busy putting on his shirt and trousers. 'Lovely!' he cried. 'And a beautiful voice, Lisa. You Quakers should sing more. I can't understand what you have against singing.'

Thou hast not noticed anything at all, not noticed this desire gnawing away at me all the time? If I were to come over to thee now and take thy face in my hands, and kiss thee on the lips, I'll wager thou wouldst keep on treating me like a mother or a sister.

But Lisa did not move from where she was. Sion was whistling now, tying the laces at the neck of his smock, every sinew of his body vibrant from the last splash of water, and filled with energy.

'Where art thou going now?'

'Home. To the cabin.'

'It's early yet, I'll made thee some food.'

But he insisted on going, and she felt jealousy seize her throat. He wasn't tired; it wasn't late. Why was he going? She added salt to her wounds:

'Lowri will be here soon.'

Oh, please don't let him change his mind now. He was hesitating. Damn him.

'Well—'

'No, perhaps she won't come after all. If th'art tired . . .'

But Lowri arrived before Sion Ifan had time to say that he had changed his mind, or Lisa to persuade him to go.

'Oh, you're out here,' she cried, lifting her skirts and stepping carefully so as not to wet her feet. Then she stopped, staring from the tub, to Sion's tousled hair. Then she turned to Lisa.

'Tomos not home yet?'

Only Lisa and Lowri recognised the bite in this innocent-sounding question.

One of the first things Thomas Lloyd did was to release Amos Howel who had been in prison for several months. But he did not dare disregard the Founder's instructions to the extent of allowing him to start running his ferry again. Thomas had soon learnt that there were men around watching him like hawks. Penn called them 'councillors,' but Thomas began to feel that 'spies' would have been a more appropriate word. Thomas Holme, the Irishman, for one, had been given unlimited powers. This man was not only Surveyor for the whole of the State, but also the Deputy of the Council — and took good care that nothing was done without the Founder's permission. Then there was the Deputy Surveyor, Charles Ashcombe. Every time Thomas tried to suggest to him that it was time the boundaries were settled, he was reminded that some of the Welsh had still not come over to claim their lands — a weak enough excuse in Thomas Lloyd's view since they had paid for them.

It was the same with the other bone of contention, the mills. Thomas had hoped to be able to smooth the way for the Welsh to be allowed to build their own mills in their Tract; but Holme showed him a letter from William Penn reminding him to be diligent in the collection of the rents, the payment from the ferry and the mill, saying he trusted him to see that no changes were made. Thomas Lloyd felt completely helpless. He was beginning to suspect why Penn had given him the office of Deputy. Had he remained as he was, and given all his attention and energies to the Welsh Tract, he could now have gone ahead and ignored the Founder's orders. As it was, he, Thomas Lloyd, was Deputy Governor of the state. He had given his word that he would be loyal to the instructions of the Governor, and a Quaker's word was his bond. He was caught.

And caught in so many unexpected ways too. Before the Governor left, Penn had explained that he expected every one who became a member of the State Assembly to swear his allegiance to the King, to the proprietary and to the Provincial Govenment, promising to fulfil his duties faithfully. Although the expression 'take the oath' was not used, Thomas Lloyd saw no real difference between this and the great principle for which hundreds of Quakers back in the old country had suffered imprisonment. When he attempted to argue about it, he was at once given to understand by Penn that it was one of the King's conditions for letting them have the colony in the first place.

One day Thomas Lloyd happened to go unexpectedly into Charles Ashcombe's office. As he appeared in the doorway he heard the sound of papers being hurriedly removed, as if the Deputy Surveyor were trying to hide something. But Thomas Lloyd did not remember this until later, for his attention was immediately taken by a strange man sitting in the chair opposite Ashcombe's desk. He was a tall man, strongly built, but Thomas Lloyd noticed particularly his cold blue eyes and their fish-like lids.

'Daniel Croft.' Ashcombe introduced the man, looking confused, and then in a voice full of unctuous respect — which grated on Thomas — added: 'His Excellency, The Deputy Governor.'

Thomas Lloyd nodded to the stranger. He would have postponed his business with Ashcombe for the time being, had he not realised suddenly that the Surveyor was longing for him to leave. He became curious, and thought he would like to learn more about Daniel Croft.

'Hast thou just arrived in Pennsylvania, Friend?'

The man's chest swelled with pride at the graciousness of the Deputy Governor in deigning to speak to him.

'Yes sir. On the *John and Sarah* last week.'

A man from Devon or Cornwall, thought Thomas, judging by his accent.

'Welcome then. Are all the arrangements to thy satisfaction?'

The man was most enthusiastic.

'Excellent. Most excellent. Friend Ashcombe has been extremely kind.'

Thomas Lloyd was surprised. New immigrants usually complained.

'I'm glad to hear it.'

'Is there any matter you wish to discuss with me, Friend Thomas?' asked Ashcombe. His face was red.

'There's no hurry.'

Thomas looked with interest at Daniel Croft who was combing through the papers in his hand.

'Oh, here it is,' he said. 'Here is the map, carefully drawn by Friend Ashcombe here. See how skilfully every field and stream has been noted. Really, sir, you are fortunate in having such a thorough officer.'

'The Deputy Governor does not want to be bothered with trifling little maps,' said Ashcombe hurriedly.

'On the contrary, I should very much like to see the map.'

The man smoothed the paper out on the table. Thomas Lloyd leaned over his shoulder and scrutinised it carefully for a long time. Finally he lifted his head slowly, and turned to the Deputy Surveyor.

'But this land is in the Welsh Tract, my Friend,' he said quietly, but in a voice of steel.

'In the areas of the land not yet possessed by the Welsh,' announced Ashcombe defiantly.

Thomas took a deep breath. He was not going to quarrel with Ashcombe in the presence of this stranger, but he was not prepared to let the incident pass without saying something. True he had heard Holme threaten to sell land inside the Welsh Tract to Englishmen, and he, Thomas Lloyd, had spoken out strongly against it. He had hoped to be able to exert his authority slowly and cautiously, but no one could have mistaken his wishes in this particular matter. Ignoring Ashcombe he turned his attention to Daniel Croft.

'I am sorry thou must be disappointed, Friend,' he said, 'But there has been some mistake. These lands are already sold.'

The man kept opening and shutting his mouth before being able to utter a word.

'Mistake? H—How could that be? — I don't understand.' He turned angrily to Ashcombe: 'Were you trying to deceive me?'

Ashcombe's colour changed from red to white.

'I am not the one to do the deceiving,' he said coldly. 'It is those people who buy land without any intention of occupying it who are the deceivers. By doing so they forfeit their right to the land. That is the law.'

'If that is the law,' said Thomas Lloyd, still looking at Croft, 'then it is odd that the Council did not acquaint me with the fact. No, Friend Daniel, I am afraid thou hast been misled. But it shall not be thy loss, I promise thee. Look here.'

Thomas was drawing circles with his fingers on the map, looking for a piece of land on the lower reaches of the Delaware in the Country of Newcastle.

'Here, where the Susquehanna runs into the Delaware there is plenty of fertile land. Only very little of it has been sold as yet. It is a better bargain than the other parcel since it is nearer the harbour. The big ships sail right past Newcastle and call at Uwchlan long before they reach Philadelphia. These lands therefore are worth much more than those hast there in thy hand. I am sure our Surveyor will be ready to sell thee the same amount of land in the Newcastle area for the same price.'

The man calmed down, and took a long look at the map. He was perceptive enough to realise that what the Deputy Governor said was true, and that he was going to have a unique bargain. Now he was in a hurry to seal the contract before anyone could change his mind again. Ashcombe was instructed to make a new map, and Thomas Lloyd went away feeling that he had succeeded this once anyway in keeping the Welsh Tract intact as promised at the Conference in London five years before. But for how long would it remain so?'

CHAPTER FIVE

Rowland Ellis and the others did not arrive until April of the following year. The journey lasted six months because of the great storms, which had forced them to put in for shelter at Barbados for six weeks. They were very relieved to reach dry land for their water was getting short, and although plenty of salt meat was available, most of them were kept alive by water and biscuits as they were too weak to eat anything else. Beti Prys, Rowland's niece, who had insisted on coming with them, had died on the way — of the same fever that had killed Morris Richard, the tailor.

But at least they had not been troubled by pirates or Frenchmen, unlike Owen Robert's company, who had been within sight of the Delaware when their ship had been attacked by the French and they themselves taken prisoners and sent to Martinico and Guadalupa. And even after they had been freed by the English, some of the young men were no better off for they were press-ganged into service with the navy, Wmffra William of Dolgellau among them. And no more was ever heard of them.

At last the *Amity* came sailing up the Delaware, just after the river had been freed from winter ice. The snow had turned into sleet, and every sign of winter was gradually melting away.

The first view the Dolgellau settlers had of their new home was the rain pouring down on the lowlands of Philadelphia, exactly as it did on the homesteads around the Marian and the River Wnion. But here every building was larger than anything around the Marian, and the river looked more like Lake Tegid than the Wnion. It was only the mountains that were smaller. In the distance they could see hills that were not nearly as high as Cader Idris. Rowland knew that there were higher mountains to the north, the Blue Mountains, but these were far away over the horizon and well out of sight . . . To live without rugged mountains as a background to their homes would be a strange experience for the Dolgellau Quakers. Rowland turned to look at Ellis beside him, wondering what effect the new land was having on him, but he could read nothing in the remote eyes.

The night before sailing from Milford Haven, Ellis had had a dream. A voice warned him there would be tragedies on the journey, and that he, Ellis Puw, would have to return again to Wales because the Lord still had work for him to do there.

Sinai was looking at Ellis too, but there was no anxiety in her eyes, only love and complete trust. Her remaining children, now grown up, had come over with their mother and step-father, eager to make a new life for themselves. Next to Lisa the eldest, was Gutyn, who would soon be marrying Lleucu, the daughter of Dewisbren, who had also come out. Ellyw, the youngest, was fourteen and very like Dorcas in appearance. She was her step-father's favourite.

Rowland looked around for his seven year old son, Rol, wanting to show him his new home. But Rol was too busy helping his friend, one of the sailors, to tie the ropes. Rowland smiled. How quickly children forget, he thought. But Rowland could not forget the pain on Marged Ellis's face as she had said goodbye to her husband and son on Milford Haven harbour. She had stood there, fighting back the tears for she must comfort Beth and Robert, who knew that something strange was happening. Her dry eyes had upset Rowland more than any tears could have done. Perhaps he should sell his land here to someone else and return to Wales. That was her secret hope, he knew. As he looked at the strange plains before him with the little hills in the distance, he promised himself that he would do just that. I'm glad I came over to see the place, he thought, but I shall not stay.

Lisa and Tomos were on the quayside waving their handkerchiefs. It was a sweet reunion as Lisa looked wonderingly at the three strapping young men, who were her brothers Gutyn, Dafydd and Huw, and at Lowri and Ellyw who had blossomed out of their childhood. Only Sioned had remained behind. She had married a farmer.

Lisa greeted her mother warmly, amazed at how young she looked. She appeared to be only a year or two older than Ellis, although she was in fact fourteen years older. And Ellis . . . Ellis looked exactly the same, as quiet and shy as if he had never moved an inch from the foothills of Cader Idris. She felt a great affection for him.

As Tomos had hoped, Rowland Ellis was delighted with the house. He walked around the outside first, examining woodwork and windows. Then, taking Rol by the hand, he crossed the threshold for the first time. Bryn Mawr. His link with the old world. He wandered from room to room, climbed the stairs, walked up to one of the windows and looked out on the land around. Then he turned to Tomos:

'Thou hast done well, Tomos Owen.'

The servant's eyes glowed with pleasure. Rowland took a deep breath. It would be a shame if Marged were never to see the place. Before him the meadows stretched out, soft and gentle after the rain. A cold breeze blew in his face. The wood burning in the great chimneyplace smelt sweet, and the house was warm through and through. Not even his longing for Marged spoiled the feeling of satisfaction which was beginning to possess him.

He questioned Tomos closely. There were six hundred acres near the house, and almost another five hundred in Gosen. How far away was Gosen? Oh, some miles, towards the wild lands of the west. Tomos told him that it was possible to buy more land to the west, at least a hundred and ten acres. And what about the seventeen acres near the city? Tomos looked surprised.

'But, master, thou hast sold those.'

'Sold them? Certainly not.'

'Yes,' insisted Tomos. 'I have received the money for them, I can show thee the receipt.'

He went to look for the big book in which he was slowly learning how to write down correctly all the sums of money spent and received by him. Here it was plainly recorded that Tomos Owen had received twenty pounds, through Charles Ashcombe Deputy Surveyor, on behalf of Doctor John Goodson.'

'I heard nothing of this until this very moment,' said Rowland. 'Who is this Doctor John Goodson?'

'Ashcombe said quite definitely that he had settled everything with the owner,' said Tomos, feeling bewildered. 'Several parcels were sold at the same time. And Ashcombe said thou wert lucky to get such a good price, for it was feared that these lands would be occupied without re-payment.'

Rowland could see that he and Tomos had been tricked by someone. Who was this Ashcombe?

He was soon to find out. A few days after his arrival he and Tomos were out examining the ditches on the furthest boundaries of his land in Meirion when his attention was drawn by three men in the next field. One of them was kneeling down holding a yard-stick, and another was walking backwards and forwards making notes in a book.

'Who are they, Tomos?' he asked.

Tomos lifted his head, knitted his brows, and then said, under his breath:

'Ashcombe's men.'

'The Surveyor?'

'Yes.'

Rowland hesitated a moment, and then walked slowly across to them and greeted them. The three looked at him quite politely and having returned his greeting continued with their work.

'You have quite a lot of measuring to do, Friends,' said Rowland, having watched them in silence for moment or two.

'Yes,' said the man who was kneeling down, 'four thousand acres in all.'

One of the other men called to him to bring the yard-stick over. He got up and as he started to walk away pointed to the hills over the west.

'Right over there — beyond those hills. It'll take weeks, I'll warrant.'

Rowland followed him as he began to walk away.

'And who is to be my new neighbour?'

The man stood still, pursing his lips thoughtfully.

'I don't remember — Hi, Samuel! What's the name of the

man who bought these lots?'

The man called Samuel turned over the pages of his book and shouted back:

'Thomas Barker and Company.'

Rowland felt his anger risings.

'And where does Friend Barker hail from?' he asked, trying to keep his voice natural.

Samuel consulted his book again.

'Thomas Barker, gentleman. Weir Farm, Chilton Polden, Somerset,' he read.

The three men then went on with their work completely unaware of the mixed feelings their words had aroused in their listener. Rowland enquired no further. These men were only servants after all; it was not their fault that their master was behaving so strangely. He decided to make enquiries of his immediate neighbours, his uncle John Humphrey and the young man, John Eckley. From what he had gathered from the land-measurers, this land within the Welsh Tract which had been sold now to an Englishman, also bordered on theirs.

'Well, of all the rascals!' exclaimed John Humphrey when he heard the news. 'The lands beyond that point belong to other Welsh Quakers. This is going to separate us. It's being done on purpose, you can be sure of that.'

Rowland could not understand. He had not yet had time to digest the problems of the Welsh Tract.

'But why?' he asked. 'It's not as if he couldn't sell the land. There are plenty of us ready and willing to extend our lands gradually, given the opportunity. Why is the man in such a hurry?'

'The answer is plain,' said John Eckley, who had taken all this to heart even more so than the others. Where John Humphrey was annoyed, and Rowland Ellis confused, John Eckley was white with a cold anger.

'I've seen this sort of thing happen before,' he said. 'My home in Wales was on the border between Hereford and Radnor, and the old hatred between Briton and Saxon was still very much alive there. When the English saw a Welsh community grow and flourish as an independent community, they would not rest until they had split us up. How did they do that? By buying land in pockets here and there all over the community. That's exactly what is happening here now. They are jealous of our independent community and of our success.'

'But that Ashcombe man. What authority has he to do this?' asked Rowland naively. 'He is only a petty official. What can he do without Penn's consent?'

'There never was any real agreement,' was John Eckley's bitter rejoiner. 'An agreement is something written down on paper, something which can be shown as proof, and used as testimony in court of Law. All the foolish Welsh had was William Penn's word.'

So, Marged had been right. She had never thought much of the promises. What would she have to say now, he wondered.

They had to act quickly and carefully. Their anger lent new purpose to their fight — for fight it was, they knew that now, a fight to keep the unity of their Tract. The first thing they must do was see Thomas Lloyd. Did he know anything of Ashcombe's activities? Thomas Lloyd was, after all, Deputy Governor, so why had he done nothing to stop it before things had gone so far? Huw Roberts set off next day for Philadelphia.

As he walked in to the Council Hall he remembered the last time he had been there, and his futile interview with William Penn. A nasty suspicion struck him. What if Thomas Lloyd had changed too? He had not seen him for some weeks, and new authority had a way of changing a man profoundly, in a very short time. It needed an exceptionally strong character to withstand the temptation and there were so many who found it all too easy to forget their first idealism.

But he was greeted warmly by Thomas Lloyd. 'Huw Roberts! I am glad to see thee.'

Then, noticing the expression on the other man's face: 'What is the matter, Friend? Is anything wrong?'

Huw Roberts said what he had come to say, staring hard at Thomas Lloyd as he spoke. He did not have to explain much before being convinced that the Deputy Governor knew nothing of this. The latter rose from his chair and started to pace angrily backwards and forwards.

'Ashcombe again! He will have to explain himself before the Land Commissioners' Board.'

In one sense, Thomas Lloyd was glad the man had over-stepped the mark to such an extent as to enable him to challenge him openly at last. Until now he had done no more than offend a few people here and there, but this time he had deliberately and quite clearly offended against the Charter of the Welsh. This was an opportunity therefore for the Deputy Governor to prove once and for all that the Welsh had special rights. Now, who were these Land Commissioners? Only one Welshman among them. He ran over the names in his mind. Dr. John Goodson. It was to him that Rowland Ellis's land had been sold, without Rowland's knowledge. But, at that time, Goodson was unaware it belonged to anyone else. He knew now. Perhaps his conscience would force him to make compensation. On the other hand, he might possibly try to justify his action by supporting Ashcombe. Thomas Lloyd did not know enough about the man's nature to decide. So he could not be sure what attitude Goodson would take. Then there was another doctor. Doctor Nicholas Moore. A straightforward man, who had criticised the Frame of Government and called it treachery. But how would he look at the Welsh desire to keep their independence? Samuel Richardson. This man had already supported the rights of the Welsh in the Assembly. They were grateful to him for this, for there was no Welsh representative on the Assembly as yet and this was something which Thomas Lloyd intended to change. George Keith. A very doubtful man. A schoolmaster, fickle of temper and ideas. And then there was Patrick Robinson the Clerk to the Court, an amiable Irishman. But Thomas Holme was an Irishman too, so . . .

'The first thing I shall do,' he told Huw Roberts, 'will be to ask Ashcombe to prepare a map outlining the borders, and bring it before the Board . . .'

He went on to explain another part of his plan, and Huw Roberts's eyes lit up for the first time.

'If I get a good price for wheat in the autumn — eight shillings

103

say — I shall have enough to risk buying a horse.'

Tomos was sitting on the side of the bed, half undressed, with an account book in front of him. He was looking intently at the paper in the light of the candle. From where she lay in the shadow, Lisa could see lines running down from his nose to his mouth.

'My goodness! Sheep are unbelievably expensive here. About twenty shillings each . . . it's ridiculous . . . if only I knew of a way of getting some over from Wales . . .'

Oh! It was so hot. Lisa sat up and threw the upper blanket to one side. She opened the buttons of her nightdress and felt the sweat under her breasts. The wainscote bed was stifling her tonight. She could hear Tomos muttering to himself. Figures, acres, prices . . . If I get so much, I'll do this, that and the other . . . land, money, work, land, money . . . Heavens above, for what? Now is the time to live, Tomos, now.

'Tomos . . .'

'Eh?'

He did not even turn round. He no longer saw her. What if she were to take off all her clothes now, this very minute. It was hot enough tonight, goodness knows. Would he notice? If she did that, and Tomos did *not* notice, it would be his fault then, wouldn't it? She would not need to feel so guilty thinking about Sion Ifan. And what harm was there in *thinking* anyway? Sion Ifan wasn't likely to take any notice of her. He had eyes for no one now but Lowri. Lowri herself said so. "Sion says my eyes are like Lake Tegid on a fine spring afternoon, Lisa . . .'

'Tomos . . .'

'. . . art thou listening to me? That lout Ashcombe is thinking of selling that lot of land that I've had my eye on. But all *he's* been able to do is to call a meeting of the Land Commissioners Board.'

He got up at last and put the papers away in the wall cupboard. He then took off his shirt and breeches.

'To be honest, that land would have been too expensive for me anyway. I've got my eye now on a little piece further north. Not such good land perhaps, but with good husbandry . . .'

He had climbed into bed beside her now and put out the

candle. Lisa tried to pull his hand towards her, but Tomos turned on his side, with his back to her. She stared into the darkness until bright circles danced before her eyes. Rhys coughed in his sleep but did not wake up. If I were to have another child, she thought perhaps I should not feel like this, so empty, so useless, and with this hunger gnawing inside me like a bad apple. 'Wait until my term with Rowland Ellis is at an end, until I've collected enough to buy another cow, until the crops are harvested, then perhaps we can think about it. But at the moment we must be careful.'

Once when they were out in the fields she had tried to tell him how she wanted to feel his arms tight around her, tight, tight, out in the open air just as they were, to feel the red stubble sharp on their bodies and the sun envelop them. But Tomos only looked uncomfortable, and started to warn her, quite gently, not to give in to the desires of the flesh. She accepted his rebuke remembering what her terrible desires had led to in the past. But she loved Tomos — had loved him — and wanted to express her love. And if he did not want her she was lost . . . *any man who looketh upon a woman to lust after hath already committed adultery with her in his heart* . . . Perhaps it wasn't as wicked for a woman to desire a man. The Bible said nothing about that, concerned only with the man's sin. Perhaps other women were not tormented so. Perhaps she, Lisa, was different from all the others. O God, why didst thou make me thus? O Heavenly Father, what is to become of me?

Dorti too was lying awake in her bed. Earlier she had opened her window wide and looked at the moonlight silvering the trees. The fragrance of the night was like wine. It was almost as light as day, everywhere quiet and still, an oppressive heaviness foretelling thunder. She was on the point of turning away from the window when she suddenly noticed two figures move from the shade of the oaktree towards the house. They walked very slowly, very close together. She drew back quickly, not wanting to be seen, but not so far back as not to be able to see who they were. A strange hope surged through her. Was it she? The woman was small and wore a hood, but it was

105

difficult to make out the face. Was the man Sion Ifân? Yes, she could swear it was. The woman lifted her face suddenly to look at the moon and a thrill of relief flooded through Dorti as she saw the small teeth and heard the familiar low laugh. As the two figures kissed each other she smiled in the darkness and went quietly to her bed. But not to sleep.

The Council Chamber was filled with the bustling coming and going of officials and clerks. They were talking to each other quietly and quickly, with much waving of papers and shaking of heads. They had been there for an hour before the enquiry was due to begin, arranging chairs at tables, placing paper and quills tidily before each empty chair to be occupied by the Commissioners, and now there was nothing more to do but wait for them to arrive. The deputation had already come, and had been told to wait in a back room. The seven of them sat there in silence, listening to the sounds of the clerks on the other side of the door.

Rowland Ellis understood by now how important this day was. It would see the confirmation − or the rejection − of separate identity of the Welsh Tract. He looked from one to the other of the quiet men around him. To a stranger their silence would have appeared passive, the silence of men ready to accept whatever might be. But Rowland knew the iron determination behind the apparent quiet, the determination of men who were certain of the justice of their cause . . . Huw Roberts, always so conciliatory, now as fierce a defender of their rights as Edward Jones and John Eckley; John Bevan, the gentle man from Trefyrhyg; Henry Lewis from Narberth; and a new powerful supporter − Doctor Gruffydd Owen, Dolserau. His arrival had been an important event, for this was a man who had been to London with John ap John and received the original promise from William Penn.

Gruffydd had been accompanied by his elderly parents, but his father, Robert Owen, had been very ill on the journey and the previous week his body had been laid to rest in the Quakers' Burial Ground in Meirion. Rather than stay at home to mourn, his son was now anxious to work for the rights of his fellow

106

Welsh, as if by doing so he could channel his sorrow for the old man into practical force.

On the other side of the door, the muttering had stopped as the Commissioners walked into the Council Chamber. Thomas Lloyd called for the seven Welshmen to be brought in to listen to the testimony.

The sun shone directly on to Thomas Lloyd's head and Rowland was reminded of that time in Dolobran when the idea of coming over to Pennsylvania had first been noted among a group of Friends. He remembered the eagerness in the handsome face, remembered the confident voice, the long arguments. The voice was still confident, but the eyes were now wary. Did Thomas Lloyd regret his decision that day in Dolobran? Had their coming to Pennsylvania all been a mistake?

The Deputy Governor was explaining the case to the Commissioners, and Rowland looked at them with interest. Samuel Richardson was the one sitting at the end, a short man but quick-witted, they said. He had been ready to argue with Penn on the matter of the mills, so he had some sympathy obviously with the wishes of the Welsh. The one next to him must be Doctor John Goodson. So this was the man to whom his land had been sold. A fair complexioned young man, but that was all he knew about him. He was playing nervously with the quill on the table in front of him. Next to him, Doctor Nicholas Moore, a huge man, with a habit of letting his head sink on to his breast and then raising his eyes suddenly to look intently at everyone around him. He was a completely fearless man, who had called William Penn a traitor to his face. Apart from Patrick Robinson, the clerk, George Keith was the last of the row. Rowland had heard that he was a very self opinionated man − able and better educated than most, but inclined to be quarrelsome.

'As things stand at the moment,' Thomas Lloyd was explaining, 'The Welsh Tract consists of several townships, Meirion, Radnor, Haverford − those are the biggest − and then a number of smaller ones like Gosen, Tredyffryn, Uwchlan . . . Doctor Gruffydd Owen, wilt thou explain to the Commissioners the nature of the promises made to the

107

Welsh Quakers by our Founder, William Penn?'

Gruffydd repeated the familiar words, and finished by saying:

'We have come here today on behalf of all the Welsh Quakers to put before you the complaint that William Penn's guarantee has been disregarded by Charles Ashcombe, Deputy-Surveyor of this State, and that we are thus being prevented from enjoying in tranquility the Tract which was made over legally to us.'

When he had finished, Thomas Lloyd called Charles Ashcombe.

'Friend Ashcombe,' he said quietly, 'wilt thou place before the Commissioners the map of the Tract prepared by thee?'

Ashcombe walked over and pompously thrust the map in front of them. Untidy lines and letters betrayed undue haste and bad temper. It was passed from one to the other and then on to Thomas Lloyd.

'Friend Ashcombe,' he said in the same quiet voice, after taking a long look at the map. 'I see here that thou art still giving four thousand acres within the Welsh Tract to Thomas Barker and Company. Why dost thou insist on being so stubborn?'

Ashcombe stared defiantly at him:

'Excellency — I was instructed that all the land was to be cultivated and sown and treated in any other way thought necessary to make the maximum use of it. How could that be done when it is left to run wild and remain unproductive. Good men with plenty of money are arriving here every day claiming that they have bought land from Mr. Penn and his bailiff in London. Am I to tell them that there is no land for them, knowing that that is a lie? It is impossible to share out the land fairly unless we give a proportion of that which is called the Welsh Tract to Thomas Barker.' After a moment's silence, he added slyly: 'Are the Welsh language and law so weak that they are afraid of a few good English Quakers here and there?'

Thomas Lloyd let him finish, then without commenting on what had been said he turned to the chief clerk.

'Call David Powell, surveyor.'

A young man stepped forward, a pile of maps under his arm.

'David Powell, thou, too, art a surveyor by profession, and newly arrived here in Uwchlan.'

'Yes.'

'And although thou hast only just arrived here thou hast nevertheless had sufficient time to make a map of the state.'

'Yes. I have a copy for every member of the Commission.'

'Excellent.'

The young man handed every one a map. It was simple and well drawn, the Welsh Tract clearly marked to the west of the Schuylkill. Other parcels of land had been clearly placed on each side of the four rivers that ran into the Delaware below the Schuylkill, and the three rivers above.

'You will agree, Friends,' said David Powell, 'that rivers are necessary for land cultivation, and that it is reasonable that every township should be set as close as possible to a river. If the Welsh Tract becomes too crowded some people will be without a river near their land. Others will have more than enough water. My suggestion therefore is this — look at the maps, Friends — the banks of these tributaries should be developed before there is any more interference with the Welsh Tract. It is true that these rivers are smaller than the Schuylkill, but they are possibly easier to make use of. Gradually the woods to the north west will be cleared and then there will be more than enough good land for all newcomers.'

The maps were indeed finely and carefully drawn and the young surveyor's words had obviously made a favourable impression on the Commissioners. George Keith was the only one to voice a doubt.

'These maps are possibly an improvement on Ashcombe's. I've nothing to say about that. It is the basic principle of the thing that worries me. Even if these promises were made to the Welsh by Friend William in a moment of weakness, William isn't here and we are in charge now. I fail completely to understand why it is necessary to fragment the state by leasing some of the most fertile parts to minorities no matter how loudly they shout.'

He was staring at the members of the deputation as if they belonged to some primitive tribe. Rowland noticed how tight the flesh was on his bony face and how his mouth drooped at the sides — as if someone were pulling it down.

'We have not come here today to discuss the principle of minority rights, Friend George, but rather to see that those rights are upheld,' said Thomas Lloyd. Then turning to the Welsh deputation, he said: 'I am going to ask you formally now, Friends: do you agree with the plans of the Deputy Surveyor to lease these four thousand acres in the Welsh Tract to Thomas Barker and Company?'

'No,' answered the seven men clearly. Thomas allowed a good few seconds to pass in silence to stress the decisiveness of this reply, and then called on Thomas Holme the Surveyor, to step forward.

'Thou hast seen the map by thy deputy. Look now at David Powell's map. Which one, in thy opinion, makes better use of the colony land?'

Before turning his attention to the map the Surveyor took a quick look at the face of the Commissioners, and came to a quick decision. If Ashcombe was to sink, he should sink alone, and not take Holme with him.

'Oh most certainly Thomas Lloyd — David Powell's map. No doubt about it.'

He did not look at Ashcombe as he spoke, but everyone felt the growing hostility between the two.

'I must admit now that I have had cause more than once to complain about the Deputy Surveyor's work. I should have liked to have had a more suitable man in his place, but what could I do? I was given explicit orders by Governor Penn to keep him on. There was a personal instruction as well as a written one. I had no choice.'

Thomas Lloyd gave Ashcombe an opportunity to speak in his own defence, but he had withdrawn into his shell. So barefaced was Holme's treachery, Rowland found himself beginning to feel sorry for Ashcombe. After all, the man had only been carrying out Penn's wishes.

They all left the Council Chambers while the Commissioners discussed the case. They did not take long to reach their verdict, and everyone was called back in. Thomas Lloyd read it out:

'We, the Proprietary Deputies, having taken into consideration the request made to us by several persons in the Welsh

110

Tract, found that what land had been so surveyed there was done by Charles Ashcombe, Deputy, without authority of the Surveyor General. Against which encroachments the persons concerned in the said Tract have craved justice from us that their rights may be maintained according to the true intent and meanings of the aforesaid warrant granted therein . . .' How fortunate, thought Rowland, that Thomas Lloyd is Welsh too. This was the second time he had been the means of securing justice for him and his fellow Quakers. Only this time he had been able to act from a position of more authority. And yet, how easy it would have been for him to have become nothing more than a petty servant to William Penn. Was that what Penn expected?

As for Charles Ashcombe, no one was surprised to hear the Deputy Governor announce his dismissal at the end of the speech.

It was a great victory. All the Welshmen in the Tract could breathe again and forget worry and uncertainty. The law of the land had at last seen fit to acknowledge their rights. They were free now to go ahead with their farming in peace.

Rowland looked at the ripe golden-yellow corn swaying in the wind and realised that this soil was more fertile than any he had ever seen in Wales. Hope reached out in front of him far into the future. It would be foolhardy to leave all this now when the foundations of the Welsh community had just been firmly established. This was an ideal place in which to rear children — Marged must be made to see that. It was a land of peace, its people safe in God's love, awaiting the mercy of Jesus Christ and life eternal.

He spent a great deal of time in the company of his bailiff, and it would have been difficult to say which of the two men was more enthusiastic about the rich yield opening out in front of them. Rowland Ellis approved of Tomos's desire to have land of his own. He knew that he could be trusted to look after his master's own lands at the same time, and there would be ready aid and assistance from Ellis Puw and Sinai's sons too.

He smiled as he reflected what a man for a bargain Tomos was. He had had his eye on a strip to the north in the uncultivated lands where as far as was known none but the Indians had previously lived. That land could be got for next to nothing, he had told Rowland. So far it had been too distant and too wild for Ashcombe's men to lay their hands on it.

Tomos was quite right, of course, and Rowland wondered at his new perceptivity. But he must take care to give the Indians a fair price. 'What's a fair price, wouldst thou say, Master?' Tomos had asked slyly. 'It's not money that the Indians want.' In a quandary, Rowland had suggested to him that he should enquire of those Friends who had already done business with the Indians, and Tomos had promised to do that.

For a moment doubt niggled at Rowland. Were he and Tomos attaching too much importance to earthly possessions? He forced himself to admit that there was something lacking in himself at Quaker Meetings these days. Sometimes he had great difficulty in fixing his mind on spiritual matters. A mist would cloud the picture and he would find his thoughts running over his lands and his plans for improving them. And yet . . . if husbandry failed, the experiment would fail too. One had to put one's own house in order first. Once the early difficulties were overcome, he would be able to experience again the bliss of those first Meetings. He must impress on Tomos again the need to treat the Indians justly.

'I saw Robin Wynn this afternoon,' said Lowri in an unconcerned tone of voice, holding her needle up to the light to thread it. But it was at Dorti she was looking, not the needle.

'He looked worn out.'

After her first quick, instinctive reaction, Dorti kept her eyes down on her work. She had been caught once too often.

'His hair was all over the place, and his trousers looked as if he'd just fallen into a pigsty like any old country lout. Who would have thought that a man could change so much? . . . It's getting dark; its impossible to thread this needle . . . Strange how men change, isn't it, Dorti?'

Dorti concentrated on her work and quickened her stitching.

'I wish those lazy girls would bring the candles in.'

Lowri let her work fall on to her lap. She leaned back in

her chair, her face in the shadow.

'He was very friendly, I must admit. "Where's that hat with the roses, Lowri?" he asked. He's never forgotten that hat. And dirty as he was, there was still something remarkably charming about him. Dost thou think so, Dorti?'

Dorti sat with her face to the window. Enough evening light was still coming through the panes to outline her cheeks and chin and the least possible tightness around her lips.

'But there it is. Thou never noticed these things . . . I can see I shall have to be more careful with Robin, or Sion Ifan will get mad . . .'

Dorti held on to the other name like a drowning man clutching at a straw.

'Will Sion Ifan be calling here tonight?'

'Yes, probably.' The self—satisfied sigh came from the shadows. 'He won't give me a moment's peace until I've given him an answer.'

Dorti kept her voice calm.

'So he has asked thee?'

'Hundreds of times!' laughed Lowri, waiting for Dorti to ask the next question — but it never came.

'I don't quite know what to do. There's not much choice here. All the unmarried men are so uninteresting.' Her voice was monotonously thin. 'Sometimes I can't help noticing how . . . coarse he is, how . . . illiterate — especially compared with Robin Wynn. Almost primitive one would say. He is certainly primitive in his appetites anyway. He reminds me of poor Thomas Llwyd in that. In his appetites I mean, not that Thomas was illiterate, of course. Thomas had the same sensuousness, the same passionate desire to embrace me all the time. Strangely enough Sion calls me his little swallow . . . Thomas used to call me his little wren . . . Oh, Dorti! I'm so sorry . . . I'm hurting thee . . . I'm so selfish, not thinking of anybody else, only of Thomas and our love for one another.'

But Dorti's face betrayed no emotion. It had become too dark to sew; she put her work aside, saying quietly to Lowri:

'If thou dost think to accept Sion Ifan, thou shouldst tell him so at once.'

113

Lowri's face came out of the shadow, and Dorti was reminded — not for the first time — of a beautiful ginger cat.

'So that *thou* may be rid of thy promise and responsibility? Oh, Dorti Llwyd, it's not so easy to atone for a sin, thou shouldst know that.'

Although she was not looking at Lowri, Dorti was aware of the little foot winging backwards and forwards, backwards and forwards. This always happened when Lowri was excited about something, and provoking somebody else always gave her pleasure. Dorti knew that.

'No. It's not so easy.'

She must try to learn charity and humility. In the past her suspicious nature had led to tragedy. Had Lowri ever swerved in the slightest from the paths of respectability — either now, or at the time? She must make herself believe that the answer was 'no,' because that was what Thomas had believed. Not a single act of Lowri's could earn the disapproval of the strictest of Quakers. And yet . . . Dorti sighed quietly. She was letting her instinctive dislike get the better of her again. Was it not this which had led to her present enslavement? She repeated in her mind: I *must* learn a spirit of charity towards Lowri.

She go up from her chair as if to escape from her thoughts. One of the maids came in to light the candles. Dorti walked over to the little table on which the Bible always lay, and opened the heavy cover. She turned the pages over slowly, knowing that Lowri was still watching her, but she had to have some help from somewhere to be able to remain calm.

. . . And have no fellowship with the unfruitful works of darkness, but rather reprove them. For it is a shame even to speak of those which are done to them in secret . .

She closed the Bible and, making an enormous effort, turned again to face Lowri, although she could hardly see her. The words came quietly and evenly, as if she were making confession to an invisible priest.

'I gave Thomas Llwyd my word on his deathbed that I would stay with thee, and care for thee and cherish thee as a sister.

114

I did this because I was guilty of misleading him, and because that led to his fatal illness. I shall keep that promise as long as I am required to do so. I am not trying to be rid of my responsibility . . . But thou shouldst not play with Sion Ifan's feelings.'

Lowri laughed — a short, humourless laugh: 'Nor Robin Wynn's either?'

They heard the door open — Dorti with relief. Huw Roberts came in, followed immediately by Sion Ifan.

'Ah,' said Huw, 'I'm glad you're both here. Here's a visitor.'

'I had promised Lowri Llwyd that I would call tonight.' Sion began. 'Is she . . .?'

'Yes, she is. Here I am Sion.'

Lowri got up from her chair and walked across the room to Sion, who stood there smiling uncertainly. His eyes lit up immediately when he saw her. He took her hands and gazed down affectionately at her, towering over her from his height of more then six feet. Dorti noticed that Lowri was smiling sweetly back at him, and making no effort at all to release her hands.

'Lowri Llwyd,' said Huw Roberts a serious expression replacing the paternal smile on his face. 'Sion Ifan has requested my permission to ask thee for thy hand in marriage. If thou art of the same mind, I shall put the request before the next meeting. I am glad to hear, Lowri, that Sion has adopted our faith, so there should be no hindrance.'

Dorti straightened her back. Had Lowri been expecting this? It dawned on her suddenly that Lowri had known very well that Sion was coming here tonight with this purpose in mind. She fought back her anger at Lowri for teasing her with lies, and gradually felt a warm glow at the thought that her penance would now be coming to an end. She crossed over to Sion and grasping both his hands, said quietly, 'May heaven bless the two of you.' And only Lowri knew the true significance of her words. By now other members of the family had heard the news and were gathering in the room. Sion Ifan had been popular among them all although he had been so slow to join the Quakers. But now Lowri Llwyd, through the Grace of God, had been the means of gathering him into the fold, and great was their gratitude. Lowri had been faithful to her late husband's vision, they said, and was not prepared to marry outside the faith.

In her new freedom, Dorti could relax sufficiently to regard Lowri and her motives more objectively. She knew perfectly well that her husband's widow was not the devoted Quaker she appeared; she believed that Lowri knew nothing of that spirit which had sustained Quakers in the face of persecution and suffering. Lowri had been forced by circumstances to come over to Pennsylvania, and having come, all she wanted was the approval and respect of the society in which she found herself. Not for her the wild love that would dare convention and risk everything. If Sion Ifan was to have her for wife he would have to discipline himself and conform.

Dorti could hear Sion's hearty laugh as the neighbours gathered around them − too loud a laugh for a Quaker. She noticed the curly locks falling untidily over his forehead, the vivid, restless eyes accustomed to piercing the dark of the forest. But what about human darkness? Suddenly she felt a prick of conscience, for had she not wanted this splendid creature to be caught in a net so that her own mind could be at rest. And yet, it was not her fault that he had been caught. All she had done was to wish it silently. If Lowri had but realised how deeply Dorti wanted this marriage, she might not have accepted Sion so readily. She remembered her sister-in-law's sharp voice as they both lay in bed one night before going to sleep.

'If Lisa had half a chance she'd jump into bed with Sion Ifan like a shot. Sion is too simple to see it, of course, but her desire is so obvious, so shameless . . . Ugh!'

Dorti had forgotton these spiteful words until this minute, but they came rushing back at her now like water breaking through a dam. Was that what had attracted Lowri to Sion Ifan? If Lisa had not betrayed her feelings, would Lowri have noticed Sion's existence at all? She thanked God that Robin Wynn was now safe from her clutches. And yet, was he really safe? The old suspicions came flooding back. The same thing cannot happen twice, she told herself passionately. Don't, oh don't let it happen again.

116

'Thou wilt miss Lowri,' said a voice in her ear. She turned round to see Huw Roberts smiling at her. 'Thou hast been very good to her, Dorti. No sister could have done more.'

Dorti shook her head hastily.

'I hope they'll be happy,' continued Huw Roberts. 'Sion was pretty wild in the old country, but coming here has steadied him I believe.'

They both looked at the engaged couple, both with their doubts, both unwilling to express them. Dorti recollected something else she had had on her mind.

'Huw Roberts, who were those strangers at our last Monthly Meeting?' she asked.

But Huw Roberts had not noticed any strangers. About four hundred people attended the Monthly Meetings in Meirion now, so it was difficult to notice everybody. Dorti however, had happened to be sitting near the door, so she had seen the two men and two women walk in quietly after the Meeting had started, and just as quietly walk away immediately the Meeting was over. Nothing wrong with this, of course, but visitors were rare in Meirion, especially visitors who were not known to the Friends, and who did not stay to introduce themselves afterwards.

'I'm sure they did not understand one word,' said Dorti.

'Perhaps they like hearing the language. There are people like that. It's good that folks should come to visit us.'

Dorti knew that the instinctive suspicions she had about these people were foolish. She could not put her finger on anything out of place in their behaviour, but their presence had troubled her.

'If they come again,' said Huw Roberts, 'we must make a special effort to welcome them.'

117

CHAPTER SIX

Lisa knew that Tomos had something to tell her. Usually he swallowed his breakfast hastily, obviously longing to feel a scythe or a spade in his hands, pushing his chair back almost before she had started to eat hers. But today he was chewing his food carefully and thoughtfully, looking in her direction every now and then out of the corner of his eye. Well, for once at least he *was* looking at her. Lisa felt uncomfortable, as if a strange man was sitting there. And yet, this was Tomos, her husband. She blushed for him because she knew that he too was feeling awkward, she could no longer get through to him. Over the last few months, a wall had been growing steadily between them, built by a resentment she could not express.

After a time Tomos got up, but he was in no hurry to leave the cabin. He walked up to the fire and poked it unnecessarily. All she need say was: 'What's the matter Tomos?' But she could not bring herself to say it. She turned, took the pitcher, and started to walk towards the back to prepare the pig food, and, seeing his opportunity disappear, Tomos at last managed to open his mouth.

'When my year's work is finished, we might as well move nearer our own land.'

Lisa stood still. Was that *all* that was bothering him? They had discussed this matter many times, and she had always known that their present cabin was only a temporary home. It had always been their intention, once Bryn Mawr was finished, to start building a house of their own, a proper house this time, not a cabin. True, there had been no direct mention of this for some time now, but Lisa had been consoling herself by thinking about the number of rooms they would have, dreaming about the sort of furniture she would have. When

Tomos first bought the land, they had both wandered over it looking for the best position for the house. They had finally chosen a sheltered valley at the bottom of a field about fifty yards from the river, not far from their present home and all their friends in Meirion. Lisa did not allow herself to name any of these friends. If Tomos was thinking seriously of getting started, this was good news indeed. Why the uneasiness?

'Thy work for Rowland Ellis doesn't end until next year,' she said carefully. 'When dost 'ee think of starting? It's no use doing much before spring.'

'No of course not,' he agreed hastily. 'We're quite comfortable here aren't we?'

His words came out quickly, too quickly, as if she had said exactly what he wanted to hear. And yet, he had just said 'we might as well move nearer to our own land.' Lisa looked at him, waiting for the explanation. Tomos continued in some confusion.

'Quite honestly there are far better places to build a house than that silly little field with the noise of the river in our ears, day in, day out. I've been having a look a bit further west, and there's a lot of good land there.'

'Wild land.'

'Well, yes. But all land is wild until it's cultivated.'

Lisa thrust out her lower lip.

'I don't know what thou hast against building a house exactly where we have already decided. It's sheltered there, not too far to carry water, right in the middle of the land thou hast bought. I'd rather keep to that — much rather.'

Tomos kicked a log until the sparks flew.

'Well, we're not the owners of that land any more.'

Lisa put down the pitcher with a thud.

'What dost thou mean? Thou hast bought that land and paid for it — *and* worked on it, goodness knows!'

'I've sold it.'

'But — why? And to whom?'

Tomos walked across to her and took hold of her by the shoulders. Suddenly in spite of the tension it occurred to her that this was the first time for a year that he had touched her

119

'Listen. I'll tell thee what happened.'

But he did not find it so easy to explain. She had to encourage him with questions.

'Why did 'ee have to sell it?'

'Lisa, I was made an incredibly good offer. With that money I can buy twice as much land elsewhere, thou'lt see.'

'But to start from the beginning again?'

'No. This time it will be different. I have money behind me now. I can get a servant to help me. Even buy a slave perhaps.'

'But who has bought the land?'

The answer was rather slow in coming. 'Someone called Dawson.' When he saw the look on her face he added quickly, 'It's all right. They're Quakers, Dawson, his wife and a cousin, Richard Hull and Priscilla. Very nice people.'

'Do they speak Welsh?'

'No, of course not, but they get on very well with the Welsh so they say. They were at the last Monthly Meeting. Very pleasant people.'

'But what will Rowland Ellis say? And Huw Roberts? And Edward Jones?'

'I cannot understand them, all this fuss about keeping the Welsh together. If they're Quakers what difference does it make? They're wealthy too, and ready to pay a good price without quibbling about it.'

Lisa sat down slowly. She did not have the arguments which would answer Tomos. Perhaps it was he who was right after all, that what was important was being a Quaker, not being Welsh. But she knew instinctively that the others would look upon Tomos as some sort of traitor.

'Thou shouldst at least have discussed the matter with Rowland Ellis,' she said unhappily.

'And have to refuse this excellent offer? No fear. No. Once the others get to know John Dawson and his wife, and see what nice people they are, they will welcome them with open arms, thou'lt see.'

But Lisa continued to shake her head. Without being able to analyse her reasons, she knew in her heart that Tomos's action was going to segregate them from their friends one way or another.

'And where is this new land thou art going to buy?'

'Well, it isn't as far away as all that. Of course we shall have to cut down trees first, and clear shrubs, but that will soon be done. And thou'rt stronger now than just after Rhys's birth and can lend a hand as well!'

A great suspicion began to dawn on Lisa.

'This land. It's not outside the Tract?'

By now, Tomos looked very uneasy indeed.

'Well, yes. To tell you the truth, it is.'

Lisa turned on him. 'Tomos Owen — who owns this land?'

'Nobody. Nobody really. Well, the Indians do I suppose.'

'And they are willing to sell?'

'I haven't spoken to them yet. I was thinking Sion Ifan might come with me to help strike a good bargain. He knows how to get on with the Indians.'

'And thou hast already sold this land, *our* land, without even being certain of the other?'

'Goodness! Don't be so cross, Lisa. I am only trying to do my best for you and the boy, that's all.'

Her temper melted away. Tomos sounded like an injured child, and what he said was perfectly true: he never spared himself. She could so easily have married a lazy, useless husband; instead of that, she had Tomos who was happy to start all over again. Another man would have broken his heart at the thought. Then she remembered their master, and felt sick at heart wondering what he was going to say.

'What if the Indians don't want to sell? We'll be without any land at all then. The prices around here now are much too high for the likes of us.'

'I haven't heard of an Indian who couldn't be charmed by a cask of rum, even if he did not want beads. There'll be no trouble there. But we have to make sure that no one else gets wind of it or it'll be goodbye to a reasonable price.'

Lisa suddenly thought of Ellis Puw. This sort of talk would be incomprehensible to him. Not for the first time in her life she longed to be able to turn back the clock to the days of her innocence, the innocence that Ellis still retained. And yet, she thought, with a deep sigh, how far back she would have to go. Perhaps there was some sort of pattern to everything that had happened to her up till now. Perhaps there was still a pattern even now, only that she could not see it. Perhaps she would have to be exiled from the old community, and that exile would be for the best in the long run. She would not then have to suffer the torture of seeing Lowri and Sion Ifan together all the time. Yes, the best thing for her to do was to take things as they came.

Thomas Lloyd felt uneasy. He was in his coach, the heavy wheels rolling over the stony road from New York to Philadelphia. Two liveried servants rode on either side of him, their eyes searching the woods, pistols ready for bandits who might be lurking in the dark shadows. But it was not this that was worrying Thomas. For a whole fortnight he had been arguing with Colonel Bejamin Fletcher, Governor of New York, who had instructions from the King to muster a defence force from each one of the colonies. Since this struck at the very roots of Quaker belief, Thomas Lloyd had thought it better to go to New York to explain to Colonel Fletcher in person why Pennsylvania was unable to comply with the request.

He had soon discovered that to try to have a discussion with a man of Fletcher's temperament was a mere waste of time. They did not speak the same language, either as Christians or as gentlemen. Fletcher's attitude alternated between threats and bullying; he seemed to believe that the best man was the one who shouted loudest. In vain had Lloyd tried to explain to him quite calmly, that the Quakers could not raise an army for the simple reason that, as Quakers, they did not believe in killing under any circumstances. And when Fletcher mentioned the oath of allegiance, it had been useless to try to explain that Quakers did not take an oath of any kind. When he realised finally that it was impossible to communicate with this man, Thomas decided to cut short his visit to New York.

All the way back, some little thought had been gnawing at the back of his mind, and his uneasiness grew. It was not

Colonel Fletcher who worried him now. Thomas Lloyd was used to the blindness of men of his sort and knew that there was no point in continuing to struggle with them. He was remembering instead something Thomas Holme had said to him before he left. Lloyd had been busy with his preparations for the journey and had not taken too much notice of it at the time, but now the words came flooding back. Thomas Holme had been appointed to act as Deputy in his absence, not by Lloyd himself but by William Penn. When he was handing the papers over to him and trying the while to hide his dissatisfaction, he had heard Holme murmur.

'This is really the best time for thee to go. There's not much demanding attention at the moment, only a little tidying up of the Mill Creek matter . . .' He was speaking so quietly that the rest of the sentence had been lost, and something else had claimed Thomas Lloyd's attention.

Mill Creek . . . Mill Creek . . . the name had slipped his mind till now, but he had suddenly realised its significance. In all the discussions about the boundaries, the possibility had been mooted of drawing the boundary line between the County of Chester and the County of Philadelphia starting at Darby Mill Creek and bearing down towards the Schuylkill. Very convenient for a surveyor, but the idea was soon scotched, for as Thomas Lloyd had explained to the Provincial Council this would mean cutting across land belonging to some of the Welsh Quakers, leaving the township of Meirion on the east in the County of Philadelphia, and the townships of Radnor and Haverford on the west side in the County of Chester. In a word, the Welsh Tract would be split down the middle. The Councillors had accepted his argument and the matter had been dropped. Why then did Thomas Holme mention it again? No two ways about it, he was an old fox. If his intention was to bring the matter again before the Provincial Council in Thomas Lloyd's absence, he could claim that he *had* mentioned it to Lloyd before his departure for New York. By mentioning only Mill Creek, and omitting the word 'boundary line' he had hoped that Lloyd would not notice what he was up to. His strategy had been only too successful.

Thomas Lloyd looked out of the window of the coach at the land around him that was passing by painfully slowly. He knew the postillion was doing his best to hurry, for now and again he was hurled against the side of the coach as it bounced over a boulder in the road. This at least served as a painful reminder that it was impossible to drive more quickly. He tried to control his uneasiness and wait patiently for the journey's end.

When at last he arrived in Philadelphia he did not waste time by going to his house but instead went straight to the Council Chamber. When he opened the door he saw that Councillor John Symcock was on his feet. He had his back towards Thomas Lloyd, so the latter sat down quietly in a back seat without being seen, intending to move forward at the end of the speech. Looking around him he realised, not for the first time, that there was not one Welshman on the Provincial Council. It was partly their own fault of course, he thought with a quiet sigh. They were all so concerned about their own Tract and so busy planning its administration that they tended to trust to Thomas Lloyd alone to care for their welfare in the Council. Friend Symcock was rather long-winded at the best of times. For a while Thomas Lloyd had been unable to follow the trend of his reasoning, nor indeed did he know the nature of his subject. But he suddenly heard the name 'John Eckley.' Symcock was enjoying himself now, stressing his words slowly and deliberately.

'. . . his land divides conveniently to add to the fifteen plantations of Radnor, and the same is true of the lands of . . . Um . . .' looking down at the paper in his hand — 'Rowland Ellis and John Humphreys . . . The line, therefore, is a straight one, cutting right across country through land earmarked by William Penn for his own children and stretching up to the Schuylkill where it takes a turn to the north—west . . .'

John Symcock sat down to murmurs of agreement. Thomas Lloyd felt himself become cold with anger. He got up and walked across to the middle of the Chamber, ignoring Thomas Holme who had jumped to his feet on seeing him.

'I came back too soon for some of my friends here I see,' he said. 'But clearly none to soon to save injury to my Welsh friends.'

124

In the stunned silence which followed, he turned his sharp, penetrating gaze on Thomas Holme.

'May I ask, Friend Thomas, if the Welsh were warned about the intention to raise this question today?'

Holme muttered that there was nothing in the Constitution stipulating that a warning should be given.

'And since when have Quakers searched the Constitution to administer justice and brotherly love?' thundered Thomas Lloyd. 'Strange indeed that the Lord led me back here today just in time to spoil your plans.'

Some of the Councillors rose in protest at the harsh words.

'The Welsh have been shouting long enough for the boundaries to be fixed,' complained Holme. 'Honestly, there is no way of pleasing them.'

'Thou, Thomas Lloyd, art one of those who have been pressing for getting things in order,' said John Symcock in a mild enough voice.

'Yes, but what order is there without justice? You all know well enough that unity is very important to the Welsh, and that our gracious Founder recognised this and gave his word that their wishes were to be respected. But for that promise, these Welshmen would never have left their homes.'

George Keith was on his feet now, his eyes surly in his strong face, his school-masterly bearing giving one the impression that he believed he and he alone was right.

'I, for one, am tired of hearing over and over again of William Penn's promise to the Welsh. We are the ones who are in charge now, we, the Councillors, elected by the freeholders of this state. Our concern is for the good of the whole state, not the whim of a small group of people who insist on keeping themselves apart from the rest of us. We all have to learn to live together to avoid divisive actions; and our only yardstick should be the welfare of the majority.'

Thomas Lloyd answered very quietly, but the emotion in his voice was there for all to hear.

'When an Englishman speaks of us living together in peace and understanding, what he really means is that others should conform to his standards. Friends, try to understand our point of view. Among us are hundreds of people who speak no English at all. Welsh was the language of their upbringing, Welsh is the language of their homes, Welsh is the language of their prayers. They saw no need to learn English to come here. If you split up these people among strangers, they will wither away like uprooted flowers. As for the rest of us, those of us who are fluent in other languages, why, for us, too, the Welsh language, and our own customs are the very essence of our existence. Should the day dawn when the Welsh themselves decide that they want to be swallowed up in a larger state, then, and only then, will you have the right to run your boundaries through their lands. But until that day dawns, your intention is a cruel encroachment on their rights.'

An uncomfortable silence fell on the Chamber. Then Doctor John Gordon rose.

'Friends, if these promises were made to the Welsh by William Penn, then what has just been said by Thomas Lloyd is right. It is possible that the difference in language between us has caused some misunderstanding. There is only one way to settle this matter once and for all, and that is for us to write to William Penn himself and ask for his ruling.'

Thomas felt the tension ooze out of him. In spite of everything that had happened, his faith in the Founder still glowed warmly deep inside him. He had such vision, his humanity was so all-embracing. He had clung so fixedly to his early idealism. The Welsh would have a ready ear when Penn heard of their difficulties.

The Provincial Council accepted John Gordon's proposal with alacrity, albeit against the wishes of Thomas Holme and George Keith. Thomas suddenly realised how tired he felt, and left without waiting to speak to the other councillors. As he came down the wide staircase outside the Council Chamber he was greeted in Welsh by a young stranger, a man of about thirty, who had obviously been waiting for him.

'I must apologise for my inadequate Welsh,' he said with a smile, adding in English: 'I've been living in London since I was very young. My name is David Lloyd, one of your relatives from Manafon.'

Thomas studied the rather wide face, the honest, brown eyes, the strong mouth and the short sturdy body. He noticed that the young man wore an attorney's suit.

'Rebecca's son!'

The young attorney's eyes lit up.

'Yes, Rebecca's son. And you are my great benefactor.'

So he knew. Thomas Lloyd had never intended that anyone should know of the assistance he had given his cousin and her child, when she had been abandoned by the child's father. Her own family had refused to forgive her for bringing dishonour on them, and although Thomas was only a very young man at the time, he had been unable to bear the look of despair on Rebecca's face. So he had given her all the money he had, which was little enough − he was only sixteen at the time − and later on had been able to do more for her. When the boy was nine, Thomas had paid for him to go to London to receive instruction in law. Rebecca died soon afterwards, and he had heard nothing more of the child. But here he was now, in Pennsylvania. What a strange world it was.

'I was waiting to speak with you before you went into the Council Chamber,' explained David. 'I have a letter for you from William Penn.'

This was surprising news.

'Oh, so thou art acquainted with the Founder?'

'I worked in his lawyers' offices in London for many years. With some success.' The young man tried hard not to sound too boastful. 'His decision to send me here was taken very suddenly. Our being related probably had something to do with it.'

Thomas read the letter which explained that William Penn was sending this brilliant young lawyer, David Lloyd, to the Colony to be its Attorney General. The Founder apologised for not having given prior warning of his intention, but since the new Attorney was related to Thomas Lloyd, the latter would scarcely doubt the good intentions of his friend William Penn.

Thomas's mind was a turmoil of conflicting emotions. On the one hand he was truly happy to see his young cousin, proud of his success, but . . . why send an Attorney General all of a sudden? He found it difficult to believe that David Lloyd of all people was just one more spy, but he could not comprehend why anyone should have been imposed upon him in this way without warning.

'On the whole this is a trouble-free state. Did Penn give thee any indication as to what thy first duties might be?'

The young man answered openly enough.

'During the last three years my work has all been to do with the legal side of this colony — matters like drawing up deeds, warrants and land transfers. And of course we had to examine the different governmental measures which were of particular relevance to Penn in his dealings here. To be frank, he felt, that Pennsylvania lacked a legal representative sufficiently versed in English law.'

But Thomas Lloyd was not listening to this last sentence. He was thinking of something that had been said earlier.

'What governmental measures would be likely to be of interest to Penn?' he asked carefully. 'For example . . .?'

'Well, the law of *quo waranto* for one thing.' The young man hastened to explain, when he saw that Thomas Lloyd did not understand. 'Some of the colonies are extremely unruly — you would be surprised! *Quo waranto* are the measures taken to strengthen their dependence on the crown.'

The curfew bell struck nine above the market, and a night watchman hurried past on his way to make sure the seven taverns were closed.

'It's obvious there's no lawlessness in Pennsylvania,' laughed David Lloyd. He turned to look down the Delaware to where the *Amity* lay at anchor.

'There are one or two matters, nothing very serious, but nevertheless they are important enough in Penn's eyes. I arrived here on that ship yesterday — and it seemed quite possible that casks of wine and rum arrived at the same time and never went through the customs. And who can swear on oath that there is no vast cargo of tobacco down in the bowels of the *Amity* this very minute, ready to sail tomorrow? There has been a dangerous degree of laxity in the administering of trade and transport regulations here. That is my first task — to see that these things come under definite control.'

128

David said all this without any hint of reproval in his voice. Both men knew that the Founder himself had been too tolerant of such things in the past, and that it was only natural that his successor should be equally tolerant. Now things had changed, and Penn was anxious to get his hands on every ha'penny. It would be much easier for a stranger to tighten things up than to leave all the responsibility to the Deputy.

Thomas could see that David had no idea that his arrival could cause any disquiet to the Deputy Governor. His conscience pricked him for having allowed such thoughts to enter his mind, and he gave the young man a warm invitation to his home. During the conversation they had that night Thomas Lloyd learnt that the lawyer had been trained in the Chambers of Judge Jeffreys, and that his work there had attracted the attention of William Penn. His admiration for Penn was sincere and absolute, and he was unequivocally on Penn's side in his attempts to secure his taxes and his rights. The law, he said, had to be administered severely against those who refused to pay. It was a very thoughtful Thomas who went to bed that night.

Sion Ifan and Lowri were married in the splendid autumn of that year. The red maple trees glowed in the warm sun. Lowri wore a grey dress of fine wool striped with green. With her own hand she had embroidered silken silver flowers along the hem and on the sleeves. On her head she wore the straw hat, temporarily bereft of its roses, but adorned instead with grey ribbon. It was a less plain bridal outfit than that worn by most Quaker women, but yet not so showy as to attract undue attention from even the most orthodox of friends.

Sion Ifan looked very unnatural in his Quaker hat and his dark sober suit, thought Robin Wynn. Poor man, poor in every respect. He remembered Lowri on the ship, a bundle of sea-sickness, wrapped in a woollen shawl, with hardly a word to say for herself. Fancy my thinking she was the weaker of the two, he mused, wryly. What this one wants she gets — if that is what strength is. And then he laughed quietly savouring the humour of the moment, for there was one thing that Lowri had failed to get and that was Robin Wynn himself.

He realised that she had made every effort to attract him, short of offering herself to him outright. There was that time when she had insisted on Robin accompanying her home from Meeting, taking hold of his arm, with a pretty fuss because she was afraid of slipping on the ice. What was Sion Ifan doing, he had asked jokingly, neglecting his duty and allowing his sweetheart to venture out on the ice alone? Oh, he preferred to go after some old wild pigeons in the woods — and the big eyes turned upon him as innocent as an angel's.

'To tell thee truth, Robin Wynn, Sion is a bit of a lout, isn't he?' Then why in the name of all that was reasonable was she marrying him, he wanted to know.

'Oh, I'm so weak. Really my greatest fault is that I have too soft a heart. Sion Ifan was so insistent, and I . . . so lonely . . . And, Robin, it's so easy for a woman who is used to having a loving husband to say yes — and to regret it afterwards.'

They had reached the gate to her house now, and Lowri stopped for a moment, standing very close to him, her head reached his shoulder.

'Have you heard his laugh? It's like a . . . like a dog barking. Not at all gentlemanly. Then, there's the way he eats . . .'

The tears came easily to her eyes.

'*Thou* art different.'

He managed to take a step back, and, opening the gate, said in a light-hearted manner: 'Not as different as all that, Lowri. Remember I'm a farmer too now.' And then felt bound to add: 'I'm very fond of Sion Ifan. He deserves . . .'

He was going to say 'better' but his innate courtesy made him change it to 'the best.' But Lowri was intelligent enough to see that she had made a mistake and, with a slight shrug, left him rather abruptly. After that he had hardly spoken to her.

Where is Dorti? He searched for her among the crowd of people milling around the bride and bridegroom.

It was not the custom of the Quakers to indulge in celebrating, even after a wedding, but today about half a dozen young men stood joking with Sion Ifan and then started to race with each other. They had looked very self-conscious to begin with, as

130

if they were doing something very daring — as indeed they were. But they were not all Quakers, nor the children of Quakers, and to be forced to refrain from old marriage customs was for them an unnatural curb, especially with such a fun-loving man as Sion Ifan as bridegroom.

The bridegroom himself was now calling for a tankard of beer for everyone, and his healthy laugh could be heard above all the noise. Robin saw that Lowri was not denying him this today. She was smiling sweetly at everybody in general and Sion Ifan in particular. Someone found a broom and one of the boys started to dance a traditional clog-dance. If Huw Roberts and some of the others had their doubts about all this merry-making on what ought to be a sober occasion, they must have decided to ignore their feelings for the time being.

'Have you seen Dorti Llwyd?' Robin asked Tomos Owen.

'I think she's gone to see Lisa,' replied Tomos.

'Why? Isn't Lisa here?'

'No. She woke up with a bad headache this morning, so I had to leave her behind. Dorti asked about her, and said that she'd go and call.'

Strange that she had left the wedding when she was related so closely to the bride. Perhaps she felt that this wedding had come too soon after her brother's death. Or were the memories of that marriage still too painful for her? He swore at himself quietly for letting such thoughts lurk in his head even for one moment. That was the measures of Lowri's poison, and the sting had gone deep. But Dorti was difficult to know — not at all his sort of woman. He told himself angrily that he did not care for these clever, deep, intense women. All too often there was a humourless condemnation of everyone and everything in their whole attitude and bearing . . . But he kept on gazing towards Lisa's house with a strange pain inside him.

'. . . There'll be no other man in Dorti Llwyd's life. Dost thou understand what I'm trying to say . . .'

But he had put those thoughts out of his mind. He knew that they were malicious lies. Was he not experienced enough to know whether a woman was interested in him as a man or not?

131

That secret glance, that ready blush on her cheek? She liked him; he could swear to that.

And yet she was always very unwilling to discuss things on a personal level. Was this simply the natural modesty of a Quaker girl? Perhaps. No, hardly. There was some mystery here, and this pain would be with him until it was solved.

The merry making came to an end. When Sion Ifan himself tried the clog-dance with the others, Huw Roberts felt impelled to remind him that Quakers did not care for frivolity before, during or after the marriage ceremony. Sion accepted the reproach, and returned to Lowri's side. Everyone was preparing to leave.

It's only natural for a sister to love her brother, especially when they both had so much in common. That's perfectly reasonable. And if that brother dies, why, again, its only natural the sister should feel the loss profoundly.

'. . . There'll be no other man in Dorti Llwyd's life . . .'

'Damn that woman!'

Robin Wynn did not know if he had said the words out loud or not, but he started off in the direction of the cabin called Red Pass.

Dusk was falling and the trees were taking on strange magic shapes. It was good to have the night come to hide the darkness of his thoughts. His heart was beating uncomfortably, and when he put his hand to his forehead he could feel the sweat heavy on his brow.

Tomos and Lisa's cabin stood before him like Pandora's box holding all the world's secrets. As he reached it he hesitated briefly, then with new determination knocked at the door.

Dorti herself answered. She stood there, the lamp-light in the room behind outlining her body. When she saw who it was she opened the door wider and invited him in.

'It's Robin Wynn, Lisa,' she called over her shoulder, and he was delighted to hear the note of pleasure in her voice. 'Lisa has a headache,' she explained.

'It's you I've come to see,' whispered Robin. 'I don't want to worry Lisa. I'll wait outside until you're ready to leave.'

Dorti glanced enquiringly at him. Where was the debonair

132

young man? The teasing smile had disappeared, so had the lazy bearing and the flippancy. Something serious was worrying him.

'I was about to leave,' she said softly. 'Rhys is sleeping quietly now. He will not trouble Lisa any more. Wait a moment.'

She went into the bedroom and Robin could hear the women whispering quietly so as not to wake the child. Then Dorti came out, wrapping a shawl around her shoulders.

'Tomos will be home soon. I'm ready to come now.'

They both walked quietly out of the house and continued in silence for a while. Dorti tried to guess what it was that Robin Wynn wanted with her, though her thoughts kept on returning to Lisa's pale tearful face. Although the reason for her sorrow was not discussed, Dorti could sense what was wrong with her friend. She felt strangely united with her that evening. Lisa too had had to hide her true feelings.

Robin glanced at her from the corner of his eye. How can I find out? Dorti should be free now of her secret obligation to her brother's widow. There's nothing left to prevent my asking her to marry me. He realised suddenly that that was what he wanted. What if she were to refuse him? What if she were to accept him? How would he know that he wasn't just second best? If he were not able to discuss Lowri's insinuations openly with her now, those insinuations would rise like some apparition to plague him every time he had cause to doubt her. And how was he to broach it? Before long they would have reached Huw Roberts's house and the chance to speak would be lost. What a quiet girl she was. She was walking beside him now like some wraith. What was she thinking about? Not about him, he was sure of that. Her distant thoughts had nothing whatsoever to do with him.

'What are you thinking about?'

He was surprised how hoarse his voice was. It sounded strange in his own ears, but Dorti replied as if she had noticed nothing.

'About Lisa.'

The blood rose in him, he grasped her wrist till she winced.

'Don't you ever think of me?'

It was not yet too dark for him to see the surprise in her eyes. She looked at him as if he were a stranger.

'Thou art hurting me . . . Robin . . .'

'Don't you know how much you are hurting me?'

Suddenly his arms were around her and his body pressed tightly against hers. She tried to draw back, but there was an unusual strength in his newly developed muscles, a strength which surprised and pleased him. He closed his lips clumsily on her unwilling mouth, so hard that he could feel his teeth biting the soft flesh. She tried to turn her head away — first to one side, then the other to escape his greedy tongue, but more than anything to escape the wild look in his eyes.

'Robin . . .'

Her reluctance and the strangled scream drove him almost out of his mind.

'Stop it!'

He pushed her away suddenly, and shouted, almost in tears: 'You prefer the dead arms of your brother!'

Dorti fell to the ground, and his passion disappeared as if someone had thrown cold water over him. He stood there staring at her, a cold fear beginning to take hold of him. What had he done? What had come over him? He felt himself shake all over. He had never intended to lose control like this . . .

'Dorti . . .'

He fell on his knees beside her. She lay as she had fallen but her eyes were now open. He saw the fear in them.

'What . . . what didst thou say?' she whispered, staring at him as a frightened animal stares at its captor.

'Dorti, I implore you . . . forget what I said.' Dear God, why did I have to open my mouth? What came over me?

'Dorti . . .'

That was all he could say. He could not bear the bruised look in her eyes.

'What didst thou say?'

Robin shook his head and closed his eyes.

'Forget . . .'

But neither of them would never forget. She had turned away from him, and was staring into the forest.

'What did Lowri say to thee?'

Robin stretched out his hand and gently turned her face towards him. This time she let him, as if she had no will of her own left.

He spoke softly.

'Lowri is a malicious lying vixen.'

She shut her eyes, forcing herself to speak. 'She has every reason to hate me.'

'I don't believe it.'

'Thou must.'

Her voice was tired.

'Since she has already told thee so much . . .'

'She hardly said anything . . . honestly.'

'I'm free to tell thee everything now.'

'I don't want to hear.'

'But thou must. There's no choice.'

She rose painfully, and went to sit on a tree stump.

'No—' when he moved forward to help her. 'I can speak more easily if I'm not too close to thee.'

There was a long silence, and then slowly Dorti began to speak.

'We lost our parents when we were very young, Thomas and I, we were brought up by an old aunt. I suppose one reason we were both so close was because of the difference in age between her and us. I always knew what was in his mind before he'd say a word, and it was the same with him. Quite often I would say something and he would break in — "That's exactly what I was going to say." '

Dorti glanced up briefly. 'I'm explaining all this to stress that I know — *know* — there was no deception in him. The only real difference between us was the pure innocence of him which made him believe the best of everybody. I wasn't like that I'm afraid. I am sceptical by nature, and this has caused me much unhappiness.

'His poetry was my delight, right from the start. It was I who copied out his work and accompanied him to poetry contests. We would meet other poets and learn the history of the Britons and their ancient poetry. What wonderful days

135

they were! We felt that we, a band of young poets, were keeping alive the flame of independence in our country . . .' She drew in her breath as if drawing in reins to curb herself from continuing along those lines. Then she went on in that flat emotionless voice.

'Lowri was the daughter of one of the servants at Cefn-dderwen, the farm next to ours — not that she was any the worse for that,' she added quickly, misunderstanding the look of surprise on Robin's face. 'Her mother had died and her father had married a woman from the next valley. The two women did not get on at all and Lowri used to complain that her step-mother was very unkind to her. I was inclined to think at the time there must be fault on both sides. However, Thomas got to hear of it, began to feel sorry for her and invited her to call. There were strange rumours, very unpleasant ones, going around about her in the village, and when I saw that Thomas's sympathy was developing into something deeper, I was very unhappy. Didn't I say I had a very suspicious mind? Thomas used to reproach me about it. He himself never had a bad thought about anybody, and when I ventured to hint at what I had heard, he lost his temper completely for the first time ever. I couldn't bear that, so I decided not to say another word against her, unless I had absolute proof.

'When the local people heard that Thomas was going to marry Lowri, many of them came to me to beg me try and persuade him not to, and I heard all the bad stories about her all over again. In the end I saw that the only way I could regain my peace of mind was to go and ask Lowri herself if there was any truth in what I had heard. So one evening when Thomas was out I ventured to do so. She burst into tears and said that her step-mother was responsible for spreading those lies about her. It was her step-mother, she said, who gave welcome to all the drovers who passed through the village, and her way of hiding this was to put the blame on Lowri. She reproached me for listening to such slander. I had no idea, she said, of the suffering she had to endure at home.

'I felt dreadful. I knew that she was only a flighty butterfly of a creature and that she could never be worthy of my brother,

136

but I was sure now that she had been misrepresented by everybody, and I accepted that the marriage was something that was to be. Oh, I admit I wasn't over fond of her, that we had nothing much to say to each other, but I tried my best. What I found most difficult to bear was the way she belittled Thomas's poetry behind his back, and the grumbling every time we went together to a poetry contest. But Thomas saw no fault in her, and if he was happy, I was content . . . well, at least I kept quiet. But at times it was difficult, for Lowri tried to turn Thomas against me in every way possible. I was bad tempered, I was jealous — there was nothing right with me. Perhaps she was right too — but it was hard to watch Thomas grow away from me.

'After he had been converted by John ap John, *she* pretended to be converted too. No . . . I'm being unfair again. She *was* converted. But she lacked Thomas's deep convictions, and she kept on complaining to him that he no longer took her to fairs or dancing. But on that score Thomas stood absolutely firm. His new faith forbade it, much as he desired to please his wife.

'I should not have listened to the new rumours that reached my ears. That was where I went wrong. Perhaps,' Dorti continued her painful self-analysis, 'perhaps I was too eager to listen. Perhaps I was avid for proof in order to convince Thomas that it was I who had been right from the start. I heard the name of Jack the mole-catcher, from more than one person. He was a great hulk of a man with a name for beating his wife when drunk. Another of the step-mother's lies, I told myself, when I first got to hear his name coupled with Lowri's. I could hardly imagine her demeaning herself so far as to go with such a brute of a man. But the rumours kept on growing. The whole thing disgusted me . . . Thomas was being cuckolded, Lowri was sharing his bed. I would wake up in the night thinking — is she with Thomas, or with the mole-catcher? Canst thou understand my feelings? It was a sin, wasn't it, feeling like that? I hated her — that was my sin. I was ready to do anything to open Thomas's eyes. But what *could* I do?

'Then he decided that they should both go over to Pennsylvania. I was determined to find out the truth before they

137

left, and one night, about a month before they were due to leave, I decided to follow her.'

The silence was so prolonged that Robin began to doubt whether Dorti could go on. He was afraid to move in case she changed her mind and refused to say any more. He knew now that he had to have the whole truth. Now she was speaking again — her voice once more under control: 'I had chosen a moonlit night so that I could follow her from afar without her seeing me. Thomas was away at one of his poetry meetings — he no longer allowed me to accompany him. When I saw Lowri getting ready to go out, I knew that this was the time to test her.

'I'm going to call on Tabitha Sion,' she said as she left. 'She's got a fever.'

She was the last person to want to visit the sick, and this added fuel to my suspicion, I followed her down the path, as she turned towards the village, and for a while I had no trouble in keeping her in sight. But the shadows of moonlight are very deceptive, and before long I had to admit that I had lost her. I went straight to Tabitha's house. Lowri wasn't there. I thought — either she had not yet arrived or she had no intention whatsoever of coming here. So I stayed for a while to talk to the old woman, just to make sure. But Lowri did not appear. Then I started back, certain by now that she had gone to meet Jack the mole-catcher. That was all I could think of. If only I could see them with my own eyes, I thought — well, I did not really know what I should do but I had to *know*.

'On my way home I had to go past Cefndderwen barn, and as I drew near I heard voices, and low, muffled laughter. I could have sworn that one of the voices was Lowri's. As if someone else were urging me on I crept to the door of the barn. The moon's rays were strong enough for me to be able to make out two figures lying there in the hay — one very small, and the other a giant of a man. I had to stop looking, I wanted to vomit. It was then that I ran and ran, until I reached home. It had started to rain heavily and all I wanted to do now was to get to my bedroom and shut the door on everything and everyone, so that I could just cry. I knew I could never tell Thomas after all.

'But he was there, in the kitchen, come home hours earlier than I'd expected. The first thing he asked me was "Where's Lowri?", and I felt angry with him for not noticing my wet clothes and my dishevelled hair, and the bruise on my face where I banged myself against the barn door. I replied that she had said she was going to visit Tabitha Sion. Thomas knew immediately from my tone of voice that I had not believed her. He began to scold me, saying I was always unfair to Lowri, that she was right when she said I was jealous of her . . . he went on and on . . . it was horrible. I cannot repeat all the hurtful things he said to me that night. Then I began to shout at him: "Thy wife is a slut! If thou dost not believe me go and see what's going on in the barn at Cefndderwen!" As long as I live I shall never forget his face. He became so pale I was afraid he was going to faint. Then without waiting to put on hat or coat against the rain, he rushed out of the house. In that moment I saw that he too had his doubts, but that he was refusing to admit them even to himself.

'Of course there was no one in the barn. Whoever it was had probably heard me — they had plenty of time to leave in any case. Even now, I don't know who I saw there. But it could not have been Lowri.'

For the first time Robin Wynn interrupted her:

'How can you be so sure?'

'Thomas came back wet through, but refusing to change. He was like a man demented, striding backwards and forwards, refusing to say a word to me. When I was just beginning to feel that the strain was more than I could bear, Lowri came back, smiling and looking very neat and accompanied by her father. It was he who said she had called at her old home on the way to see Tabitha Sion, and he had brought her back now since the weather had turned so bad.'

She turned to look searchingly at Robin, as if challenging him to deny this.

'So she could not possibly have been in the barn with the mole-catcher.'

She went on: 'Thomas was like a man whose treasure had been returned to him. He couldn't do enough for her that night . . . and I was glad to see him happy once more.'

'And you, Dorti Llwyd?'

'Oh . . . the shame . . . the guilt . . . And then, next morning, Thomas had a fever. He was never robust and his constitution was not able to withstand the wet clothes and his cold. By evening he was worse . . . and it was all my fault . . .

'When . . . when he knew he was going to die he called me to him. He said, "Dorti thou art strong, and Lowri is as delicate as a violet in the wind. Thou must promise to take care of her . . . to stay with her . . . Promise?" And then those awful words of judgement on me. "Do this . . . to make amends for the harm thou hast done her . . . for my sake . . ." '

She was sobbing now. Robin felt a wave of impatience with the brother — and such stupidity, to enslave his sister on his deathbed.

'Well, you are free now.'

'Yes,' but her voice was uncertain.

'Tell me one thing . . . you are absolutely certain that the father was not protecting his daughter that evening?'

She turned on him fiercely.

'Do not *say* such things. Of course I cannot be sure, but I *have* to believe it because Thomas believed it . . .'

Robin looked at her strangely, but it was dark now and Dorti did not see the look. Much later that night he asked himself what had prevented him from asking her to marry him, as he had fully intended to do.

140

CHAPTER SEVEN

The great bird was black against the clear winter sky. It flew gracefully over the snow towards the door of the barn, its wildness tamed by hunger. A grail, thought Ellis, how strange to see one in winter. In Wales it would, in the order of things, have flown far away by now. But here, in this huge strange land, nature could not expect to be the same as anywhere else. This spendid frightening country was stronger than nature itself. Stronger than a man's nature too.

The bird hopped nearer the fence where the wind's direction had prevented the snow from piling high. Ellis noticed that Lisa had carefully put out chaff and grain for the birds, the one to feed them, the other to prevent their feet from freezing to the earth. He smiled to himself. That was one thing Lisa had been consistent in over the years, her love for the 'beasts of the field and the birds of the air.' Sometimes it was difficult to guess what was in her mind. She was certainly calmer now, but that was not always a sign of happiness. We all change as we get older, some of us become more sober, some more sour, and the devil always at hand to bend man to his own intentions.

The devil had walked beside him many times, hissing bitter words in his ear, offering him the escape of depression. His soul had shouted out for the relief of tears. But Dorcas's voice was in his ear too, supporting him, girding him, giving him strength to renounce himself. Her love threw a revealing light on the devil's intentions. Oh, Satan had a strong foot in this fair land. Ellis had seen fine men transformed. No sooner had they reached here than they had become obsessed with schemes to swell their material wealth. God had set a feast before them — abundant plains, gushing waterfalls, streams to irrigate the soil, orchards whose like had never been seen in Wales, woods calling out to be used for the good of man. And then the Devil would come and set a veil between the eye and the soul, whispering 'Take, take . . . more, more, more . . .' Giving no hint that one day he would come to claim payment. Could the Old Man prosper in this paradise, where prison and pain had failed in the days of their adversity?

Ellis raised the latch, opened the door carefully, and called out 'Lisa!' Her answer came from the back, and in a moment she was hurrying forward to greet her step-father.

'Ellis Puw! Come on in. It's freezing . . . go to the fire to thaw out . . .' She spoke warmly, but Ellis noticed, not for the first time, the watchful eyes trying not to betray true feelings.

'I've called to see why you two were not at Meeting today.'

Rhys ran in from the back and climbed up on Ellis Puw's lap. 'I've got a bow and arrow of my very own. Uncle Sion gave them to me.'

'Where's Tomos? Is he ill?'

Lisa poked the fire fussily, her words deliberately unconcerned.

'He's gone up to the northern forest to have a look around. He heard there was good land available there.'

Ellis spoke slowly. 'Isn't he venturing a bit? They say the Indians up there are rather wild.'

Lisa laughed, but Ellis discerned an uneasiness in her voice.

'Oh, Sion Ifan understands the Indians. They're easy enough to deal with if you give them a few beads and baubles.'

'So Sion Ifan has gone with him?'

'Yes.'

Lisa turned round to stir something in the pot behind her. Her hair was partly hidden, rather untidily, under her cap.

She's getting to be very like her mother, thought Ellis, smiling. But there were bony hollows where the rosy cheeks used to be. He only half-noticed this for his thoughts were on something else.

'I'm not sure I like the way we treat the Indians.'

'Why?' Lisa rounded him sharply. 'Sion Ifan would never

142

treat anyone badly,' she said, adding more slowly 'nor Tomos neither.'

'No, of course they wouldn't,' said Ellis calmly. 'But it is so easy to strike a bargain with such simple people, we must guard against taking advantage of them.'

'They're not so simple. Haven't they been stealing and killing Huw Roberts's pigs?'

They all quoted this when trying to justify deceiving the Indians, but Ellis remained silent for fear of rousing Lisa's temper again. Was is not their duty as Quakers to show primitive people the highest standards and not measure behaviour by the Indians' own yard stick. So many things to disappoint one in this land, he sighed for the hundredth time. He still recalled the shock of seeing black slaves for sale in the market in Philadelphia.

'But Friends treat them compassionately. If *we* had not bought them they would have fallen into the hands of bad masters . . . They would suffer much more if they were set free . . .' It was so easy to find moral excuses. As easy as it was for a poor man like him to criticise the rich.

'Tomos was saying that Rowland Ellis bought another hundred acres.'

'So he really has bought them, has he?'

'Why? Is this news to thee?'

'No. I did not realise he had already done so.'

The previous week Rowland had been telling Ellis about the interest in this land. Ellis had ventured to mention something he had on his mind for a long time. He flushed now, realising how presumptuous his words must have sounded. Rowland however was not only his master but also his spiritual brother, so that he had to speak out about his concern at the way so many Quakers were allowing themselves to think only of possessions.

'I, too Ellis Puw?'

Rowland had not held the implied rebuke against him. That was his great strength. He did not consider his behaviour above the criticisms of men such as Ellis Puw.

'But if I do not buy the land it will fall into the hands of another Englishman like Thomas Barker. The Welsh must buy as much land as possible within the Welsh Tract, we have to close our ranks to make sure that thou and others like thee can live here faithful to your roots, and to your own language.'

Ellis Puw was honest enough to admit the validity of this argument. From now on he must try not to doubt his master's motives. But where was the money coming from to pay for this new undertaking? Ellis did not know the details of Rowland Ellis's estate as well as Tomos did, but one need not be a genius to know that it took time for land to pay for itself. Ready money was in short supply here. Indeed it had been rumoured that money was so short that some of the Colonists had started minting their own, but Ellis knew nothing of such things. All he knew was that he was concerned for Rowland Ellis.

'When dost thou expect them back?'

'Oh . . . they could arrive tonight, or tomorrow perhaps, there's no telling when they go out like this.'

But Lisa's voice was trembling, and Ellis looked at her more closely. He almost asked 'Is Lowri willing for Sion Ifan to go off like this and they so recently married?' But he changed his mind and asked instead:

'When did they go this time?'

The effect of this simple question was astounding. Lisa ran up to him and fell on her knees hiding her face in his rough coat. Rhys began to cry, but Lisa took no notice.

'Oh Ellis, I'm so worried.' Her voice was low. 'The two of them have been gone for three days. They've never been away as long as this before. Dost 'ee think something could have happened to them?'

'Lisa dear, 'ee should have told me sooner.'

She lifted her face and looked at him, searching his eyes greedily for consolation. 'It was Tomos who told me not to tell anyone in case someone else got there first. Ellis . . . I was all right until 'ee started talking about the Indians. Dost 'ee think some harm can have come to them?'

'I cannot say, my dear.' He could not tell a lie even to comfort her.

'The snow came so quickly. It didn't start until last night.'

144

'It's not too thick. Possibly they've gone to shelter in some cabin somewhere.'

Ellis got up. 'But I'd better go and tell Rowland Ellis.'

'No, don't.'

Lisa was torn between her promise to Tomos and her worry. His temper had been uncertain of late, especially when anything stood in his way. If she were to send men after them now, she had no idea how he would react, especially if his personal plans were to be spoilt as a result.

'Sion Ifan knows those forests like a beaver,' she said, regaining her composure. 'He can speak to the Indians in their own language, did 'ee know that?'

Come to think of it, thought Ellis, if there were any real cause for concern, Lowri would already have missed her husband and spoken to Huw Roberts or someone. And had he not just seen her walking from the Meeting House with Siencyn Morris's son, and heard her light-hearted laughter as he he helped her over the snow?

He should go home and tell Sinai he was going to keep Lisa company for a while. He would not mention Tomos's absence – although he did wish he could tell Rowland Ellis. But Lisa was so insistent, Ellis got the impression that Tomos did not particularly want Rowland Ellis to know of his plans. He wondered why.

None of the Quakers had ever hidden anything from each other in the old days. For a moment, Ellis Puw hated this new country with all his being. It was contaminating them, cooling their ardour, encouraging greed . . . much better for all of them to have stayed in Wales in spite of the poverty and the persecution. He remembered his dream at Milford Haven when the Lord told him that there was still work for him to do in Wales, and his heart leapt joyfully at the thought of seeing the quiet Wnion again, the clouds above Cader Idris and Rhobell Fawr, the buckbeans and sundrew on Tir Stent . . . This land would stretch out its claws to grab his soul too if he stayed too long.

If Sinai suspected there was something wrong when Ellis told her he was going straight back to Lisa's house, she did not show it.

When he returned to Red Pass Lisa was still pacing backwards and forwards restlessly. Taking hold of her hands, he gradually felt her calm down. He threw a log on the low fire and the two of them watched the little flames begin to lick at it. The twilight was closing around them but Lisa did not bother to go and light the lamp. It would have been a cosy picture had not the place been full of Lisa's mute anxiety.

'Dost 'ee think it is possible to stop loving someone?' she asked suddenly. Ellis knew instinctively that his reply was of the utmost importance to her, and he delayed answering for a long time.

'I believe that all human relationships change – they either deepen or they fade away altogether. The only thing which remains constant is God's love.'

But Lisa did not want to speak of God's love. She threw Rhys a hurried glance to see if he was listening. She did not want him to start crying again. But he was playing happily with Uncle Sion's big bow.

'Ellis, dost 'ee think a wife can help it when she stops loving her husband?'

He looked troubled. 'What art thou trying to say, Lisa?'

She was looking down at her apron and when she spoke he could hardly hear her. He noticed again how thin she was, her shoulder blades were sticking out and there were new lines on her forehead and around her eyes.

'Ellis, I've tried my very best. I wasn't going to admit even to myself that he had changed, that everything had changed . . . Perhaps I've changed too. Oh – I don't know . . . it's difficult to find words . . .'

She got up suddenly and started walking around the room, betraying openly now how agitated she was.

'Don't say that thou hast not noticed how much he has changed. Don't say it's all my fault. Ellis! . . . When he begins to talk of the cattle he is going to buy, and how many cheap acres he hopes to get his hands on, and which is the most worthless of his possessions that he can palm off on the Indians . . . hast 'ee noticed how his face becomes like one of his own cows? Dear God! When he talks like that I begin to feel that

146

my head's full of fleas. And I don't get one red cent for myself. Oh, I too, was keen enough in the beginning. Somehow this country makes one hard doesn't it? There's much here for the taking . . . hast 'ee not seen what is happening?'

Lisa stopped suddenly, and then smiled wryly at Ellis.

'What a question to ask *thee* of all people! If this country were to destroy thee, Ellis Puw, I would begin to think that the devil was stronger than God.'

'Lisa . . . don't talk like that.'

'It hasn't destroyed Sion Ifan either. He always says that if a man has enough to keep him from starving and enough to buy warm clothes against the cold, what more could he want? All possessions are a nuisance he says.' Lisa laughed more easily for the moment, but suddenly her face clouded again, and Ellis heard her say: 'At least, that's what he used to say.'

She turned suddenly and came near him. She took off her cap, and her fair hair fell loosely on her shoulders. Stretching to her full height, and smoothing her hands over her body slowly, she said:

'Dost 'ee remember how I used to be, Ellis Puw? There were plenty who wanted me once, weren't there? Perhaps some still do. Look! My waist is as small as ever. My breasts as white and strong and shapely. I'm twenty-eight . . . and that's not old. A little grey in my hair, that's all.' She closed her eyes and moved her head sensuously from side to side, like a cat wanting to be fondled.

'Ellis . . . look. Tomos doesn't see me . . . dost 'ee understand? I might as well be an old, yellowed one-eyed witch as far as he's concerned . . . All he sees in front of his nose day and night is soil.'

What could Ellis say? Who was he to blame Lisa for her carnal desires? He had not failed to notice how obsessed Tomos had become with his love of land. She had fallen on to her knees beside him again. 'Help me Ellis Puw . . . the devil knows my weaknesses so well.'

He still looked so young, he was so good. How could Ellis Puw understand her when he himself had never suffered this gnawing need? But he was her only hope. Her mother depended

147

on him, and Lisa too wanted to draw comfort from his virtue. Ellis searched for words. He would have liked to have been able to tell Lisa that only she herself with the help of God, could overcome this, and then only if she really wanted to. But everytime he tried to form his sentences they seemed hollow, for her feelings went beyond anything in his experience. He and Sinai had never had any bodily intercourse, and they had been able to live together quietly without making demands on each other. If Dorcas had been allowed to live perhaps . . .

But how could he now, in his virginity, advise Lisa? He stroked her hair mutely. Patience, my little one. These things pass. The next world is a richer one, there is no end to understanding . . .

All he said was:

'When Tomos returns I'll speak to him.' But as he spoke he felt her stiffen. She raised her head, listening. He too turned to listen, but could hear nothing.

'What's . . .'

'Listen!'

She jumped to her feet, ran to the window and threw it open. Eagerly her eyes searched the landscape, and then she gave a shout — almost a scream. 'Here he is, Ellis! He's back!'

'Tomos?'

Ellis rushed to the window.

'Sion Ifan!'

She was transformed. She rushed to the door, held it open wide, shouting and laughing with the tears running down her cheeks. She had forgotten all about Ellis.

'Sion! Where on earth hast 'ee been?'

'Hola!' he shouted back, waving his hand. One foot dragged after the other wearily through the snow, but he was smiling broadly.

'A blazing fire and a bottle of mead for a weary traveller!'

The words rang in Lisa's ears like bells across the snow.

'At thy service, sire,' she answered, her voice half laughing, half crying.

With a great stamping of feet to release the snow from his boots and clothes Sion Ifan stepped into the cabin. His eyes

148

were narrow as he tried to see in the darkness so bright had been the snow's reflection even at night. Peering at the man standing in the corner he gave a sudden shout of joy:

'Well, damn me, I *thought* you might have got here before me, you old devil!'

The other two looked at him in surprise, Lisa still laughing:

'Sion Ifan, don't be such a fool! That's Ellis Puw.'

Sion's eyes became serious immediately.

'Ellis Puw? Where's Tomos then?'

Lisa's smile disappeared. 'Isn't he with thee? When I saw thee laughing I thought . . .'

Sion rushed back to the door and stared out searching the darkness. He shouted out loud: 'Tomos!'

Nothing, not even the howl of a wolf answered him. The soft quilt of snow stretched out into the forest, silent and frightening.

'I could have sworn he was walking ahead of me.'

He remained standing at the door, his eyes like two arrows ready to shoot out into the darkness. A soft oath escaped him.

'The silly fool. I told him not to go back . . .'

On seeing Lisa's face he stopped, but he could not hide his anxiety.

'I must go back at once.' And he began to fasten his cloak again.

'Wait and have something to eat first,' pleaded Lisa.

'I'll come with thee,' said Ellis Puw. 'But Lisa's right, thou must eat first.'

'What is it, Sion?' asked Lisa, searching his face for some explanation. 'Something is worrying thee badly. Tell us.'

She turned towards him imploringly, and he suddenly gave in and agreed to sit down for a while.

'He couldn't have been far behind me. He should be here before I finish eating. All right then — just a crust and a drink.'

But Lisa was already heating the soup, and pouring out beer for him.

'Where have you both been all this time?'

Sion took a long draught from his tankard. 'Over towards the Blue Mountains.' He spoke rapidly. 'There's no time to explain properly now, but the Indian, Waneha, that was his name, he wasn't too satisfied with what Tomos was offering him for the land. You see, they're beginning to understand the value of things now. It developed into a bit of a row between them, and in the end Waneha refused to strike any sort of a bargain with Tomos. So I persuaded him to give up for the time being. I know these people — they're very stubborn, but they can be won over in time. It's patience that's needed. But Tomos was furious. He had set his mind on having that particular piece of land. On the way home he got the stupid idea of going back to Waneha's land and firing a few shots from his musket just to frighten him, he said, and show him who was the stronger. I thought I had managed to convince him how crazy that would be.'

Seeing the terror on Lisa's face he said hurriedly:

'I'm sure I did succeed too. It was just a stupid idea he got into his head in the heat of his disappointment. He wasn't serious!'

But in spite of his comforting words Sion left his food uneaten and began to put on his cloak again. He grasped his gun and stepped out into the darkness. Ellis Puw had lit a lantern, and he followed Sion while Lisa, with fear in her heart, stood at the door watching them disappear into the forest.

They scalped them. That's what they did to their prisoners. Everyone had his own story to tell of the horrors perpetrated by the Indians of the North. What had happened to some of the first colonists had become legendary by now. But these tales were always about things which happened to other people. Never to the Welsh, the peaceful Quakers. God would look after Tomos.

What did they *mean* by scalping? She tried to push the question to the back of her mind, but her imagination insisted on seeing the bloody knife cutting a line above the eyebrows, above the ears . . . she saw the strange, devilish face of the Indian at his work, heard his victorious scream as he held the sticky hair up in his hand . . . heard Tomos shouting . . . and shouting . . . Lisa felt everywhere go black around her.

As the first, clear silver light of dawn began to spread from the east, they found the body of Tomos Owen. He was lying on his face, his musket beside him. He had tripped over his gun, Sion Ifan said hurriedly to Ellis Puw. But in his heart he could not be sure. The footsteps in the snow were facing northwards. Of the Indian, Waneha, there was no sign.

CHAPTER EIGHT

A great change had come over David Lloyd in the two years that had passed since his arrival in Pennsylvania, although he himself had only gradually admitted this to himself. During the long conversations he had had with William Penn before coming over, his imagination had been fired by the splendour of the Founder's vision. He admired this gifted man who possessed all the resources and virtues needed to bring about the fulfilment of a noble dream. News of his patron's financial worries saddened and annoyed him for was it not Penn's own people — those who were benefitting from this vision — who were the cause of his worries?

Being connected with the law can make people either more devious, or more just; David Lloyd belonged to the latter class. Having come over to Pennsylvania and having seen for himself how things stood, he was shaken. Perhaps because he himself had come from an impoverished background, perhaps because he was independent by nature, he had come to realise how difficult it was for most of the colonists to pay Penn the feudal dues of quit rent out of their scanty earnings. He had also come to realise that it was still harder for them to accept the idea of paying the rent of any sort for land they had already paid for. He had gradually become less severe with culprits, and by now had come to disregard the transgression altogether. There must be a better way of getting money, he thought, than by milking the poor.

On the other hand, he was well aware of the fact that he had been sent there by the Founder to look after the Founder's dues, and when Patrick Robinson, Clerk to the Philadelphia court resigned, following Doctor Nicholas Moore's example, because of what they regarded as the oppression of the Frame of Government, David Lloyd agreed to take his place. As David's sympathy with the Welsh and their difficulties grew, so Thomas Lloyd became less suspicious of him. Whatever Penn's intention had been in sending him to Pennsylvania, Thomas quickly saw that David Lloyd himself was completely sincere. The two cousins became close friends.

The Attorney had just bought almost a hundred acres in Meirion, with a handsome two-storied house with a wide pentroof over the second story window. Thomas Lloyd liked nothing better than to call on his cousin and his wife, Sarah, to relax in the tranquility of their library.

But he did not look relaxed tonight. He was striding backwards and forwards like a caged leopard, his thin aristocratic hands restless, his cheeks and forehead unusually red under the silver hair.

'Had I not seen the signature myself,' he said, showing a letter to the Attorney, 'I would not have believed it possible. Even now, I have to believe that there is some mistake somewhere. Someone could have forged his signature. But — read the letter thyself . . .!'

David Lloyd had already started to do so. It was a short letter from William Penn saying that His Majesty, King James, was urging the establishment of a military guard in every colony in view of the danger of attacks from the French in Canada. Would Thomas Lloyd be good enough to put the matter before the next meeting of the General Council?

'Why should I waste my time?' Thomas Lloyd had never looked more disturbed. Opposition, persecution, the violence of enemies — all that he could face with equanimity and dignity. But for William Penn, the Chief Quaker after George Fox himself, to send such an instruction . . .

'William knows very well that the Friends will refuse. It's incredible. It's completely contrary to our basic beliefs . . . it's one of the reasons why we are here today. Why on earth does he ask me to carry out such an idea?' David Lloyd was re-reading the letter, as if by doing so he would discover the secret behind it. He sat down in his chair, and said slowly:

'I think you have hit the nail on the head there, Cousin.'

'What dost thou mean?'

'I believe our Friend knows exactly what the reaction here will be, and what the reaction of all Quakers will be to such an instruction. Have you not just said "William Penn knows very well that the Friends will refuse." Well, he is depending on that, I believe. But since he mentions His Majesty — does not that suggest there has been some command from higher up?'

The Attorney raised his head.

'Everybody knows that he is in serious financial difficulties. But did you know that he was also in political trouble?'

Thomas shook his head.

'Well, he has always been friendly with King James — a strange friendship, if ever there was one. James is in trouble with his Bishops who are suspicious of his friendship with France. The King wants to see England Catholic again before he dies, that's what they're saying. Therefore to retain his throne, James has to prove his enmity to France, and his friend, William Penn, has to prove at the same time that he is not a secret Jesuit. That is why you have had this letter. I'll warrant Penn is hoping that the instruction will be opposed by Friends, but he will have proved his trustworthiness and his loyalty.'

Thomas Lloyd was calmer now. He stared at his cousin in disbelief. Could this be true? His mind was seriously troubled. On the one hand, he was glad to think that Penn did not really want them to bring in military powers to undermine the whole purpose of the Holy Experiment. On the other hand, he found it hard to believe this great man capable of wallowing in secret politics, who had suffered so much for truth and light in the past. What could have happened?

He began to think of the first time he had met Penn. The Founder was only a young man at the time, turned out of his home by his father, Admiral Penn, for his Quaker preaching and writing. Thomas Lloyd had to admit that he himself was not always an accurate judge of character, but he remembered now how it had occurred to him as he heard Penn speak of his father, that there was something defiant in the attitude — almost as if it were important for him to prove that his father could not force him into following his own way of life. Had the father not been such a tyrant . . . Thomas sighed. William was a complicated man, a man of many personalities dwelling within the one body — dreamer, practical soldier, religious idealist, shrewd, arrogant, sensuous, generous, compassionate . . . and now the politician playing a dangerous game.

'I'll write back at once saying that the Quakers cannot possibly comply. If his secret intention is what thou dost suggest . . . Well, we shall see what his reaction will be.'

Thomas Lloyd shrugged his shoulders in perplexity.

Some months later Dorti was sitting near the open door staring at the pattern the shadows from the trees made on the ground as they moved slowly in the sunlight. No one in the Meeting had spoken yet, everyone waited for the stillness that must come before they could centre down.

Ellis Puw and his family were sitting in a row, their backs to the wall on the right. At thirty-two Ellis looked better than he had done in his youth. The bony hollows had filled out, and perhaps he had lost something of his other-worldly appearance, But his face still shone with a deep serenity, a warm mantle for Sinai and her children.

In the seat in front of Dorti sat Lisa, holding Rhys tightly by the hand to stop him from slipping under the bench. No one was now more diligent than Lisa in attending Meetings. She rarely smiled, and sat, a motionless statue, head bowed, no matter who was speaking. With her pale, emaciated face, and clothes unusually plain even for a Quaker woman, she looked more like a nun who spent hours doing penance. That was Robin Wynn's observation, Dorti remembered, not her own. Where was he this morning?

If Lisa's clothes were sombre, Lowri's were completely the opposite. She was sitting with Sion Ifan immediately in front of Dorti, her cloak placed over the back of the bench, so that Dorti could gaze at the cherry red silk lining. She had bowed her head, and Dorti could see between the white collar and cap of fine lace, the prettily curled yellow ringlets, carefully parted on either side of her white neck. Sion Ifan sat beside her, his wild black hair imprisoned uneasily under his hat.

John Bevan got up, a gentle man from Morgannwg, with a strange turn of speech. Dorti tried to fix her mind on what he was saying, but today her eye would keep on wandering from one person to the other.

Huw Roberts and Catrin his mother, Robert Jones, and his wife and their two children, all of them from Penllyn like herself. What strange stroke of fate had placed them all here in this far land, instead of in their own homes around Llyn Tegid, like their fathers and grandfathers before them? John Humphrey from Llwyngwril and Catrin his wife, Rowland Ellis and his son Rol, full of the inquisitiveness of his nine years. She caught the boy's eye and smiled at him. He blushed, and bowed his head, as if she had guessed all his secrets.

All Merioneth people, but John Eckley was not from Merioneth. He talked a lot about his home in Herefordshire just over the border from Radnor, his pride in his roots, an umbilical cord tying him for ever to his old home. His Welsh had a slight English accent to it, but he was never heard to speak English, not even when Ben Dawson or Richard Hull tried to have a word with him on the way out of Meeting. Of course *they* were there, and their wives with them. A flash of anger swept through her, followed almost immediately by shame. They were all Quakers and ought to be embraced with open arms. Had not Ben Dawson already shown how kind he was to Lisa and Rhys after their sad loss. The least he could do, whispered a small voice inside her, for had he not gained admission to the Tract by buying Tomos's good land, and benefitting from his careful husbandry?

Some of the Welsh had gone out of their way to welcome them, especially those who could speak English. Others tended to keep away, mainly because of shyness and their lack of English. No one could deny that they were pleasant enough people, but that only complicated the issue. As John Eckley had said:

'If they were openly hostile to us, like Thomas Holme and George Keith, it would be easier. Where there is fierce opposition, there are always two camps — us and them. But these people are not like that, and there lies the danger. They are completely harmless, everyone likes them. For all that, they are dangerous people, for they undermine our community with their English ways.'

Ben Dawson was often moved to speak in Meetings. Because he did not understand what had already been said, his testimony was always the fruit of his own meditation, and almost always unrelated to what had gone before. There was no ruling against his speaking in English of course, although his words were not understood by one half of his fellow-worshippers, and the spirit of waiting together and experiencing together, so essential to their way of worship, was lost. Had Friend Ben been of a silent nature, it would not have mattered so much, but he was an eloquent speaker always ready to contribute, who felt it his duty to offer testimony on every possible occasion. A third of the Meeting had been turned into English.

One evening John Eckley and Robin Wynn quarrelled over this.

'The sooner all the Welsh learn English the better,' was Robin's sharp comment. 'They'll have to, sooner or later.'

Dorti could hardly believe that Robin was really serious. It seemed as if John Eckley's fervour about his Welshness was beginning to get on Robin's nerves, so that he sometimes pretended to make fun of the Welsh urge to be considered a separate unity. She could not understand why, but these two always seemed to be at each other's throats.

'Why dost thou say that, Friend?' asked Eckley just as sharply.

'Because this is a big country and English is now the language of the majority of people who are pouring over here, no matter how it was in the beginning, and it is always the majority who win. One must learn to accept the undesirable if it is inevitable. It's no good arguing about it.'

'As the Cecils and the Salisburys did in the last century?'

'And the Wynns in this?' Robin laughed, but for once there was no laughter in his eyes.

John Eckley chose to ignore this remark. 'There were other families too who chose not to follow the majority. The Kyffins for instance.'

Dorti could not help breaking in eagerly:

'Thou art right John. I remember Edward Kyffin's words: "How much more should we cherish our own language, which Almighty God has protected in this one spot in the Kingdom for twenty-seven hundred years, among the quarrelling of so many different nations . . ." '.

As she paused, Eckley finished the sentence for her . . . ' "who came among us at that time with intent to ravage and destroy the language and the people completely." '

'I suppose it was from your brother you learnt that.'

Dorti still felt hurt when she recalled the unkind tone of Robin Wynn's voice. There were times when he looked at her coldly and suspiciously, at other times, far more often, she felt him warmly close to her. Yet that odd feeling of estrangement came to the surface too often, and she noticed that he did not try to touch her now as before. Where was he today? She felt empty and disappointed because he was not where she expected him to be. Once again she tried to turn her attention back to the Meeting, but Ben Dawson was on his feet now and her whole being was irritated by all this everlasting English.

Later, on the way out of the Meeting House, groups gathered together speaking in a seemly but eager manner. How many of them had come here today hoping, like her, for a tranquil, inspiring meeting, and had come away disappointed. Or was she the only one? Could it be her own fault — was she lacking tolerance and charity? Then she remembered that John Eckley must surely feel the same way and she turned and smiled at him.

'Where's Robin Wynn today, Dorti?' asked Rowland Ellis as he passed. She blushed, pleased to think that people associated her with Robin — but annoyed because she did not know the answer.

There was no need for her to answer, for at that point, Robin himself came galloping towards them on his horse, without waiting to dismount at the gate and tie the animal to a post. He pulled so roughly at the reins that the horse bucked. Everybody rushed up to him, sensing he had important news.

'Calm down!' smiled Sion Ifan, taking the reins and patting the head of the sweating beast to quieten it.

'What's the matter?'

'Thomas Lloyd has resigned!'

'What!'

'Never!'

'It's true. I had to go to Philadelphia this morning to fetch the farrier for one of the cows, and happened to meet David Lloyd. He was furious!'

'Furious with Thomas?' asked Huw Roberts in surprise.

'No. With William Penn,' said a new voice. Dorti had not noticed the absence of Doctor Edward Jones from the Meeting until that moment, but he too had only just arrived on horseback.

'I had a note from Thomas himself asking me to go and call on him,' he said. 'He wanted the Welsh to hear the news at once.'

'But . . . Why?' asked Roland Ellis.

'Why did he have to resign?' said the Doctor bitterly. 'What could the Deputy Governor of the Quakers' New Jerusalem do when faced with the fact that a military defence is to be forced on the colony?' His words were sharp, as a sword's edge. 'For that is what Friend William is doing. Thomas had believed that he was only pretending in order to please the King – but it was not so. Not only has William accepted the resignation – "with regret," as he says, – but the new Deputy is already on his way here.'

'Who is it?'

'A man called Captain John Blackwell – a soldier through and through. One of Cromwell's old army treasurers, married to the daughter of General Lambert. We are in trouble, are we not Friends? Rumour has it that Friend William met Mistress Blackwell in London and that she talked him into giving her husband the post. William expected Thomas to be willing to co-operate with Blackwell if you please. And well – there it is.' The Doctor shrugged his shoulders. 'We are losing Thomas's leadership and courage and as for this man who is coming to take his place, he's not even a Quaker.'

They looked at each other in dismay. What on earth had come

over William Penn? They felt as if a great rock had been turned into sand under their feet. It was not only the coming of the military which troubled them, but the fact that it was William Penn, the Founder, who was sending them. How was it going to be possible to live in peace with soldiers among them once again. The presence of soldiers always encouraged fighting and oppression. Rowland Ellis was the first to speak.

'It is the King who is forcing Penn to do this, of course,' he said. 'We must not be too hard on him. Let us rather pray for him. It is a terrible thing for a man to be forced by circumstances to sell his principles. Friends, let us pray for our friend William Penn. Let not the spirit of bitterness and hate grow out of our disappointment and our fears for the future. Let us consecrate our hearts and keep faith with each other in a spirit of love and unity, keeping out as far as we are able every argument and disagreement . . .'

'Amen,' said Ben Dawson, not understanding one word.

'David Lloyd said many other things too,' said Robin Wynn to Dorti later when they were nearing Huw Roberts's gate. 'You know how he had always supported Penn all along . . .'

'Like thee!'

'Like me, if you say so,' agreed Robin with a smile. He loved to gossip, thought Dorti affectionately.

'David Lloyd cannot understand why Penn does not come back to the colony to face people, since he is forcing something so distasteful upon them. He has had a letter from some London Friends saying that they were concerned because William was spending so much time with the King at Court, living in great style in Holland House, and travelling all over the place with the King and those two Jesuits, the Earl of Sunderland and Father Petre. It is even being rumoured everywhere that he has been converted to Papism. Penn himself claims that he acts so in the interest of the Quakers. But how can this be? That's what David Lloyd wants to know, while he demands more and more money from his fellow-Quakers so that he can sustain his present way of life. George Fox is very ill just now, but Margaret his wife is very critical indeed of Friend Penn's behaviour.'

'Art thou critical of him?' asked Dorti.

His answer was important to her. She could see he was in very good humour, despite the bad news he had bought. He pinched her arm playfully, touching her for the first time since she did not know when.

'We don't know all the facts,' he said lightly.

William Penn's second letter from Worminghurst really added salt to the wound. Informing his Attorney General of Captain Blackwell's appointment, Penn wrote:

'I hope very much that the Assembly will receive this person with kindness, let him see it, and use his not being a Friend to Friends' advantage.'

David Lloyd was amazed at the obvious meaning of the last part of the sentence. Blackwell was there to keep King James quiet — that proved his first suspicions correct. He was also there to show that Friends, like everybody else, were ready to compromise and administer the law according to the demands of the Crown, no matter how contrary to their beliefs this might be. David was now forced to believe the rumour that this was the only way William Penn could keep hold of his government in Pennsylvania.

He was glad Thomas Lloyd had still retained one office in spite of his immediate inclination to resign completely. He still remained Keeper of the Seal and Master of the Rolls — a position almost as important as that of the Deputy Governor. Perhaps the time will come when we shall be glad to make use of the position, thought the Attorney. After all, the Keeper of the Seal had to approve of every law passed by the Deputy Governor.

'First we have to show Brother Blackwell quite unmistakably that he is not welcome here,' said the Attorney to Thomas Lloyd and some of the other Councillors.

'The best thing to do is keep away,' said the Englishman, Samuel Richardson.

'But are enough of us ready to do that?' asked Thomas.

There was nothing for it but to ask publicly at the next meeting of the Assembly.

It was found that ten of the Councillors were ready to support the Lloyds and eight to welcome Blackwell. As for the rest they were either absent that day, or not ready to show which side they were on. Although most of Blackwell's supporters were not Quakers, it was a great grief, but no surprise to Thomas and David to find that Griffith Jones, the only Welsh member of the Assembly, was one of them. 'You are opposing the authority of the King,' he said, 'and no good ever came of rebellion.'

Well, ten was enough to make a token protest, and they could count on many more supporters from among the two hundred members of the Senate. What worried the Lloyds was that the number of colonists who were not Quakers were now beginning to have a say in government. In the southern counties the representatives were all Anglicans, and already their administration of the law was causing dismay to the Quakers.

It was a hot summer's day when Captain Blackwell came to Philadelphia. He had arrived two days earlier on the *Welcome*, and was staying in Pennsbury until his own house was ready. Robin Wynn found an excuse for going to Philadelphia that day, for he was anxious to see this cuckoo in the nest. He wrote to his uncle:

' . . . *a great crowd had turned out to see the Captain. Indeed I was surprised to see that there were so many people in Pennsylvania! The population must have increased enormously since you left. I was allowed to stand at the head of the stairs leading to the great door of the Council Hall and could therefore observe the main street. I could see the coach approaching in the distance, only five minutes before the Senate was due to be opened. It was being drawn by six black horses, with twelve soldiers in red uniform riding each side of it. Such a splendid and ceremonious sight had never before been seen in this colony. In exactly two minutes the coach had come to rest at the bottom of the steps and the Captain descended in all his sweaty glory. He was wearing a bright red and white suit − the better to show off the blue ribbon of office across* his chest and stomach. A wide body, a large head, with thicker lips than I have ever seen on any man before — that was Captain Blackwell. He took a full minute to parade up the steps and I expected to hear the sound of pipe and drum at any moment — but perhaps even he did not dare to perpetrate any act of such impudence (if indeed he is capable of understanding that such it would be in Quaker country). I am perfectly certain that he did not understand why he was not given the usual huzza by the people. My curiosity overcame my shyness and I succeeded in slipping into the forefront of the public gallery in the chamber, and I must admit that William Penn would have been very shaken to see the half empty room. Exactly as the clock struck the hour the Captain took the chair, precise soldier that he is. He called first for the Attorney General, but got no answer. Then he called the keeper of the Seal and Master of the Rolls; again no answer. He started then to call out individual names reading from a parchment before him (and it was devilish amusing to hear him stumble over the Welsh names!) Some answered, but for the most part there was silence. Then one of the officials ventured to inform him that they did not have a quorum of members present and that therefore nothing could be done that day. For a moment the Captain looked around him in perplexity, and I'll warrant that no one had warned the poor creature of the feeling prevailing against his assumption of office. Then he squared his shoulders, lifted his head up and barked out as if on a field of battle: 'Let everyone attend here tomorrow at the same hour.' Such a different way of behaving from Thomas Lloyd as I have never seen, dear Uncle. I know you will be glad to hear the story, and I am grateful that you are far away over the sea, for I forsee that such a storm will follow these events as was never envisaged by Friend Penn in his plans for us. I hope my aunt is well, and you too, and all the family. I need a new pair of leather shoes for the ones made here are very rough. Could you please send me two pairs? It would be wiser to put them in a wooden case to keep out the damp and mildew. If you do this you will receive the sincere thanks of your nephew,

ROBIN WYNN.

Nevertheless, to make protest sufficiently powerful, it is necessary to get the majority to join in, and the unpleasant truth was that the southern representatives were ready to welcome Blackwell, and that by now, they represented a substantial proportion of the Government. The Quakers saw the danger of remaining outside the Council when dozens of other people were longing to have the chance to take their place. What would happen if the voice of the Quakers were silent in the highest courts? The case of Peter Ludgar was only one indication of what could happen.

Peter Ludgar was an insignificant little thief, but as sometimes happens, the most insignificant person is sometimes destined to play a role of importance. Sussex was one of the southern counties and it was there Ludgar had appeared before the court charged with stealing twenty sacks of flour from a neighbour. He was given a prison sentence, ordered to be publicly whipped, and to do hard labour until his neighbour felt satisfied. Ludgar appealed to the Supreme Provincial Court, and under David Lloyd, the judgement was reversed.

The southern counties were indignant. An appeal on their behalf was sent to Captain Blackwell to restore the original sentence. That day there was better attendance at the Council Hall than there had been for some time. The Captain read out the appeal in his biting military voice, and then from under his bushy eyebrows he glared at the stony faces before him, his lips jutting out aggressively.

'What I see here on all sides is lack of discipline, lack of respect for law and order, weakness on the one hand, treason on the other. To restore respect for the law, it has to be administered unflinchingly. I uphold the original sentence.'

A murmur of surprise and dissatisfaction went through the Council Chamber. Samuel Richardson jumped to his feet:

'But the Deputy Governor does not have the right to give his verdict before the Assembly has discussed it.'

Blackwell turned a cold eye on him.

'Right? What is this talk of right? According to English law, the Governor has the right — and indeed the *duty* to administer that law.'

Samuel Richardson's face went puce.

'If I may remind thee — thou art not Governor here. And in the view of most of us neither art thou Deputy Governor.'

A roar of support went up from one side of the floor, and Blackwell banged on the table in front of him.

'I shall not listen to such impudence. Leave this room at once, Sir.' Then, when he saw that Richardson was standing his ground:

'Captain Markham, command your men to *help* the Councillor to leave!'

The Quakers could not believe their ears — or their eyes. For the first time ever, there were soldiers standing around the hall. For the first time, force was being used to keep order in the Assembly. Thomas Lloyd rose to his feet slowly and with dignity.

'Excellency,' he said, and if there was the slightest tinge of mockery in his voice, no one could tell whether Blackwell was aware of it or not. 'The first verdict cannot stand until it receives the Seal of State, and cannot receive the Seal of State until it receives first of all the approval of the majority.'

Perhaps that was the moment when Blackwell at last sensed the strength of the opposition to him. An oppressive silence fell over the enormous room, while the soldier sat there trying to sense the thoughts of the men in front of him. The task proved too much for him. 'Let us look once again at the documents from the Sussex Courts,' he murmured, almost failing to get the words out. Then he snapped at the officer who was standing behind his chair: 'The box, man! Don't go to sleep!'

The next hour was spent trying to study the documents but at last Blackwell threw them down in despair.

'Half of them are not here. Where's the Attorney General?'

David Lloyd had been sitting all this time at the back of the hall. He got up immediately.

'Excellency!'

'These Sussex papers are not in order. We shall have to examine the minutes of the High Court. The details will be the same. Be so good as to ask your officers to bring the papers here.'

David Lloyd had been waiting for this moment.

'I regret, Excellency, that they are not available.'

Blackwell's head shot up.

'What! What do you mean by "They are not available?"'

David Lloyd had now moved to the middle of the stage. All eyes were upon him, and obviously he was enjoying every moment of the attention he was getting. He walked slowly from the back of the Chamber up to the Deputy's table, head held high under his sparkling white wig. Raising both hands slowly he held his black gown away from his chest. His timing was perfect.

'Those documents are the property of the *Supreme Court,* Excellency. And there is no higher authority than that court. They are not available to the Assembly.'

They all knew that some crisis had been reached. In standing there and challenging Blackwell, David Lloyd was also challenging the authority of the absent Governor, if not indeed the authority of the King himself. Blackwell now chose to ignore the figure standing before him. He took a deep breath and then lifted up a parchment lying on the table in front of him.

'Here is a letter, gentlemen, which I received from William Penn this morning.' His voice rang out around the courtroom. 'I shall read it to you, and then you can decide for yourselves what the authority of the Deputy Governor is.'

His voice rose still higher as he continued:

'Here are the words of the Founder of this colony: "I enjoin thee to deny the Assembly the right to do anything buy say ay or no when you come to pass bills for laws. The Assembly no longer has the right to debate, amend or alter legislative bills. If the Assembly is allowed to turn into a chamber for debators, judges or complainors its partisans will overthrow the Charter quite in the very root of the Constitution".'

He allowed the parchment to fall through his fingers, and forced himself to turn and look at David Lloyd.

'I restate my request. Ask your officers to bring the documents here.'

'And witness the end of an administration of law and justice which is a model for anywhere in Europe? God forbid!'

David Lloyd's voice was equally as loud as Blackwell's. The

latter now jumped to his feet and pressed forward as if to grasp at the Attorney's throat.

'I'll strip you of every office you hold here, you treacherous villian,' he shouted. 'From this moment on you are no longer Attorney General. Away with you, out of my sight immediately.'

They were all on their feet now, and the noise could be heard out on the streets of Philadelphia. In the end it was Thomas Lloyd, and not Blackwell, who was able to restore order. He turned to Blackwell, his voice like a razor: 'You are quite right. The Deputy does have the right to sack the Attorney General, but the Master of the Rolls has certain rights too, among them the right to appoint his own Deputy. I now appoint David Lloyd Deputy Master of the Rolls, Clerk of the Peace, and Clerk to the County Courts of Philadelphia.'

The situation had become almost comic, as the smile on David Lloyd's face proved.

'Completely out of order!' Blackwell was shouting, now totally out of control. 'I have never in my life seen such quarrelsome, factious, turbulent creatures!'

And he stamped out of the Court, shouting that he would be preparing criminal charges against Thomas Lloyd.

CHAPTER NINE

At last, after staring long and uselessly into the darkness, he got up from bed, walked over to the window and opened the heavy curtains. It was still dark outside, but even as he looked, a thin strip of silver light began to break across the sky in the east. He thought he could hear a wolf howl in the distance, but inside the house all was quiet.

Over there, where the silver strip was slowly spreading, was Marged, and there was Bryn Mawr, as far away from him as the north star. What was he doing here, Rowland Ellis asked himself, with all this vast distance he had set between himself and those he loved? For the hundredth time since Tomos's body had been brought home, he reproached himself for allowing this Jezebel of a country to seduce him. He suddenly felt very angry with himself. Why should everything he did always lead to the destruction of others — not to his own destruction but to the destruction of those for whom he was responsible? His conversion had destroyed Meg; his decision to buy land in this country had destroyed Tomos and brought the hardness back to Lisa's face.

He pressed his head against the window pane and felt the cold against his hot forehead. He should have warned Tomos more earnestly not to allow greed to get the better of him. Yet, how could he, when his own heart leapt at the thought of all those green acres? That last venture had emptied his coffers, and he had no ready money left now.

How complicated are one's motives, he thought. Layer after layer had to be removed before one could get as much as a glimpse of the truth. Even then, it seemed a bottomless pit. Oh for the simple straightforward trusting faith of a man like

Ellis Puw. He owned nothing. He did not have that Goliath to conquer.

Even now his mind was busy trying to decide on which side of the new land he should start clearing the brushwood and what he should plant there first. He was worried too by the need for more servants, servants from Wales. The flood of immigrants from the old country had eased off, mainly because news of the quarrels and disappointments had now reached Wales. He fiercely opposed the decision of some of his fellow Quakers to buy slaves in order to solve this problem. He could, of course, buy slaves now and set them free later — had not Penn himself ordered Quakers to do this when the slave had completed fourteen years' service? But quite apart from his innate dislike of the idea, where was the money to come from to pay for the slaves? He had nothing but land.

The outlines were sharper now. The tops of the trees looked like spiders' webs on the horizon, and the pines near the house were black. The dark earth was hidden by a crystal frost and the fences stood upright against the whiteness like black guardsmen. He could hear movements downstairs and Rol was beginning to call for attention in the bedroom next door.

And attention he could have, thought Rowland with a smile, for the nine year old boy was the apple of his eye. Rol loved to play around the farm, but most of all he loved going to the fields with his father. Last year Ellis Puw had made a chair for him and screwed it on the cross bar of the plough so that the boy could be with his father while he turned the soil without getting overtired. But that was last year. Rol now scorned the 'baby chair' as he called it and insisted on walking with his father until his little legs could no longer hold him.

Rowland got dressed ready to go to Philadelphia for he had heard that the *John and Sarah* had arrived from Bristol and he expected letters from Wales. It was afternoon by the time he arrived at the Exchange; he glanced quickly through the bundle which had been put aside for the Meirion Quakers, found the letter which was the most important to him, and started to read it immediately.

Bryn Mawr.*
The Ninth Month, 1688.

My dear husband,

I received thy letter, the only thing my soul was aching for. Thou knowest that I am with thee every moment of every day, with nothing but the Lord's pure strength to sustain me. The children are in bed, and Elin, Catrin and Besi (a new maid) have gone upstairs. So here I am, taking advantage of the silence to write to thee.

Thy letter arrived yesterday, three days after Winter's Eve, having been three months on the way. But to receive it, no matter how long after it was written, brings thee back to Bryn Mawr, which is what my heart longs for more than anything else. It is good to know that God is giving his support to the venture in the Tract, in spite of the rumours that arrive here from time to time, and that the farm is flourishing.

We had a good harvest here this year, better than last, says Lewis Owen, Tyddyngarreg (who has been a very good neighbour to me during these last months). He paid me six pounds for one of the horses we did not need any more according to Ned the bailiff. This is because so much of our land has been distrained. And the end is not yet in sight, I am sorry to have to tell thee. Cae'r Gog was taken last week, and the justices are threatening to take more cattle this time. Do not imagine I tell thee this merely to worry thee, but I believe it is better for thee to know what is happening to thy property.

There is one other thing which has caused me to pray hard for guidance: thy daughter, Ann, is now sixteen and she has been blessed with extraordinary beauty. I pray everyday that this blessing will not turn into a curse, for I fear that modesty has not accompanied that beauty. I am not saying there is any harm in her, but she is self-willed and insists on going her own way, asking the advice of no one. I am afraid I failed to stop her going to the revels at Bryn Adda. I tried to convey to her your opinion of such festivities and how Friends had suffered

*imprisonment and persecution and death for forty years trying
to bring testimony against such frivolities. But she would not
listen. Her father was not here to forbid her she said. I want
thee to know that I would not be troubling thee, knowing how
I was hurting thee, had something else not happened as a result.
At the revels thy daughter met the new curate of the parish a
man called Richard Johnston, who lives in Doluwch-
eogrhyd, and she now meets him at every opportunity. I myself
have never seen him, but I know very well what thy feelings
must be for he belongs to those who shattered thy life. Lewis
Owen told me that the whole town is talking about it, but
I can put up with this. My only fear is that I have failed
in my charge.*

*Sian is a very obedient girl, thank the Lord. She is taking
care of the hens and the geese now. I trust Rol is company and
comfort to thee. Knowing that, my longing for him becomes
less. Bet and Robert pray for their father every night before
going to sleep. As I do, my dear love,*

Thy wife,

Marged.

He folded the letter carefully, not seeing the market crowds
surging around him, not hearing the cries of the merchants
offering their goods. On the quay the sailors were loading cargo
on to the *John and Sarah,* and he stared up at the tall masts
which for a short time lay bare of sail, and down into the still
green water where the anchor rested.

When he was a child his grandmother used to warn him not
to go into the middle of Cae'r Gog. 'Keep to the side, my boy,
or you'll be sucked down into the bowels of the earth by
the goblins.'

But grandmother lived at Dyffrydan and knew nothing of
the exciting thrill of placing one foot carefully in front of the
other in the wet earth and watching the water lick at his shoe,
and cover it completely — and then jump back quickly. Cae'r
Gog was of little use to a farmer. If they had taken that, there
could not be much good land left. The thought of Ann was
too painful at the moment. He walked over to the nearest sailor.

171

'When will you be sailing back?'

'Back to Bristol, Sir?'

'Yes.'

'With the tide tomorrow morning, Sir.'

'Where's the captain?'

The sailor nodded his head in the direction of the Blue Anchor, and lifted his little finger with a suggestive wink. 'If you want to catch him before he falls under the table you must go there immediately. He's been there two hours already.'

Rowland thanked him and directed his footsteps towards the tavern.

Back again in the Welsh Tract he went to see his uncle, John Humphrey, and told him the news at once.

'I have to return to Wales immediately. I know that thou wilt take care of my property here until I return. I can leave everything safely in Ellis's hands — but I am sure he can come to you for advice when necessary.'

His uncle looked at him in amazement.

'I'll do what's needed. But is anything wrong?'

Rowland took Marged's letter out of his pocket and showed it to his uncle.

'Yes, I see,' said the latter when he had read it. 'When dost thou sail?'

'Tomorrow morning, at dawn. The *John and Sarah* leaves then. I shall not get another ship for a month if I delay now. I am going to leave Rol in thy care, and in Aunt Catrin's. He'll be safer here. Lisa will help look after him — he will not be much trouble.'

Rowland spoke quickly and quietly. John Humphrey could see how worried he was under a veneer of calmness. He knew as well as his nephew that what had not been said by Marged in her letter spoke more eloquently than any words actually written down — she was not one to complain over nothing. If John Humphrey was worried that Rowland Ellis was leaving the Tract at a time when every Welshman was needed to safeguard his lands from the greed of newcomers he did not say a word. That was one of the difficulties of trying to keep roots in two places, he reflected, for he himself had turned his back for ever on Llwyndu and Llwyngwril. But neither John Humphrey nor Rowland Ellis dreamt how important the following year was to be in the history of the Welsh Tract.

Strange things were happening in London. Bewildering news reached the Tract that King James had fled to France two days before Christmas, and that his daughter Mary and her Dutch husband William had been declared King and Queen towards the end of February. But Thomas and David Lloyd now felt the distance between them and London to be so great that the news in itself could not affect them at all, except as an interesting event taking place in a far country. *This* was their country now, this was where their loyalty lay. What happened in London was no longer of any importance to them. Yet, the close friendship between William Penn and the ex-King found them wondering about possible repercussions such an event could have on the colony.

'Blackwell's position has certainly been strengthened,' said David Lloyd.

'How so?'

'James did not really fear France, that's obvious. There's only an excuse of a militia here in spite of all the fuss made at the time. Only a handful of men act as a guard to the Deputy Governor himself. Calling for soldiers was all show, as I intimated at the time. But things have changed now. William and Louis of France are sworn enemies. There will be much tightening up here thou shalt see.'

'It's pretty tight here already,' said Thomas with rather a bitter smile. They had both been forbidden by Blackwell to attend meetings of the Assembly. Legally they had no right to oppose him. The Deputy had the right to do this, for the post of Keeper of the Seal and Master of the Rolls belonged to the Court only. After that eventful day on which the authority of the Deputy Governor had been brought into question, the two Lloyds, and Samuel Richardson as well, had been forbidden to set foot inside the Chamber. To find out what went on there now, they had to depend on Doctor Gruffydd Owen, who had just been elected after a by-election as representative for part of the County of Philadelphia.

'There are two distinct groups forming,' he said. 'And the two are at loggerheads and becoming more so every day. There is the Quaker group, and the administrative group. The latter is the weaker at the moment, but since more and more land is being sold in the County of Chester to non-Quakers I am afraid that the Quakers have only a short time left to remain in the majority.'

He laughed abruptly. 'When the Welsh were complaining that their Tract was being swallowed by the English, they didn't get much sympathy from the Quakers as a whole. But now that the Quakers themselves are in danger of being swallowed by Baptists and Anglicans and even by people who have no religion at all — there is much wailing and gnashing of teeth.'

'There will be still more before that man Blackwell has run his course,' said David. 'But never mind, the Election is in sight. In April the county of Philadelphia will be choosing six members for the Senate. We must take care this time that we have strong representation in Philadelphia. We have been much too lax up to now about sending anyone to the Assembly and this has weakened our voices in the highest places.'

The other two knew this was true. With their emphasis on governing the Tract from the Meeting House, and ignoring the central government as far as possible, the Welsh Quakers had acted according to George Fox's fundamental principles. Slowly they had come to realise that the colony Founder's way of administration was very different from that intended by the Founder of the Quakers, and that the real power was vested in the Assembly and not in the Meeting House.

It was Dorti Llwyd who suggested that John Eckley should stand for the Tract in the election.

'You won't find a more single-minded man to look after our rights. I know his whole life is dedicated to preserving the separate entity of the Tract.'

None of the others had thought of John Eckley until she spoke, for he was a serious young man, quiet until excited over some injustice or other. But Dorti knew that he had a solid layer of practical ability. When they thought about it they all realised that what she said was true, and much to the surprise of some of them, it did not prove difficult to persuade him to allow his name to go forward. David Lloyd then suggested to Thomas Lloyd and to the Englishman, Samuel Richardson, that they too should stand for election in their own districts.

'I am convinced this is the only way to break Blackwell's hold on the Council and challenge his authority there. I would give much to be able to see his face when he hears who his new councillors are.'

But the election was not to be held until April. It was only February now and much water was to flow down the Delaware before that fateful election took place.

On the 20th of March, that is, the first month of the year 1689, Doctor Gruffydd Owen came rushing to Thomas Lloyd's house arriving completely out of breath. The high colour on his cheeks was still burning as a result of what he had heard in the Assembly that morning, and he was glad when he saw that David Lloyd was sitting with Thomas in his library.

'I had to come here at once to tell you. What do you think has happened? They are starting to interfere with the boundaries again. Because I don't happen to live in the Tract the fool is too stupid to realise that I'm still a Welshman and he came out with his plans as bold as brass. If he expected me to remain silent . . .'

'Perhaps he mistakes thee for the other Griffith, and believes he can buy thee.' David Lloyd's smile was somewhat crooked for the fact that Griffith Jones had sided with the owners against them still rankled with the Welsh. The Doctor snorted.

'Anyway, Blackwell announced today that the Welsh Tract was to disappear as a unit: Radnor and Harford are to become part of the County of Chester, as well as a strip of land in Meirion, and the rest of Meirion is to be included in the County of Philadelphia. The proposed boundary line will cut through the Tract like a hot knife through butter.'

Thomas Lloyd felt an overwhelming weariness. He realised suddenly that the perpetual fighting over the rights of his fellow countrymen was exhausting him.

The Doctor went on: 'And we believed that the question of the Boundaries had been settled once and for all four years ago!'

Thomas slowly shook his head.

'Not once and for all, Friend. I realised the peace was only temporary when Penn ignored the letter I sent asking him to give his verdict one way or the other. He never answered, so I knew that this was bound to come up again sooner or later.'

'And they have good reason for raising it now,' said David Lloyd. The other two looked inquiringly at him.

'Don't you see? Blackwell and his gang have somehow got wind of the fact that Thomas here and John Eckley intend to stand for election. By moving more than half the Tract to the County of Chester where he has so many supporters — the intervention of our candidates there will be a mere flea bite. He is at the same time weakening the vote against him in the County of Philadelphia. And what does it matter to him if the Welsh Tract is destroyed in the process?'

It was all manifestly clear to them. Not only would they be losing a voice in the Assembly, they would now be losing the right to make their own laws, collect their own taxes and to carry on the administration in their own language. The whole fundamental reason for the existence of the Welsh Tract was being undermined.

'I suppose it's the same old plan resurrected again?' asked Thomas. 'The one that has the boundary going through the property of Rowland Ellis and John Humphrey.'

'And John Eckley's too,' Dorti reminded them. 'They are going to make sure that John stands in the County of Chester. His chances of being elected there are slim indeed.'

There was no time to lose. The following morning Thomas Lloyd went to the Council Hall and insisted on seeing the Deputy Governor. The official at the door looked very doubtful, but seeing the look on Thomas's face, he rushed to tell the Captain that the former Deputy was waiting to see him. Blackwell could not easily refuse, neither did he wish to, for he felt certain now that his own personal standing in the state had improved during the last few weeks, and he wanted Thomas to know this.

'Yes, Mr. Lloyd? What can I do for you?'

His voice was patronising and at the same time over-conciliatory, as if he were speaking to some wild, unreasonable creature, trying to calm him down. Thomas did not mince his words:

'I hear there is a move afoot to change the boundaries to the disadvantage of the Welsh,' he said. Blackwell looked uneasy, but shook his head, as if such an idea were repugnant to him. He invited his visitor to sit down. Thomas Lloyd refused. He is playing for time, he thought.

'No, no, Mr. Lloyd. You have been misinformed,' said Blackwell in some confusion. 'Nothing definite has been put forward, I assure you. If anything comes up which the Welsh should know about, you will be given plenty of warning.'

Thomas looked at him in amazement. Had Gruffydd Owen made a mistake? Or did Blackwell have the nerve to tell a blatant lie? For years now Thomas Lloyd had been used to dealing with Quakers. There had been disagreements of course, and even quarrels from time to time, but he had always been able to depend upon their telling the truth. This was fundamental to Quaker principles. Was it not for such principles that the Quakers had suffered imprisonment and persecution? For a person like Blackwell to lie to his face was an experience which belonged to another world. Maybe Gruffydd Owen had been misled in some way. Who was he, Thomas Lloyd, to call the Deputy Governor a liar without being absolutely certain? He stared long at Blackwell, and saw the arrogant self-confident look return to his eyes, to perplex Thomas more than ever.

'I hope we shall, John Blackwell,' he said slowly.

There was nothing to do now but leave. He felt uncomfortable and very ineffectual as he walked out of the great door, though to all the intents he should have been feeling confident at having succeeded in his purpose. A vague fear began to worry him, a fear that unknown powers were working against him. He saw the Doctor hurry across the square to meet him.

'What did he say, Thomas?'

Thomas Lloyd looked intently at him.

'Art thou certain thou wert not mistaken Gruffydd? He denies that anything has yet been proposed.'

Gruffydd gave a low whistle.

'Well, the shameless liar! I certainly did not misunderstand either his words or his intentions. The matter is to be brought up again this afternoon.'

Thomas thought for a moment, then—

'Go to the Assembly this afternoon,' he said. 'I shall try to get as many people as possible from the Tract to gather outside the Council Hall. As soon as Blackwell starts on the business of the boundaries I want thee to get up and say that Thomas Lloyd is waiting outside to come and present the case for the Welsh.'

He drew his hand over his forehead. 'I'm not sure what we can do, but we shall not give in until we have fought and fought . . .'

The first thing to do was to get the Welsh to assemble outside the Council Hall. He sent his servant Benjamin quietly to John Eckley's house to ask him to spread the word around that the presence of everybody from the Tract was required that afternoon in Philadelphia. On such short notice there was no knowing how many people would come, but the effort had to be made. He himself went at once to David Lloyd's house. The latter was filled with glee at the thought of the fight to come, but Thomas Lloyd himself now looked worn and worried. He asked himself for the hundredth time why Penn had not returned to his colony long before now. He could easily have left his commitments in London and the safety of the King's Court. This kind of difficulty would not have arisen had Penn come back, Thomas was sure of that.

Doctor Owen was in his place in time. He felt the nerves of his stomach flutter, and tried to breathe deeply to calm himself, but without much success. Looking round, he saw representatives of the County of Chester standing together, studying a large document and discussing it earnestly: John Blunstone, Randall Vernon, Thomas Usher — they were all there, men who were anxious to get a permanent footing in the Welsh Tract. He felt the blood rise to his head, and almost failed to stand up when the Deputy Governor came in to take his place at the head of the long table.

'Councillors,' the Deputy said at once, as if in a hurry to

get the work finished and go home. 'The first piece of business to be dealt with today is to listen to the petition on behalf of the justices of the County of Chester. Mister Blunstone please!'

John Blunstone got up, cleared his throat, looked around him once, and began to read from the document in front of him.

'Whereas the said County of Chester is a small tract of land not above nine square miles, and but thinly seated, whereby ye said County is not able to support the charge thereof set upon it by the Provincial Government. Upon our humble petition to the Proprietor and Governor and his serious consideration of our weakness position, he was pleased out of compassion to us to grant an Enlargement of ye same, in manner following, viz: to run up from Delaware River, along Darby Mill Creek, ye several courses thereof, until they took in Radnor and Hereford townships . . .'

At once Gruffydd Owen was on his feet cutting across the monotonous recitation.

'Before you proceed, Friends, I should like to inform you that Thomas Lloyd is outside the Chamber waiting to present the case of the Friends who live in the Tract under consideration. You are legally bound to give a hearing to those affected by any new plans.'

The three men from the County of Chester stared at him in stupefaction, and Blackwell's lower lip slipped down into his numerous chins. Gruffydd turned to the other Councillors.

'As you know, Friends, the Welsh have good reason for opposing this plan, because of the promise made to them by the Founder, William Penn, before they came out here. I am now appealing to your regard for justice to see that these promises are not broken, either now or at any time in the future.'

His words were listened to in silence, but some members exchanged glances and sighed audibly. They had all thought that the business would be completed quickly this time now that Thomas Lloyd was out of the way. They had had a bellyfull of the talk of promises made to the Welsh by William Penn. But they were not all of a mind. 'Attorney Owen is right, Excellency.'

Samuel Carpenter, a big, slow spoken man, was on his feet now.

'I believe Thomas Lloyd should be allowed to present his case.'

Blackwell's face went as black as his name. He banged on the table.

'I refuse to allow a traitor to enter His Majesty's Chamber,' he shouted. 'The matter is settled. Hearing the petition is merely a matter of form. We can waste no more time on it.'

'Excellency,' said Samuel Carpenter, his voice smooth but reproving. 'Our Founder William Penn is a Quaker. Most of us here are Quakers. We believe that everyone has a right to express his opinion.'

Friend Carpenter was right. Half-apologetic murmurs of agreement were heard in the hall. Blackwell knew that Samuel Carpenter's intervention had won the day for the Doctor. He threw his quill down on the table and shrugged his shoulders impatiently. Then with a great sigh said: 'Call the traitor in.'

John Eckley came in with Thomas Lloyd. From the moment they set foot in the Chamber they were completely ignored by Blackwell, and they were obliged to stand there waiting until Gruffydd asked one of the officials to fetch chairs for them. Blackwell had turned towards John Blunstone.

'You were saying, Sir, before we suffered this interruption, that you had indisputable proof that the Proprietor intended to extend the boundaries of the County of Chester to include the townships of Radnor, Hereford and Meirion. Let us now hear this evidence.'

John Blunstone rose once again.

'A few days before Governor Penn left this Province I was speaking to him on the bank of the river near John Symcock's house, and I asked him to decide this matter. I and others were witness to his words. He said quite clearly that the new boundaries should include Harford and Radnor. Then I asked him if he would be pleased to put his signature to this to avoid further dispute and he agreed to do so the following day.'

One could feel listeners stiffen. This was news to most of them.

'And did you get the signature, John Blunstone?' asked George Keith eagerly.

'The next day, John Symcock went to see the Governor, and came back without getting the order. What obstructed him I am not certain but two days later Penn was on his way to England.'

'Without having left any definite instruction in writing?' asked Samuel Carpenter in a dubious tone.

Gruffydd Owen jumped to his feet. 'Really, is this what is being offered as indisputable evidence?'

'There is no doubt but that was his intention, Friend,' answered Blunstone, beginning to redden. 'Randall Vernon will bear me out.'

But all Vernon had to say was that some man from Harford had told him he had asked Friend Penn which county Harford belonged to, and the Governor had been pleased to answer that it must belong to Chester.

Thomas Usher now wanted to say his piece—

'The Founder told me — "Thomas," he said, "I intend that the boundaries of Philadelphia County shall come about three or four miles on this side of the Schuylkill." That is, Excellency, exactly where it is intended to start the County of Chester. There was no mention of independence of the Welsh Tract.'

'That's only hearsay,' shouted Gruffydd. 'There is no shred of evidence for what the Friends say — nothing that would hold water in a court of law.'

'But there is sufficient, I maintain, to prove that it is time to give a final verdict in this matter without further delay. What reason have you now for doubting these men?' snapped Blackwell.

Thomas Lloyd could see that Blackwell had no intention of giving him an opportunity to speak if he could possibly help it. He would have to interrupt without being invited. He got to his feet.

'Since you were kind enough to invite me in perhaps you would like to hear the opinion of the Welsh people?'

Fearing he might be stopped he went on immediately. 'We too were given an assurance by the Founder — but a completely different one. We were assured that our Barony should not be divided, and that it should be made a County Palatine. I have

181

to remind you kindly, Friends, that we Welsh are the descendants of the Ancient Britons, who always in the land of our nativity under the Crown of England have enjoyed that liberty and privilege as to have our bounds and limits by ourselves within which all causes, quarrels, crimes and titles were tried and wholly determined by officers magistrates and jurors in our own language, which were our equals. Governor Penn knew this. He respected our wishes by promising us, before we emigrated, that we would have the same rights in Pennsylvania. If we lose our unity and are swallowed by any one of the other counties, how can we continue to hear and determine cases in the old British tongue?'

He stared earnestly at the men in front of him. Most of the faces betrayed confusion, lack of understanding, impatience, and as far as George Keith and Captain Blackwell were concerned, sheer hositility. He tried again.

'Friends, during my time in that chair' − pointing to the chair where Blackwell was sitting − 'had you ever reason to doubt either my sense of justice or my sincerity? If so, now is the time to speak up and call me a rogue who seeks nothing but self advancement. But if you remember my time there with love and affection, I ask you to trust me once again. Believe me, these requests the Welsh are making are not idle whims, but arise from a nation's longing to preserve its own identity. I implore you not to proceed with these plans to separate us.'

He knew he had touched something in them; not in all of them, perhaps, but enough to give a majority if it came to a vote. Then he heard the harsh voice of the schoolmaster George Keith.

'Words eloquent enough to charm the devil himself. But in the meantime we have to solve the problem of the taxes. The County of Chester, as it stands, is too poor to pay taxes. The Welsh Tract, officially part of Philadelphia county at the moment refuses to recognise this or to pay the taxes due. To whom then does the Welsh Tract intend paying taxes? Oh, they say, *they* are a separate Barony. They don't have to pay any taxes at all. All the others can do so on their behalf! They ask for justice. But what justice is there in that, Friends? I maintain that since the Welsh have always denied being part of the County of Philadelphia that the Council has the right to place them in the County of Chester.'

John Eckley now spoke for the first time.

'The Friend knows full well we already pay taxes to the County of Philadelphia. All we ask is that we be allowed to retain a proportion of the taxes for our own administration. No one can accuse us of trying to evade paying what is just.'

'There is a difference between just and just,' complained George Keith. 'It does not mean the same thing to everybody.'

'That's enough discussion,' thundered Blackwell. 'It's high time we took a vote on the matter. Since Thomas Lloyd and John Eckley have had their opportunity to speak, I now ask them to leave.'

It was best to concede with dignity. They had been given a chance to put their case forward and nothing further could be done except trust to the justice and wisdom of the Assembly. Gruffydd would be there to see they had fair play.

As soon as Blackwell saw them leave he turned to Thomas Holme who had been sitting quietly self-confidently waiting to be called.

'Surveyor Holme, I understand you have a map which will put an end to speculation about the Founder's intention four years ago.'

This was Thomas Holme's hour. Unable to refrain from glancing triumphantly at Doctor Gruffydd, he got up from his seat without a word, opening out an enormous map and held it up for the Councillors to see. They all stared at it. On the map the Province was split by a red line, a dark blood-filled artery, running from north to south. Like a schoolteacher, Holme took a stick pointing the places as he named them.

'Here is the township of Radnor. You see that there are forty plantations here. And here is Harford with thirty-two. As a manifestly natural line runs from the upper reaches of the Schuylkill down to Darby Mill Creek here, the lands of Rowland Ellis and John Eckley can conveniently be placed in the County of Chester along with Radnor and Harford; John Humphrey can stay in the County of Philadelphia.'

Doctor Owen jumped to his feet.

'On whose authority was this map drawn up?'

Holme turned towards him, a superior smile on his face.

'On William Penn's authority, Friend. This is the map prepared at his request soon after the year 1685.'

'Lies! All lies! If it has William Penn's authority behind it, why has it not come to light sooner?'

The Surveyor's voice was like grease.

'The Gentleman forgets who was President of the Assembly before the present Deputy Governor. What point would there have been in trying to present such a map to the Assembly knowing the Deputy Governor would be bound to ignore it?'

'Art thou accusing Thomas Lloyd of dishonesty?'

'I'm accusing nobody – only explaining why I had to wait for Captain Blackwell's arrival before being able to act according to the Founder's wishes.'

Something resembling a smile broke out on Blackwell's face, and he said:

'The vote, Friends! Everyone in favour of changing the boundaries according to the plan on this map which has received the blessing of our honourable Governor, raise his hand!'

Gruffydd Owen's heart sank. The map changed everything. Even if Penn had not approved it officially with his signature there was no evidence to show he disapproved of it either. Obviously he had wished to allow the Assembly to make the final decision themselves.

'Against?'

There were three against: Doctor Owen himself, Samuel Carpenter and William Yardley, who felt that the Welsh should have time to consider the new evidence. The only other Welshman, Griffith Jones, voted with the others in favour of the new boundaries.

Gruffydd dashed out of the Chamber at once to tell Thomas Lloyd and John Eckley who were still waiting outside. They looked at each other in consternation. Gruffydd gave them a verbatim report of what Thomas Holme had said. Thomas Lloyd looked puzzled. He was trying to figure out what was wrong with Holme's statement. Certainly this was the first he

had heard of the map, and there was something else too . . .
Of course! He knew now what was wrong. And he became
very angry indeed.

Outside the Council Hall, Dorti found herself with Robin Wynn
among the crowd standing half way up the stairs. A great
number of people from the Welsh Tract had gathered there
despite the short notice, farmers and their wives, menservants
and maids, carpenters and tailors, smiths, coopers, craftsmen
of all kinds as well as land owners; men and women, thought
Dorti with a flame of independence still burning within them,
all waiting to hear the outcome of a discussion which would
affect their whole lives.

'Strange to think of Gruffydd Owen having to fight there all
by himself,' said Robin. 'If only the Welsh had seen to sending
proper representation to the Assembly before now, this situation
would not have arisen. That's what comes of concentrating too
much on their own little unit and forgetting there's a big world
outside.'

Dorti's answer was sharp.

'The Welsh Quakers never expected to have to fight every
inch of the way for their rights. And who are "they," Robin
Wynn? Thou art talking about "us" not some "they" thou dost
not belong to.'

Robin laughed. Sometimes that was exactly how he felt: not
a real part of the community. He was not a convinced Quaker,
neither was he a fiery Welshman fighting for the rights of the
Tract. He prided himself on his ability to look at things
objectively, as an impartial chronicler. To him the important
things in life were to be able to keep a sense of proportion and
a sense of humour. What was the point of feeling strongly one
way or the other when justice was not an absolute and could
be changed by new circumstances at any moment? Who was
he to say that truth, the whole truth belonged to only one man
or one side? That was why he could smile at Dorti now without
anger, and his smile almost drove her mad. What a pity she
was so emotional about her beliefs . . . And yet, did he not
find her earnestness charming? She must not, of course, be

allowed to influence him and make him into a humourless zealot like John Eckley. He suddenly realised that her admiration for John Eckley was beginning to get under his skin. He, Robin Wynn, to be jealous of John Eckley of all people!

There was a rustle of excitement near the great door, and the sound of voices rose above the murmur of the crowd. Then Thomas Lloyd appeared, standing on the top step. He raised his hand for silence. Behind him, on his left, stood John Eckley and on his right, Doctor Gruffydd Owen. The three looked very serious.

'Friends from Wales,' said Thomas Lloyd. 'When I came here today, I still believed that this fair city was rightly named the City of Brotherly Love. But after the indefensible action that has just taken place inside these walls, I am afraid that another name is more suitable for the City of Philadelphia . . . the City of Betrayal.'

A murmur arose from the crowd at these unusually strong words coming from the ex-Deputy.

'When John Eckley and I left the Chamber nearly an hour ago, I was confident that I had presented our case fairly and reasonably, and I believed that my brethren had given me a fair hearing. But after our departure — *after,* note that well Friends — a map was exhibited by the Surveyor, Thomas Holme, which he claimed had received the blessing of William Penn four years ago. This map divides the Tract into fragments. Why was it not brought out while we were still in the Chamber? Because, Friends, I can prove that this latest "testimony" of the Surveyor is a complete fabrication.

'This map refers to thirty-two plantations in Haverford, and forty in Radnor. But Thomas Holme has been over-confident and therefore careless. These are figures for *this* year. Four years ago there were only thirty plantations between all the Welsh townships. This map was drawn up deliberately to deceive the Assembly. And Holme and Blackwell have acheived their aim. A few moments ago the Assembly voted to abolish the unity of the Welsh Tract; and this before the Senate has a chance to debate the matter. I ask you now: are we going to relinquish our Charter and our rights so easily?'

A great cry rose up from the crowd. 'No!'

Inside the Chamber it was not possible to carry on with other business. Thomas Lloyd's voice came in through the open window and the Councillors looked uneasily at each other as they heard the crowd supporting him. Blackwell called one of the servants to him and instructed him to ask Thomas Lloyd either to keep silent or be arrested for causing a disturbance.

'It appears to me that we have two Governors now,' he grumbled, 'one inside the Chamber, and the other outside.'

CHAPTER TEN

Not everyone from the Tract was in Philadelphia that day. Sion Ifan had fully intended going in answer to Thomas Lloyd's request and had come in early from the fields to snatch a bite to eat before starting off. As he came into the house, he saw that the kitchen was empty. Nothing unusual in that these days; Lowri liked to go visiting. To be fair to her, she had been in poor health for most of the winter, and after days of being confined by the ague it was only natural she should want to go out at the earliest opportunity. Sion had to admit to himself he was relieved she was out of the way today, otherwise it would not have been so easy for him to go to Philadelphia.

He himself had never had a day's illness in his life, but far from making him impatient with other people's illnesses, he tended to regard it as sufficient grounds for the most capricious behaviour in others. And yet, even Sion suspected sometimes that a sudden headache was a convenient way of keeping him at home, when he wanted to go elsewhere.

He lifted the cauldron to see if there was a drop of *cawl* left, but although it still hung in its place above the fire, there was only about an inch and a half of greasy water floating in the bottom. Luckily, there wasn't much of a fire beneath it, otherwise it would have boiled dry.

He started to step over a pile of clothes in the direction of the buttery, but before he could get there he heard a stifled sound coming from the bedroom. He rushed in and saw Lowri lying fully clothed on the bed. Her face was blue, and the bed shook with her shivering. She had tried to wrap the blanket around herself to get warm, and one naked leg was still weakly searching for cover.

188

'Lowri!'

Sion Ifan was terrified. She was really and truly ill this time. He saw that the nails of the hand clutching the blanket were also blue. She did not open her eyes, but kept on groaning. Sion went to fetch another blanket and put it carefully around her. Her temperature must rise very high, and she must start sweating before she could get better. He knew that much. It was the sweating that was important. He had heard of some people failing to sweat, while their temperature still rose . . . Dorti, he had to fetch Dorti. She would know what to do.

But Dorti was bound to be on her way to Philadelphia, and, in any case, it would take him at least half an hour to fetch her from Ciltalgarth. He couldn't leave Lowri for that length of time. Lisa . . . it was highly unlikely that Lisa had gone with the others. She never went anywhere now. Thank goodness she still lived in the old cabin, only a stone's throw away. But he still hesitated — Lisa's behaviour had been very strange after Tomos's death, and he wasn't sure what sort of reception he would get. She hardly spoke to anybody unless she had to. He could not be sure that she did not blame him for . . . But what could he do?

If anything, the shivering was getting worse. He squared his shoulders. He had to get help. Gently he tried to move Lowri to the middle of the bed in case she fell out.

'I'll be back soon, *cariad*. Lisa will be here in a minute, and then I'll go and fetch a doctor.'

The groaning grew louder, and Sion could not tell whether she had understood or not. He hesitated no longer, and ran as quickly as he could to Lisa's cabin.

She was sitting by the fire staring into the embers as if seeing all her past in the dying coals.

'Lisa. Come and help me.'

She turned and stared vacantly at him, as if he were only a shadow standing there.

'Lowri's ill, Lisa. She's got the ague badly this time. She's had it before — but never as badly as this!'

A single flame lit up the embers for a moment, and perhaps the flame of life which appeared in her eyes momentarily was only a reflection of this. It died away at once, and she turned her head to the fire again.

'Only for a little while, Lisa,' said Sion. 'Come with me then I could go to—'

'Dorti. What about Dorti? Does she know? I'm sure Lowri would prefer . . .'

'Please come,' implored Sion. 'Dorti has gone with the others to Philadelphia or I should not be bothering thee, Lisa. Hurry, please, I implore thee.'

But she was already on her feet, thrusting the pins firmly in her untidy hair. As it happened, Rhys was at John Humphrey's house playing with Rowland Ellis's son, so she did not have to worry about him. For that matter, she was sure she would not have to stay long. Sion fussed so when Lowri was ill. Everybody knew about the three-day agues. All the patient had to do was keep warm, not catch cold, and it was all over almost as soon as the sweat broke. Sion was like a cat on hot bricks. She had difficulty in keeping up with him along the path between the two cabins.

In the bedroom Lisa looked down at the terrible sight on the bed. She drew in her breath. This was not the Lowri she knew. Her head was swaying continually from one side to the other, and the golden hair — usually so carefully arranged — was spread out like a dark hay-stack on the pillow. There were black smudges under eyes, seeming like bruises in the blue face.

'If Ellis Puw were here he would know exactly what to do,' whispered Lisa. Lowri's head was now hanging over the side of the bed. Trying to lift her back Lisa felt her forehead: it was burning hot under her hand. So the fever was rising now. Even as they looked at her, her colour changed, and the terrible blue started to turn to yellow.

'She'll be all right in a moment,' murmured Lisa comfortingly, and went to fetch some water and a cloth to try and cool the fevered forehead. She tried to give her some water, but Lowri pushed her arm up and the water spilt all over the coverlet. Sion Ifan and Lisa looked at each other without saying a word. So many Doctors in the Welsh Tract, and every one of them away in Philadelphia today. But the shivering at least

190

had stopped by now. Lisa sat down on the side of the bed and held Lowri's hand. Why did she have to be the only one available today? She looked at Sion Ifan, and a wave of pity came over her as she saw how much he had changed. She had heard the odd rumour of trouble — how Lowri was always complaining, and expected him not only to look after himself but after her as well, how she belittled him in public. She had heard about Siencyn Morris's son . . .

But she had refused to allow herself to open the lock on her emotions after Tomos's death, refused to allow the rumours to penetrate further than her ears. But now . . .

His back was bent a little, she noticed, and the healthy mischievous look had disappeared from his eyes. Stupid lout — that was what she had called him one evening, when Lisa had been there to hear. They said she took every opportunity of belittling him. Everybody was surprised at the way she had 'tamed' him so. Suddenly Lisa realised she was gripping the hot hand lying in her own, cruelly.

'One of the doctors could be back by now,' whispered Sion hesitantly. 'Had I better go?'

In the old days Sion would never have asked anyone what to do. A flicker of impatience flashed through her, followed immediately by pity.

'No. There's no point. No one can be back yet. Sit down. The fever is running its course.'

He obeyed at once and sat down on the other side of the bed, leaning on one hairy muscular arm. If she were to let go of Lowri's hand and move her fingers just along the blanket, she would be able to touch his. The old familiar thrill ran through her again. She turned her eyes away and stared at the cup in her other hand.

. . . *A golden cup in her hand full of abominations and filthiness of her fornication* . . . Had someone cried those words out loud? She continued to stare fearfully at the empty cup. God had chastised her twice for her wantoness; and here she was again, on this poor woman's bed . . .

She let go of Lowri's hand and started up in fear from the bed. Moving over to the table she let go the cup as if it were a burning brand. She stood there with her back to him, but every sinew of her body was aware of his presence. Her love and her longing were as alive as ever, and she, poor fool, had believed she had been able to smother every emotion. Her only hope lay in concealing her love. Only then could it remain undefiled. She must leave.

But Sion was standing beside her.

'Lisa . . .'

She was afraid to look at him.

'Lisa, th'art angry with me?'

Angry? The dear fool! She roused her eyes, and had no need to answer. For the first time ever, he saw her true feelings and he was stunned. Lisa . . . his sister, his innocent companion in the forest, his friend's wife . . . his friend's widow. He saw the colour suffuse her cheeks, and her eyes become black pools shimmering in the sun. The sharp outline of her face became tender, and he saw her throat flutter like a small bird in a shrub. The white flesh shone above the black bodice. Lisa . . . his loneliness broke through the dam. He lifted his hand slowly to touch her cheek.

'What's that woman doing here?'

The two spun round, guiltily to face the bed. Lowri was sitting up. Her eyes were two great burning coals in her head. Her voice croaked, indistinctly:

'Send her away from this house this instant! She wants to take my place.'

Then she began to cry, and became feverish again. Her lips were still moving but her words did not make sense.

'I'll go now.' Lisa moved towards the door; Sion took hold of her arm.

'No. She did not know what she was saying. Don't leave me now . . . wait . . . wait until . . .'

He did not finish the sentence. He did not need to. Slowly, as if she had no will left now, Lisa came back to sit at the bedside. And slowly, slowly, she took hold of Lowri's hand once more.

That same night Ellis Puw had another dream. He saw Dorcas standing halfway across a wooden bridge over a river. She was beckoning him to come nearer, but he had turned his eyes downwards to look into a whirlpool under the bridge. He heard her voice calling, but could not hear the words because of the noise the water made as it poured into the whirlpool. Dorcas began to step backwards still beckoning to him. She was smiling, but she could not understand why he did not hear her words. A mist surged up hiding her feet, then closed around her legs, before enveloping her completely like a shroud. He woke up suddenly to hear himself shout.

'I'm coming! Wait . . .'

He sat up in bed, bathed in sweat. Sinai turned drowsily in her sleep and Ellis looked down at her anxiously. How was he going to tell her that he must leave her and return to Wales? He knew now that the Lord had work for him there, for this was the third time he had had this dream.

In the Meeting House in Meirion personal problems had to be put aside for the time being for all discussion hinged upon the fate of the community. They organised their campaign carefully. The sixty freemen of Haverford and Radnor, that is, the men with a right to vote in the Election, met, and John Eckley was adopted as candidate. Thomas Lloyd's plan was simple, but daring. The freeemen had already been warned by the supervisors of the Election that they were expected to vote now in the County of Chester, but Thomas's plan was for them to ignore this instruction and deliberately go to Philadelphia and vote there as they had always done.

'We have stated clearly enough that we are not part of the County of Chester, nor a part of anywhere else but the Welsh Tract. The Tract is ready to send its representation to the State Senate, and ready to pay its fair share of the taxes. But we still claim we are one Barony, and this Meeting House is our main centre of administration. That was George Fox's vision. That was also William Penn's . . . once. Does anyone here hesitate? Does anyone here say in his heart that we shall be challenging the law by doing this? I tell you now . . . If the law be tyrannical and councillors deaf, which man among us is ready to bow his head and say passively "We are too weak." The spirit of

Christ which leads us to truth has put in our hands a weapon stronger than the legions of the Devil himself. Let us now show that the insult to our language, the theft of our land, and the denial of our rights, have all put fire in our veins!'

He stared intently at the faces before him. Everything depended on how they responded now. He knew that the people of Meirion were of one mind about the unity of the Tract; but he was not certain of some of the men of Radnor and Haverford After all, English was the language of many of them, and it would have been much easier for them to feel closer to their English neighbours than to the monoglot Welshmen of Meirion. However, he knew he could trust to their sense of fair play, and to their patriotism. The leader of the Pembroke group which had settled in Haverford was Henry Lewis of Narberth. It was to him Thomas Lloyd appealed now:

'What hast thou to say Henry? Art thou ready to stand with us?'

In the great silence which fell over the Meeting, every eye was fixed on Henry Lewis. His answer was vital, for he was a thoughtful man and a just man in the eyes of his fellow Welshmen. The men of Haverford would be bound to lay great stress on his opinion. A whole age seemed to pass while he considered Thomas Lloyd's words. At last he rose to his feet.

'Friend Thomas,' he began slowly. 'I am ready to act according to thy plan. And I am ready to go even further. Today I had notice that I have been appointed one of the magistrates of the County of Chester. I shall be informing the authorities that I refuse the commission.'

Thomas Lloyd drew a deep breath of relief. The unity of the campaign was now assured. He could hear a quiet rustle go through the room. They all felt that something important was about to begin. A young man from Radnor was standing up now. 'I too have had summons to act as constable in the court of the County of Chester. It will be an honour for me to refuse.'

Other voices were raised now: some had been summoned to act as jurors, others as constables. To refuse was contempt of court, but every one of them insisted that this was what they must do regardless of the outcome. The fight was on.

And a fight it was to be. They were all affected in one way or other. In the market, in the taverns, on the streets of Philadelphia, bitter words were exchanged between hitherto peaceful neighbours, until everyman had to make his choice and show his side in the quarrel. The trouble grew into something far more than the refusal of a community of Welsh people to lose their independence. English, German and Dutch Quakers came to feel more and more that their own priceless independence as freemen was at stake, threatened by the new authority of the Administration. With Thomas Lloyd, Samuel Richardson and, above all, John Eckley, as candidates, they saw a way of challenging those powers which threatened their democracy. The whole glorious Quaker vision in the New Land hung in the balance.

In the Welsh Tract the English Quakers were just as much in favour of the unity of the Tract as the Welsh themselves, not so much perhaps because of their zeal for the independence of the Welsh as because of their certainty that the Tract was their only hope for the continuation of Quakerism in the Province.

Most eloquent in condemning the Administration was David Lloyd. The democrat in him rebelled against the continuous rise in taxes, which brought suffering to farmers, merchants and craftsmen alike. He objected to the compulsory exporting of beaver and leather while cobblers, saddlers and hatters were having to pay a ridiculous price for their raw materials. He objected to the cruel injustices on the part of the Surveyor in land administration. The conviction deepened in him that the Government was daily growing further and further away from the common people.

It was also growing further away from Quaker principles. Patrick Robinson had been appointed Attorney General by the Deputy Governor, and one of his first actions had been to make stealing a capital offence. This in a state where hitherto even murderers had not suffered the death penalty. But what was to be expected? Neither Robinson nor Blackwell were Quakers. Where had the spirit of peace and reconciliation gone?

To Ellis Puw all this agitation was like a storm of thunder and lightning after a quiet summer's day. He longed to return to Wales, for he knew that was the Lord's wish. But the journey back was long and expensive, and he could not yet afford it. The day would come, he consoled himself, but it was not yet. When that day came to pass, the Lord would show him the way. In the meantime he had work to do.

He was helping those poorer than himself, the uneducated. He knew now that that was to be his task here. He himself was poor and uneducated, so who better, to understand the workings of these people's minds? The Tract leaders were gifted, educated people with lofty ideas and they did their work well. But someone was needed who could tell the menservants and the maids and the widows and the least among them that they too counted in the eyes of the Lord — just as much as the important people did, and that it was not given to scholars alone to understand the Scriptures and feel the love of the Father warm them. And the clever ones could be misled. Had he not heard that one of the leading Quakers was no longer teaching the children of Philadelphia the doctrine of Inner Light? He said this ruled out the intercession of Christ. This man, George Keith, claimed that no one could be saved through his own endeavours alone, but only through Christ.

That was not how he, Ellis, had been taught long ago by John ap John. God has many ways of speaking through the mouths of his prophets, John had said, but it was the light alone which enlightened everyman who came into the world, and was a direct communication between a man and his Creator. Salvation did not depend on the intercession of a third person, otherwise many people would be denied it, not only the poor and lonely but also little children, the mute, the deaf, the slow of understanding, and the weak of mind. And it was *his* work, Ellis Puw's, to comfort and to educate such poor creatures.

One day . . . and his eyes shone at the boldness of this new idea . . . one day, he would write down a guide for the

196

uneducated Welsh poor so that they could learn about eternal life in God. He would address them through a book, and call them away from many matters to the one essential, to the salvation of their souls.

Of politics and state administration — well, those he left to the wise, and those who believed good government alone was needed to make the world a better place. But for his part, he could see that Satan lay in wait more eagerly to corrupt those who governed rather than to corrupt the simple man. Government was a quicksand. Politicians were often obliged to use worldly methods to defeat the world, and there was no time for the contemplative life which put men before causes. True strength lay in quiet watchfulness . . . *those who wait upon the Lord, shall renew their strength . . .*

Suddenly the cold of winter turned into spring. Rivers thawed and the sound of waterfalls pouring down into the valleys was heard again. Flowers appeared on the arbutus tree, and the meadows were full of wild hyacinth and columbine; perch and carp came to the surface of the lake.

The Welsh had long ignored Penn's orders about the mills, and all along the Schuylkill the sound could be heard of busy corn and woollen mills, tannery and smithy. Dams were built to utilise the power of the waterfalls, and forests yielded to wheat fields and pasture land. Their prosperity strengthened them in their resolve that John Eckley should represent them in the Assembly . . . but only as one of the Tract representatives, not as a Chester representative.

On the day of the Election, there was a strange sight to be seen in Pennsylvania, a sight that would be later described by parents to children for generations to come. They saw the sixty freemen of Radnor and Haverford set off from the Meirion Meeting House for Philadelphia to cast their votes all together for the Welshmen from Meirion. It was a quiet procession and only the sound of their footsteps proclaimed their determination.

The fact that John Jarman of Radnor and Lewis John of Haverford had been taken into prison had added fuel to their resolve. The two had been arrested for refusing to act as

Constables in the County of Chester. Behind the freemen walked a solemn orderly crowd, angered by the treatment of the two young men, even those who had previously been lukewarm.

In his Draft, Penn had instructed that every vote was to be a secret one. This was not a remarkably revolutionary idea, since it was already in operation in New England; but procedure was not the same everywhere. In some places, the system of placing black and white beans in a hat was used — a just enough method of voting in the opinion of many people, and one which the Charter itself could not fault. But it worked only when there were no more than two candidates, known to all, and the choice between them clear and straightforward.

But this was an unusual election. Only one candidate had been nominated for the Welsh Tract — John Eckley, and no one at all had been nominated to oppose Thomas Lloyd and Samuel Richardson as representative for the County of Philadelphia. An open declaration or show of hands would no doubt have shown the same unanimity beyond any shadow of doubt that every man among them was free to vote according to his conscience. So that day all the freemen had been instructed to write down secretly on paper the name of the man of their choice, and place it in the big box in the voting area.

The election officers in Philadelphia were surprised to see nearly eighty sober-looking men silently file into the big room, every one in turn dropping his paper through the hole in the box.

There was no doubt as to the outcome. Every man from the Welsh Tract had voted solidly for John Eckley, and the vast majority in the County of Philadelphia had voted for Thomas Lloyd and Samuel Richardson.

'Dorti!'

The girl moved from the window and hurried towards the bed. 'Dorti . . . this pillow's too hard, I must have a softer one.' The voice became peevish. 'Really I don't know why I have to ask and ask. This bed hasn't been made for days . . . No, be careful, thou art hurting my head now . . . you are all so hard and selfish here. I have to go down on my knees to beg

198

for every favour. You'll all be glad to see me in my grave, I know that . . .'

The plaintive voice went on and on. Dorti could almost recite the words by heart before they were uttered. By the time Lowri was out of breath the words would have turned into tears. Dorti looked down at her without answering. She saw the bony body under the bedclothes, the claw-like arms, the lips drooping at the corners in a face which daily looked more like a parchment. Pity swelled up in her throat, pity not only for Lowri, but for everything beautiful which must wither away.

'What art thou looking at?'

Lowri, aware of her haggard appearance, had raised the sheet to her chin.

'Thou art glad to see me like this, art thou not, Dorti? This one won't be here long . . . I'll be rid of her soon . . . that's what thou art saying to thyself, isn't it?' She sat up painfully. The fever seemed to have attacked her again for her eyes blazed unnaturally.

'But I'm not going to die yet. Thou art not rid of thy sin so easily — nor that stupid husband of mine either. Nor that whore who's waiting for him . . .'

Dorti bent down, and put her arms around her and very gently forced her head back on the pillow. This woman no longer had the power to hurt her. She knew that now. Years ago, there had been a terrible wound. She shut her eyes, but there was no need to do that to see the pictures in her memory — Thomas sitting at Lowri's feet listening to her sad story about her cruel step-mother; Thomas announcing half-defiantly that he was going to marry her; Thomas with pale face and stormy eyes reproaching her hurtfully, quoting Lowri's words like a ventriloquist; Robin Wynn and the question he had not been able to utter: 'Did you commit incest?' What further harm could Lowri do her?

Sion Ifan came out of the shadows where he had been standing uncertainly. He was always uncertain now. What further harm could Lowri do him? Had Thomas been allowed to live he too would have turned into this apologetic creature with the watchful eyes. She thought of the night Sion had come to ask

199

her to look after Lowri. He had barely managed to make his request, perhaps because he felt the relationship between her and her sister-in-law to be a strange one. Goodness only knew what story Lowri had invented to amuse her husband in the early days of their marriage.

For the thousandth time, she asked herself why Lowri had chosen to marry Sion Ifan. In her personal relief, she had not wondered about it at the time, but the way Lowri had treated him afterwards, made it all the more puzzling. Perhaps indeed it was a mystery to Lowri herself. She had always wanted the trappings of respectability, and resented having to live as a servant, as she put it, in Huw Roberts's household. Perhaps she had really believed she could mould Sion into any shape she chose. Perhaps she had believed that she could persuade him to secure more and more land for himself and become rich. Others had been able to do that. But not Sion; that was not his nature. And yet who knows what a man's secret amibitions may be?

'She's asleep now.'

He nodded his head thankfully on hearing her comforting whisper, and withdrew again into the shadows. Dorti bent forward and wiped the damp forehead. Nothing, nobody had ever defeated Lowri before, she was the one who did the defeating. And now — her mouth was open, and her breathing painful. But she was quiet. Dorti tried to turn her mind in another direction.

In Philadelphia at that moment men were voting for John Eckley. Dorti would have liked to have been there more than anything else in the world. Perhaps she would be able to go tomorrow to see him being triumphantly presented to the Assembly. Would Sion be willing to look after Lowri on his own so that she could go? She smiled rather wryly for a moment. Sion Ifan was second to none in hacking his way through the forest or in ploughing furrows on the open plain, but inside the house he was like a sheep dog in a hen house. Perhaps Lisa would come. But Lowri would not let Lisa near the bedroom.

She took up a sheet and started to sew. Would Robin Wynn

go with her? Despite his usual desire to know all about what was going on Dorti could not be certain how he would act this time. She did not really know how he felt about John getting so much of the limelight. He spoke scornfully of him on every possible occasion — and Dorti was not too modest to realise why.

And yet Robin had not asked her to marry him. She had felt many times that he was on the verge of doing so, his body nearly touching hers, the warmth from his clothes reaching her, his eyes full of shadows and light. The tongue need not speak of love, they say. But she longed to hear words which did not come, and he never actually touched her. Yet he sought her company on every possible occasion, and all their friends assumed they were 'courting.' Those friends knew nothing of the bitter arguments, the mockery and the hurt feelings which embittered their relationship.

It was not Lowri's insinuations that were the bone of contention between them now, but the unity of the Tract. Robin had become friendly with his neighbours, John Dawson and his wife, and Dorti had come to realise that he now looked on the Tract more and more through their eyes. True they were all in Philadelphia today supporting John Eckley, but they supported him as a Quaker against the authority of the Assembly. Their feelings about the unity of the Welsh within the Tract were very lukewarm, and Robin agreed with them that for the Welsh to insist on holding their meetings and hearing their cases in their own language was a case of whipping a dead horse. Were not more and more people buying land in the Tract? And were not some of the Welsh themselves being induced to sell them that land because they paid well, much more than they normally expected? And who could blame those who sold? Were the Welsh expected to build a Great Wall of China around themselves to keep out other nationalities? Oh, he was sorry of course for those who could not speak English, but schools were being opened all over the state now, Robin said, and before long the English of the Tract children would be as good as William Penn's own, and did not the future belong to them?

The needle slipped and pierced her finger. Dorti watched a drop of dark blood well slowly to the surface.

But there was no need for Dorti nor anyone else to go to Philadelphia on the following day. When Blackwell and his supporters in the Assembly realised that the arch-trouble makers had been elected, they were furious. At once John Eckley's election was declared null and void, as, according to them, two thirds of the freemen in the Tract had voted in the wrong county.

Thomas had already warned them to expect this. 'But even if we have a hundred elections,' he told them, 'the result will be the same every time. In the end you will see that perseverance is more powerful than the mailed fist.'

On the day of the second election, they determined to show the strength of their unity by using both methods of voting, secret ballot and public vote. All of them went to the voting hall as before and each one put his paper in the box. But this time David Lloyd stood waiting for them outside the door and shouted to the great crowd assembled there.

'Freemen of the Welsh Tract, whom do you wish to have represent you in the Senate of Pennsylvania?'

The answer came in a great shout that reverberated down the street: 'John Eckley!'

'Every one of you?' David demanded.

'Every one!'

The quiet people, that was how they liked to think of themselves. But it was hard to keep quiet as they escorted their three new representatives to the Assembly, for after the second election not a word had been heard from Blackwell.

Not a cloud scarred the blue of the sky that day, not a puff of wind. The sun spread its fiery mantle over the streets of Philadelphia and its light was reflected in the shining faces of the Quakers who walked resolutely behind the three elected men. There was no need of tabard or pipe, trumpet or song to help them on their way. The rejoicing was within. They had declared their will against the authority of the Government. Justice had been reinstated. The children ran alongside them, chattering and laughing, though they did not know why. Today nobody reprimanded them or told them to behave more decorously. Their parents just smiled. The inhabitants of Philadelphia came to their windows and out on to their windows and out on to their doors steps to watch the victorious Welshmen march by.

They had reached the Council Hall and were climbing the stairs. On the top step stood six soldiers, each one with musket in hand. Only the slightest movement of his eyelids betrayed how deeply offended Thomas Lloyd was at seeing soldiers guard the Quaker Senate House. They did not move as the three councillors walked past them. On, on across the entrance hall, until they reached the great Chamber. Thomas put out his hand to open the familiar door, but it did not move. He tried to turn the knob, but the door was firmly locked against them. He began to knock on the oak door in front of him, quietly at first and then harder and harder, continuing to knock determinedly, the other two joining in. On either side of the door were two windows high in the wall, and these were open on account of the heat. The three of them were aware that the Assembly could not proceed with all this noise going on outside.

Then Thomas made a sign to the others, and they ceased their knocking. He raised his voice and shouted through the window:

'John Blackwell! How long dost thou intend to close thine ears to the voice of justice? The mills of God will turn against those who refuse to listen to the voice of the people. Remember that. Thou, an old soldier of Cromwell, shouldst *know* that already. Open up for us, the elected representatives of the people. Open!'

The voice could be heard resounding from the ceiling as the tide beats against a rock before it recedes. Then came silence, and the three men waited, knowing that the men on the other side were waiting just as expectantly.

Then suddenly the silence was broken by the sound of someone running towards them from the direction of the great door. They saw Gruffydd Owen push past the soldiers. At his heels were Samuel Carpenter and William Yardley, two others who had opposed the new boundaries. These men had realised at once what was happening. The other councillors had plotted together to arrive early so as to be able to lock the door against John Eckley's supporters. Gruffydd's voice thundered out:

'Friends, there are more of us here now — William Yardley, Samuel Carpenter and I, Gruffydd Owen. We ask you to open this door. In shutting us out you are not only breaking the law, but also making prisoners of yourselves at the same time.'

At once came the sound of bolts being drawn. It was as if Gruffydd Owen's voice had been a sign for those inside the Chamber. The door was opened and there stood Blackwell guarded by six more soldiers. Behind them stood the members of the Assembly.

'We shall open the door for you, Doctor Owen, Mr. Carpenter, Mr. Yardley. But it is closed against traitors and unruly conspirators. A legal case is being prepared against this man, Thomas Lloyd, and I will not, under any circumstances, receive him in this Chamber.'

The look Blackwell threw at Thomas was one of pure hatred. Gruffydd moved aside and with a sweep of his arm, invited the three new councillors to precede him into the room. Immediately the soldiers closed around them, their muskets raised to prevent their entry. John Eckley made as if to challenge them, but Thomas reached out a hand to stop him.

'No John. It is the power of the gun and the sword which prevails here. These Friends have chosen to forget the words of the Lord Jesus. We know that everyone who takes up the sword shall perish by the sword. The will of the people will be stronger in the end than all the threats of those drunk with their own power.'

The Councillors shuffled uncomfortably behind the obstinate bulk of the Captain's body. From the very beginning they had been unhappy about Blackwell's personal grudge against his predecessor. On the other hand, they told themselves this was the man appointed by William Penn himself and therefore a man who claimed their loyalty. But some of them had begun to feel pricks of conscience. Was it not the duty of those who believed in the Inner Light to oppose anything which threw a veil over that Light, no matter who he was? Otherwise, they would be guilty of setting Government above conscience. It was right to safeguard the interests of the Founder and to proclaim their loyalty to the King, but the Quakers found these strong arm tactics for keeping order unfamiliar and undesirable. Thomas Lloyd's words seared their conscience.

Thomas had turned away now and was walking across the hall to join his companions. The other five accepted his leadership and followed him. One look at their faces and those outside knew there was something amiss. The low murmur turned into an expectant silence. Thomas took a step forward and started to speak.

'Friends . . . When we came here seven years ago, we had hoped we were turning our backs for ever on oppression and violence, intolerance and hatred. Our faces were turned towards the New Jerusalem. The Holy Experiment, that was how we dreamed and talked of this country, a place where we could worship God without fear, a country where we could live and work according to the Lord's will, a country where every man would be as free as the next to voice his opinion, for each man's soul is precious in the sight of God. This was Friend William Penn's vision. We followed him joyfully to this country and no one denies that we have received many privileges here.'

He waited a while, his eye moving from one face to another before him. Even the children were still.

'It is very easy, Friends, to lose privileges; not so easy to recover them afterwards. Inside this Chamber behind me, are men who are prepared to bear arms to force you to give up your right to pass your own laws, to establish your own courts, to raise money, to elect your own representatives according to your own wishes. To this end, they are ready to lock the door in the faces of those who have been elected by you in a fair election . . .'

Dorti caught John Eckley's eye upon her. He looked worried and disappointed. Yet there had never been such a welling up of support for Thomas Lloyd as there was now among the ordinary colonists, not only among the Welsh, but among Quakers of all nationalities. His words reflected the hopes and ideals of all of them, as well as their fears for the future. As she looked back at John Eckley, Dorti's eyes tried to convey all this.

Suddenly their attention was taken by a movement behind Thomas Lloyd. Outside the door of the Council Hall something very strange was taking place. While he had been addressing the crowd, about two dozen men had appeared quietly behind him. These were not soldiers, as the onlookers had at first feared, but members of the Assembly. They came now to stand behind Thomas, side by side with John Eckley, Gruffydd Owen and the others. Their intention was clear. Another two dozen out of the sixty or more members of the Assembly had felt enough shame to turn their backs on Blackwell and his supporters and had come to stand beside Thomas Lloyd. And more would follow.

Dorti turned her eyes towards John again, and this time they both smiled at each other.

CHAPTER ELEVEN

One day towards the end of the summer Rowland Ellis called on William Penn at his house in London. Although Rowland had heard him speak years ago this was the first time the two men had met, for Rowland had reached Pennsylvania two years after the Founder had left. As he stared intently at the stout figure in front of him, it was difficult for Rowland Ellis to believe that this was the same person as that handsome young man who had shared the same platform as George Fox fourteen years earlier. Over-flushed face, pot belly, white flesh, loose skin of the hands, all betrayed the years of over indulgence. Yet there still lurked in those large eyes some traces of the innocence and vision of the dreamer.

Could this dual nature of his be responsible for his present troubles? Rowland had heard from the London Quakers that William Penn was in danger of being sent to prison. There were rumours of letters written to ex-King James in France, letters which had been discovered, strangely enough, in a cave on the shores of Flintshire . . . and what was Thomas Wynn's role in all this? Rowland thrust the thought from his mind. No doubt William had been unwise in his friendship with James, but he could hardly believe, as some did, that Penn was a secret Jesuit. Throughout all the Founder's actions, there ran a strange innocence, as if he were saying to himself: If I do this, or if I say that in order to achieve just ends, everything will come right in the end.

And that is how it must have been with the promises made to the Welsh. Hand in hand with this man's great vision went a wish always to evade the unpleasant. That was his tragedy. That was why George Fox, and particularly Margaret Fox,

207

were so suspicious of him now.

Then William Penn smiled at Rowland Ellis, and the Welshman warmed to that smile. His doubts disappeared. This man was full of charity and sympathy. He could not be otherwise. With renewed confidence Rowland began to tell him about the troubles of the Welsh people in Pennsylvania, of what he knew from personal experience, and of what he had learnt from a long letter from Huw Roberts — the letter which had prompted him to come to London.

'Thou must have heard of the quarrels, Friend William. I have come here today at the request of my fellow Welshmen so that thou might hear an account personally from one of us.'

Rowland spoke of the difficulties Thomas and David Lloyd had had with Blackwell from the first; of the elections and how the successful candidates had been kept out of the Assembly by military force; of the real danger now that the state would be split down the middle setting Quakers against the Administrators.

'It's only a word from thee that can change all this, William Penn. Thou are the only one who can restore brotherly love and tolerance there. Recall Blackwell, I implore thee, and let the Councillors themselves choose their own Deputy Governor before it is too late. More and more men who are not Quakers are being elected to the Senate, and it is in Captain Blackwell's interest to increase their number.'

A frown appeared on the kindly face of William Penn. He poured out two glasses of wine, handed one to his visitor, then took a deep drink from his own glass before replying. 'Thomas has been a great worry to me, and David even more so, for he has been ungrateful and disloyal!'

Roland broke in swiftly:

'No, not disloyal to thee, Friend William. On the contrary, it was because they were so loyal to thy great and holy ideal that they had to act as they did.'

William twisted the thin stem of his glass thoughtfully. Rowland got the impression that he was having difficulty in keeping his mind on the conversation. The chair creaked under his great weight, and he closed his eyes. The Welshman was suddenly reminded of his visit to Lefi Huws long ago, a

208

comparison confirmed by the Founder's next words.

'I am surprised that Thomas Lloyd puts such stress on government and administration since the Welsh and all the others are absolutely free to run their religious meetings as they choose. Is that not the most important thing in the long run? Government is not an end in itself, only a means. It is a great grief to me to hear that some people are turning administration into a religious matter. Government is merely a human and moral institution to do with society, trade, law and public good.'

Rowland remembered sentences in the Frame of Government which completely contradicted this statement — 'Government is part of religion itself,' Penn had stated then, 'sacred in its institution and end . . .' At the time Penn had been criticised harshly for emphasising the sanctity of Government, now he had swung to the other extreme. Rowland was amazed at the way he could turn that statement upside down and use it to prevent Quakers from taking part in their own government.

'So the Holy Experiment has ceased to be holy?'

'No, no, no. It's still holy in so far as everyone is free to worship as he wishes!'

So it was to this that the great dream had come? Was it impossible therefore to combine God's church and the State? Rowland's heart sank.

'It was not only for freedom to worship that we went over to Pennsylvania, William Penn,' he began slowly. 'It is true that some people went over because they feared persecution and that some went in the hope of material gain, but the majority of them went in the purity of their hearts and in a burning desire to see Christ rule every aspect of their lives. That was Thomas Lloyd's goal, I can assure thee, and it is a grief to all of us to see Blackwell bring a legal charge against him because of it. Oh, I know I am only speaking at second hand, but if thou wert to have an hour with Thomas Lloyd himself, thou wouldst be on his side.'

He was not sure what impression his words were having on the great man before him. He even doubted whether Penn was really listening.

'How would it feel, William Penn, for thee to see Thomas

Lloyd in prison in the New Jerusalem, and that because of his unshakable faith?'

The dreamy eyes turned slowly towards him, and the two men looked at each other for a moment in silence. Then William Penn got up from his chair clumsily, and a great sadness seemed to fill the room.

'Thou dost not know half my troubles, Friend. Thou sayest I am the one with the power to change things. But that is not true today. Enemies are pressing me on all sides.'

He shook his head hurriedly, as if to shut out something from his mind, then went on:

'Thomas is an old friend. I should not like to see him going under. No . . . I thank thee for calling on me, Rowland Ellis . . .' With that, he started to walk slowly towards the door but stopped half-way hesitantly. He turned, a gentle smile on his visitor, but his mind was clearly on something else. It was as if he were listening, listening. Listening for what? Rowland wondered.

Obviously, the interview was at end. Rowland would have liked to have had a more definite answer, and he waited a few moments, questions hovering on his lips. But of what value was an oral promise after all? They had had that before. The most he could hope for now was that the seed of his words had somehow somewhere, fallen on fertile soil.

Robin Wynn signed his name on the document and threw the quill down on the table with a gesture of satisfaction.

'There you are, Richard Fenn.'

He pushed a little leather bag across the table. 'My debts cleared before I even start ploughing. What more could a farmer wish for?'

The other looked at him smiling.

'The land you have here is second to none. You won't regret buying it, I'll warrant. When does your uncle come back?'

'He's on his way already. That's why I was so anxious to complete this business. Jack the master cannot bear to think of himself as a servant.'

He laughed as he said this, but it was with very mixed feelings that he closed the door on his visitor. It had been a bitter blow to him to hear that Thomas Wynn had decided to return to Pennsylvania, this time bringing his wife and children with him. He realised of course that he was only a kind of bailiff for his uncle at present but the old Doctor had left him alone for so long he had almost succeeded in persuading himself that he, Robin Wynn, was the owner of the land and everything on it.

He had been surprised at himself for taking to farming as he had done. True he had been lucky enough to find faithful, hardworking slaves, but he had also worked very hard himself. It was pleasant to stand in the evening, and look out on the tresses of wheat blowing in the breeze, knowing that he himself was responsible for the abundant crop — with the help of God's grace, of course, he hastened to add. And now the whole family was coming over to claim their estate. So what was going to happen to Robin Wynn? Was he to return to a position of dependence again? God forbid! So at the first opportunity he had started to look around for a farm for himself.

Before long he had found the very place. Not a large farm, but there was plenty of wild land to the west which could be developed later if necessary. There was a pleasant house on a rise of land looking down over a bend in the river; around it were wide meadows of tobacco plants; and to the east, the Bay of the Delaware opening out into the Atlantic.

He was fortunate in having been able to buy this property from Richard Fenn, a farmer who had reason to be grateful to Doctor Wynn for curing him of the small pox on board the *Welcome* long ago. Robin had heard that a relation wanted Richard Fenn to return to his old home in Worcestershire, and he had at once taken advantage of the opportunity this offered.

He had not said a word to his friends in Meirion about his intention. He had not even told Dorti Llwyd. For that matter it would be more difficult to tell Dorti than anyone else, for not only was his new property outside the Welsh Tract, but it also happened to be in New Castle, one of the sub-counties populated mainly by Anglicans. He knew that these counties wanted to break free of the rule of the people of the North, the majority of whom were Quakers, and Robin could see that they were bound to succeed sooner or later, for the anti-Quaker population was growing daily. It was not this which worried him so much as the knowledge that he would lose his friends in the Tract, perhaps for ever. This was a cause of real concern to him. He did not like anyone to think badly of him, and he knew very well that the Welsh would not look with favour on anyone who chose to break away.

But time heals, he consoled himself, picking up the deeds in front of him with an owner's pride. He could see himself wandering over his own acres: Wheat and hay over here, pumpkins and potatoes over there, but most of all tobacco; and a happy band of Negro workers, singing as they lifted the sheaves. Then back to his own house to his wife sitting by the fireside, spinning, weaving, mending, giving breast to his child . . . He realised that the face of the wife at the fireside was Dorti's and he laughed out loud. Who else but Dorti? In his newly acquired confidence as land owner he could laugh at his old doubts. Really, there was a certain charm in the mystery that surrounded her. How stupid of him to withdraw, withdraw all the time. Dorti had hidden depths of love far beyond those of most women. When she loved, she loved passionately. He saw that now. And it was easy enough for him to see that her love had been turning towards him for some time now. He wanted a wife. Was not that the natural desire of every farmer since Adam? He wanted Dorti.

Come to think of it, it had been unfair of him to keep her waiting for so long without giving her the security she craved. He would make it up to her the very next day. His decision filled him with warmth. Of course she would find it difficult at first to leave the Tract, but a wife's love for her husband was more powerful than her love of anything so vague as a land or a community. A woman's concerns were always with the less abstract things. A husband, children, a home of her own, that was what every woman wanted above all else. Dorti would soon make new friends in her new home.

He went to bed that night his conscience quieter than it had been for a long time. He thanked his uncle silently for being the means of forcing him to see the hidden possibilities in himself.

The whole place was alive with the story, but no one was sure what exactly had happened. Some said that William Penn had already been in Pennsylvania a fortnight, secretly looking into matters; others said that Captain Blackwell had suffered a fit of apoplexy; others, more fancifully, that the King had discovered Blackwell to be in the pay of the French and that a regiment of soldiers was on its way down from New York to arrest him. But people tended to believe those who claimed to have seen a coach full of boxes, and a cart full of furniture, leaving the Governor's house in the early hours of the morning, going down in the direction of the quay. Of the Deputy Governor himself there had been no sign for days. If all this were true then Blackwell was already on his way back to London. And good riddance too — that was the opinion of most people. Ever since that never to be forgotten day when he had tried to use force to keep out the new councillors, a feeling of guilt had been growing in the Chamber. Through that action, more than anything else, the Duputy had betrayed a basic Quaker principle.

The three elected councillors were no longer prevented from going in. On the contrary, they were listened to with unusual respect on every side, apart from Blackwell's own diminishing circle. Gradually the Deputy had come to sense that he did not speak the same moral language as the others. Thomas Lloyd had published a pamphlet questioning the right of the Deputy to make laws on his own without first getting the agreement of the freemen of the two Houses. It had already had a startling reception from the colonists.

Blackwell had not gone yet. But in his fine house overlooking the Delaware he knew he had lost the battle. Sitting at his desk, quill in hand, he dipped it into the inkwell and started to write his letter to William Penn, a letter full of confusion and anger.

'. . . I expect now only my release. For I see it is impossible for me to serve you in this place. Thomas Lloyd is a serpent whom you have fostered. He is pushing his oar into every boat . . .'

Rowland never really knew how much effect his visit had had on the Founder. Towards the end of the year, he received a letter from Thomas Lloyd thanking him for intervening on his behalf.

'It was from William Penn himself that I learnt of thy visit,' he wrote. 'The twists and turns of destiny always work towards the same end, like countless threads on a loom coming together to form one pattern. William Penn had no need to recall Brother Blackwell; the latter forestalled him by sending in his resignation. When he accepted it William Penn forbade Blackwell to proceed with his intention to prosecute me, reproving him for behaving in a quarrelsome and contentious manner. Great is my gratitude to thee and to the Lord for sending thee there on my behalf. And now I must tell thee this: at their Meeting today the Assembly decided to re-elect me Duputy Governor. I had been praying for this, not so much for my own upraising, but in order to continue to serve my fellow countrymen and to guard their welfare. We are waiting now to receive William's assent to the will of the people . . .'

Rowland gave a sigh on reaching the end of the letter. Another knot had been untied. The future of the Welsh Tract should now be secure. And these troubles seemed so far away from Wales, and other bonds, more personal ones, were being unloosened around himself and Marged.

Looking back over his forty years he wondered why these bonds between himself and his loved ones had always been more a cause of grief than joy. Meg . . . a bond where young love tried to stifle conscience; there was the bond which slackened when minds grow apart: The bond tying him to his daughter Ann — that bond was cut cruelly that day a year ago leaving himself bruised within.

And yesterday another bond had been severed.

He climbed the stairs in the unnaturally quiet house and went into the room which had been his daughters' bedroom. Ann's bed remained empty, as it had done since that awful day when

214

the girl had stormed at him about his narrow religion, his lack of understanding, his neglect of his children. At the time he could have sworn that it was Meg, her mother, standing there, and that she would now raise her hand to strike him across the face like before. But Ann had run out of the house, away to Dolrhyd to her lover.

His eye moved now to the other bed. Sian was lying there in her white gown, the band about her head giving her the appearance of a nun. For once the Quaker in him did not mind the comparison. How silent she was now, how different from her silly laughter and perpetual purring noises. He marvelled now at the strange wisdom in the marble faces which until yesterday, had been so cruelly vacant, stupid. Losing her was even more of a blow to Marged than to himself. Over the years some strange understanding had developed between the two of them; the woman caring for the child day and night until the personalities of both had fused into each other. It was Marged herself who had said that it was time to cut the last knot, and that was Bryn Mawr itself. He was more relieved than he could say that it was she who had said it first. It was impossible to keep roots in two places — that is what she had said. So was it not better to sell what was left of the farm? Lewis Owen, Tyddynynygarreg, had already said he wanted to buy it.

Marged looked at him directly as she added: 'And we can give some of the money to Ann as a dowry.'

His first response had been bitter.

'A dowry for that English curate instead of a tithe for his church?'

But there was no real bitterness left in his heart; he was too tired. He did not know how long he knelt at Sian's bedside. Then he felt a hand on his shoulders, the hand that was always there to comfort him. What was past was past. The future lay with Marged, and their children, in that far land over the sea where a fair-haired boy was waiting for them.

Robin had gone over every step carefully in his mind. The first thing he must do was to ask Huw Roberts for permission to ask Dorti to marry him. Again he laughed out loud thinking of it. Everyone knew they had been courting for years, and to broach the subject to Huw now would only be a matter of form. He intended to do everything formally from now on. As a landowner he must say goodbye to the carefree days of living from moment to moment. He had begun to mature on the day he had felt the hardness of the mattock in his hand, and now . . . Dorti would be sure to approve of the new Robin Wynn.

As he ate his lonely breakfast, he could imagine her sitting opposite him sharing his table, elegantly straight-backed, raising her head every now and again to smile at him. He would go out to inspect the servants, and come back to the smell of bread baking in the oven, and meat turning on the spit above the fire, to the sound of his children chattering. He could see her now, in the evening, sitting with him at the fireside before going up to bed. And in that bed he would explore the mystery of her body, until they reached the sweet release.

The day drifted on until it was time for him to start for Ciltalgarth. As he had expected his news was received warmly by Huw Roberts, and if Robin felt a twinge of conscience at not mentioning the location of his new property well, sufficient unto the day . . .

She was in the kitchen, but here was no smell of bread baking, or of meat turning on the spit. Gainor, Huw Roberts's sister, was dozing by the fire. Dorti was sitting at a table beside the window, her head bowed over a pile of manuscripts. He felt annoyed for a moment: that damned poetry again! Then he smiled: Dorti had too much time on her hands. It would be different once she was in her own home.

Huw Roberts gave his sister a gentle poke to wake her up, and gestured to her to follow him out of the room. Dorti heard her sleepy fussing and slowly raised her head to see who was there. When she saw the visitor she brightened up at once.

'I didn't hear thee arrive.'

'No. You looked pretty far away. Are you glad to see me?'

She blushed, and she smiled in response to the warmth in her eyes.

'Of course I'm glad . . .' she said, adding softly, 'always.'

216

He wasn't going to waste any time on trivialities. Time was too valuable now, with the question bubbling inside him. He crossed over to her, took hold of her hands and pulled her to her feet, so that she was standing very close to him.

'Dorti . . . I've just been speaking to Huw Roberts.' The blush deepened and he heard her quick breathing.

'You know why . . . Dorti. I want you for my wife. You will marry me, won't you?'

There was a moment of silence. She hesitated, waiting for him to say more. He sensed at once what she wanted to hear.

'Dorti, I love you.'

At last he had his arms around her kissing her passionately, as if — the strange idea came into her head — as if he were challenging himself to believe otherwise. And she was yielding now, her body melting into his own, her lips soft on his. She did not reply, but he got his answer in the way her arms went around his neck like a laurel wreath around a conqueror's head.

For a long time they remained thus, then at last they broke apart and started to laugh, a laugh of pure pleasure.

In dream after dream she had heard him say these words, words always ending with the one important question. But it had not happened until today. Until now she had not even felt his hand in hers — not since the night of her confession. Sometimes she had felt that he was terribly angry with her.

But now the days of uncertainty were over. Robin was hers and she was Robin's. Something new had happened to him. The moodiness had disappeared, he had not said one mocking word. The shoulders were squarer, and there was a new confidence in his whole bearing. It was the gentle, mischievous voice of the Robin she had known before which now asked her to marry him. Dorti felt like Branwen freed after years of penance with all the grief of the past melting away. She was floating on a cloud now, the sun warming her body, melting every spot of ice inside her.

Life was perfect, thought Robin, all his doubts dispelled. How stupid they all seemed now. Somehow by insisting on climbing the steep rock, he had discovered that the rock itself had disappeared. One other rock remained, but he

217

felt now that that, too, would soon disappear.

Calmly, carefully he began to tell her about her new home.
'New Castle?'

He could expect nothing else for the moment. He heard the
fear and disappointment in her voice, and thought, it's only
natural she should feel like this about it at first. But when he
had explained everything, and described the lovely place, she
too would come to feel as enthusiastic about it as he did.

The girl stared at him and saw all her hopes trickle away
like sand through her fingers. A few moments ago she had felt
blessed among women. And now . . . she listened to the words
which sounded the knell to her dreams.

'Life there won't be so different from what you are used to
here. You'll be better off in many ways. Neither of us will be
dependants in other people's homes any more. You will have
your own house, with your own maids — I promise you
that. The children will never have to worry about where the
next ha'penny's coming from. And there's a Meeting House
near by—'

'An English Meeting House!'

'What does that matter? It's the same Gospel in any language.'

'I shall be away from my own people.'

Her voice became flat with disappointment. He frowned.

'Dorti! Dorti! You left your own people behind in Wales.'
Robin tried to laugh, but it was a poor attempt. 'The journey
from here to New Castle is far shorter than from Penmaen to
Pennsylvania!'

'I was changing my country then, not my community. A
community of people is more important than a country.'

'What rubbish! It's up to everybody to merge into the society
in which he finds himself.'

'Yes. But that only applies to the weakest. We haven't merged
into Indian society have we? Are the English trying to merge
into the Welshness of the Tract?'

'I have said it before, a hundred times, it's the strongest that
wins every time. We might as well admit it and take life as
it comes.'

With a deep sigh, she realised that he had not begun to

218

understand.

'That's where we are so different from each other, Robin. In any other community but a Welsh one I would eat, drink, sleep, breathe — but in the end it would kill me. Dost thou not see? If we have children they will be strangers to us.'

'You have to accept that as inevitable. It was your own fault for leaving Wales in the first place. Even Thomas Lloyd cannot save the Welsh Tract now. It's too late. There are too many foreigners here already.'

The darkness was beginning to close around them. She must stay, she told herself fiercely. They had been betrayed from outside, but God forbid that anyone from inside should betray them as well. For her, it was all so clear. She could not turn her back on the Tract, it would be treachery.

But there was another reason why she had to stay.

'Robin . . . try to understand this. I cannot leave Lowri.'

He looked at her in amazement.

'Lowri?' He could not believe his ears. 'What has she to do with you now. She's Sion Ifan's. Lowri is his responsibility.'

She knew that her answer sounded lame to him.

'She's terribly ill. The ague sometime turns into Black Water fever and it nearly happened last time. It could really happen next time.'

'But why you? Are there not enough women to look after her?'

'But none understand her as I do. She will not have anyone else.'

All his disappointments, his frustration, his inability to understand caught on to this one thing and he lost control completely.

'Lowri! Lowri again! Every time we come close to one another she comes between us. She must have bewitched you. God only knows you have reason enough to hate her — but here you are now, choosing her rather than me.'

He was genuinely perplexed. How could anyone choose a person she hated rather than someone she loved? Was he not young, goodlooking, easy-going, a landowner? And he loved her. What kind of woman was this who refused what other women desired above all else?

'Really, it's impossible to understand you. But perhaps I understand only too well!' His voice became hoarse. 'Lowri

Llwyd is still a link between you and your brother!'

In his anger he caught hold of the pile of manuscripts on the table and swept them on to the ground.

'So much for you and your fine brother! I'm glad I realised in time.'

Dorti stood there frozen to the spot, the words striking at every nerve of her body like poison arrows. She heard him stride away from her, and the door bang after him.

Slowly she sat down again. She should be crying, but her eyes were dry. She felt as if another Dorti Llwyd was standing outside her body, watching every emotion in herself from afar. That other Dorti spoke to her now. 'The choice has been made for thee now. Thou art free of thy doubts. Thou art free of the temptation to turn thy back . . . half thy mind does not have to run after his ideas . . . ever again . . .'

Later on perhaps her feeling would return to her. But now she could feel nothing. She went on her knees on the floor and started to pick up the manuscripts.

CHAPTER TWELVE

Lowri died one quiet morning in that bright autumn. All night long she had fought fiercely to keep hold on life. Gradually her screams had turned into sobs, and the sobs into heavy, painful breathing. Dorti and Sion Ifan had watched with terror the fear of death which clutched her. As the morning sun pushed its way through the leaves outside her window, a change had come over her; the other two had both seen the shadows that come on people's faces before they die.

When the breathing stopped, Dorti fell to her knees, but she was too tired to pray. Her mind failed to find the appropriate words. She knew that Sion Ifan was on his knees beside her, and her thoughts were mainly on him, thoughts which at last turned into prayer. She prayed that he would be able to find again the happiness and confidence he had lost. What would he do now, she wondered. How did he feel? His life would be very strange without Lowri, and no one could blame him if he behaved like an eagle suddenly released from a cage. Dorti opened her eyes and looked at him suddenly, she saw that there were tears trickling silently down his cheeks.

For the thousandth time she marvelled at Lowri's ability to attract men's love. In spite of the ravages of her illness, her unfaithfulness, her complaining and belittling of him, this big strong man could even now weep for her. Thomas too . . . No. She would never understand, never . . .

And she herself, Dorti — what about her? She was, at long last, truly free. Free in a way she had never been, even when Lowri had married Sion Ifan. She started to cry quietly — not for Lowri, but because all this had come too late. Thomas was in his grave, Robin Wynn was on the point of marrying Ben

Dawson's daughter — it was always too late, and there was no one in this world to understand the strange desires of her heart.

No, that wasn't true either. John Eckley understood, although perhaps he could not, any more than she could, put a name to those desires. She had seen very little of him recently because she had been involved with Lowri, and he was busy trying to catch up on his farm work as well as all his political work. But one day, on the way out of Meeting, he had greeted her shyly, hesitantly and pushed a little package into her hand.

'I do not know if thou wouldst like to look at these, Dorti Llwyd. It's a collection of Morris Kyffin's work which I copied some time ago. I know thou art fond of reading.' Then he added, seeing her flush with pleasure: 'There are some poems by Edward Morris too, and one by Rhisiart Phylip greeting John Davies, Mallwyd.'

She knew all about these:

> ' . . . A'th blant di—waith, blina' ton,
> Aeth i sisial iaith Saeson . . .'

> 'Woe that your unemployed children,
> Now whisper the Saxon tongue . . .'

John Eckley *did* understand. He knew the secret she had shared with Thomas. She got up from her knees suddenly, feeling that her unspoken prayer was about to be answered.

In the year 1691 the Welsh made their last attempt to keep their unity. During the months leading up to the attempt, their hopes had been dwindling rapidly. Not because they were losing faith in Thomas Lloyd — as Doctor Gruffydd Owen was careful to stress in the Meeting House — but because the difficulties of the Welsh were bound to become submerged in all the great cares of his office.

And those cares were increasing daily. The fight was now between the rights of the community as a whole and the rights of certain pushful individuals among them. What hope did a small group like the Welsh have of obtaining justice, thought

John Eckley, when there was so much else to claim the attention of the majority of the people? The question of the new harbour for instance. George Keith was on his feet now arguing fiercely on behalf of the three merchants. Everyone knew that a new harbour was needed, in addition to the one near The Blue Anchor, in order to maintain the increasing trade in Philadelphia. At the moment the perpetual delay, with everyone having to wait his turn at unloading cargo, meant great financial loss to the colonists. Thomas and David Lloyd between them had earmarked the only piece of suitable land for the new harbour; and these three wealthy merchants had beaten them to it, and bought this particular piece of land for a personal venture.

John Eckley listened with growing distaste to the nasal, school-masterly voice quoting John Locke. George Keith was trying to prove that by granting the request of these three merchants the Assembly would be upholding the freedom of the individual against the oppression of the state. The good of society versus the good of the individual – John Eckley knew that he would be supporting the Lloyds. But the rights of the greater society against the lesser? Was there a separate principle involved there, or was it all part of the same principle?

Thomas Lloyd was drawing his hand slowly across his forehead. He is growing old, John realised suddenly, a sudden fear mingled with pity. He caught David Lloyd looking at him, and knew that he too had noticed that same tired gesture.

George Keith's voice thundered on:

'These three gentlemen have clearly tried to find land in other places, and have been faced every time with stubborn opposition. They tried to buy a strip of land near the Schuylkill waterfall. And the answer? Oh no, the Welsh were there, and no one else was allowed in (although most of these same people are still in Wales, as far as I can gather). Then they sought land in the township of Haverford in the County of Chester—'

John Eckley got up immediately.

'The township of Haverford is in the Welsh Tract.'

George Keith ignored him.

'In the township of Haverford in the County of *Chester,*' he repeated emphatically as shouts of agreement broke behind him. 'But no. The few Welsh who are left there turned their faces as usual against the future. The only English word they know is No.'

John Eckley felt full of despair.

Thomas Lloyd appeared to be in a dream, and the monologue went on in a flood no one could stem. As Doctor Gruffydd Owen said to him later: "All that is needed is for someone to say that a certain thing is so, and sooner or later everyone comes to accept it. George Keith and his friends keep on referring to Radnor and Haverford as if they were part of the County of Chester, and one day there will be no further argument. If we do not do something about this soon, it will be accepted as fact. But what *can* we do? It's no use expecting any help from William Penn now.'

And this was only too true. After the Battle of the Boyne in Ireland, they had heard that he had gone into hiding to avoid arrest by Queen Mary's militia. Of all things, he had been accused of taking part in a Jacobite plot. They had to face it now — William no longer counted here.

John Eckley sighed. It was a cruel irony that gave the Welsh victory under Blackwell, and failure under Thomas. Indeed, the great victory over Blackwell was in danger of being snuffed out like candlelight.

'What shall we do then?'

'Appeal to the Land Commissioners — for the last time,' said Gruffydd in a decisive tone of voice. 'They have the greatest authority in the State. They behaved fairly towards us last time, and the principle has not changed.'

But the Tract had changed. They both knew that. Moreover many of the Welsh had returned to their homeland. The Act of Toleration had removed the strongest incentive to emigration. Everyone was now allowed to worship in whichever way he chose, without fear. Now that the danger was over, the number of Welsh people in the Tract was declining. Pennsylvania had become the land of the adventurer, the land of the easy-money man, and these were the ones who were gradually seizing power.

Gruffydd's voice broke across his reflections.

'Dost thou know he has heart trouble?'

224

'What! Thomas?'

'Yes. He had rather a bad attack yesterday, you could still see the effect of it on him today.'

John knew that Gruffydd was trying to explain to him why Thomas had allowed George Keith and his supporters to get the better of him. In the old days Thomas's eloquence would have won the day for them, but today his arguments had appeared half-hearted and obscure compared with George Keith's masterly reasoning.

John thought of the enthusiasm of the crowd, as they had ascended the stairs that day. He remembered Henry Lewis quietly announcing his decision not to act as justice in the County of Chester. He remembered John Jarman and his friend being taken into prison for three days for refusing to act as Constables. Had it all been in vain? The English Quakers who had settled among them were a Trojan Horse. They had not liked Blackwell with his flamboyant militarism, and in order to overthrow him they had been happy enough to give their support to Thomas Lloyd at the time. But when only the rights of the Welsh were at stake, it had been a very different story.

He suddenly thought of his childhood in Kimbolton, and remembered going with his cousin, Robert, to the Meeting House in Almeley for the first time. How he had looked out over the plain towards the distant mountains with an indescribable longing in his heart to belong to that country. Although he could understand Welsh when it was spoken by his old aunt Catrin, in those days he had always spoken English with Robert and others of his own age. Then one day he had come across some of Morris Kyffin's work carefully copied out on a piece of parchment. He found it in the library in his cousin's house where it had been left to become mouldy in a chest. Reading the words had given him a new pride in an inheritance he had almost lost. Thereafter he spent every possible moment in the library reading for days at a time.

In the middle of these recollections he suddenly thought of Dorti Llwyd. Throughout this disappointing year she had been the only one who had been able to comfort him.

'Even if we fail,' — he could hear her now — 'we still have

to keep on fighting. Who can tell but that our failure will turn to success in the end? A phoenix can rise from the embers of honourable failure, but never, never from servile yielding.'

He sighed again, and felt Gruffydd's hand squeeze his arm sympathetically, as if he had been following the trend of his thoughts.

The letter was finally sent to the Commissioners. It was simple and dignified, reiterating William Penn's promises:

'. . . We implore you to be tender, not only of the promises made by the Governor, but also not to deny us our main reason for coming here. We trust that you will be pleased, as is within your power, to save our land from the boundary that still threatens it, so that we shall not be prevented from enjoying our estate peacefully according to the true intention of the Governor . . .'

They did not have to wait long for an answer this time. The reply had been prepared by the Commissioners even before Gruffydd Owen had presented the formal petition to them.

John Eckley sat with John Bevan and Henry Lewis watching Gruffydd as he approached the Commissioners' table. The Welshmen felt the Commissioners' eyes upon them looking them up and down as if they were some strange creatures from another world. Oh, that Thomas Lloyd were here with them or David Lloyd. But for several weeks now both men had been in the southern counties arguing with colonists who had refused to accept Thomas Lloyd's jurisdiction over them.

George Keith took the letter which Gruffydd handed to him and threw it carelessly down on the table. Gruffydd's lips tightened into a determined line. He picked the letter up again, and gave it deliberately to the Commissioner on Keith's right. No one said a word, as this mute little drama was acted out, but one or two looked very uncomfortable. The last time, John remembered, Samuel Richardson and Doctor Nicholas Moore had been among the members of the Board, but they had long since been displaced. Today the majority of the Commissioners were strangers to the Welsh.

'There's no need for thee to behave like that, Gruffydd Owen.'

George Keith drawled out his words, like one bored with the whole business.

'There is no need for us to read the letter. We know exactly what it contains. We have heard the arguments ad nauseam. The Commissioners —' he sighed deeply before continuing, 'have spent two whole days discussing the matter. Here is their reply.'

He read from a piece of paper before him.

'The Welsh will be allowed to remain in one Barony on condition that they pay the quit rent owed by them on their properties, starting from 1682 the year of their coming to Pennsylvania.'

Nine years rent on forty thousand acres! That was almost twenty thousand pounds!

'And that they continue to pay the quit rent due to the Proprietary from now on.'

The conditions were utterly unreasonable.

'Theft, it's nothing but theft,' said Edward Jones when they met to discuss the outcome. 'One of George Keith's malicious tricks. How can any of us pay quit rent going back nine years? Anyway quit rent was not part of the original agreement nor a part of our financial estimates.'

'In any case,' said Huw Roberts, 'we did not obtain the land until 1684, and even then we were not sure of the boundaries.'

'I'm in debt already,' complained Thomas Ellis Is-Cregenan. Many of the others were just as worried, having ventured to buy more land than they could afford.

'Once we allow the expression "on condition" to slip in we might as well compromise all the way,' said Edward Jones. 'If we give an inch we shall be shaking the very foundations of the justice of our cause.'

The company fell naturally into their thoughtful Quaker silence. Then Huw Roberts raised his head and looked around. 'Do we all agree that we should refuse these conditions?'

Before anyone had time to reply Dorti Llwyd had begun to speak, her words tumbling out fast.

'Forgive me — I had not intended to speak . . . I do not own any land, and I am not a freeholder, but someone has to . . . Don't you see? This is just a cunning plot. That is exactly what they expect us to do — refuse. Then the way will be clear

227

for them, in their turn, to refuse us, to say that they have made their gesture. That will be the end of the Tract. What is the more important? To make sure of our hold on our heritage, no matter what it cost us in money, or to give them cause to bring a final verdict against us? Be cautious, I implore you. Accept these terms as they are. With the Lord's help the money will come from somewhere.'

She was right of course, thought John Eckley, feeling ashamed. This *was* a plot. He looked hopefully at the faces around him, but felt his hopes die away as he saw the hesitation in all of them. Most of them had invested all they had in their land. Where was the money to come from to pay quit rent for the years that had passed, not to mention the leases due from now on? Were they to sell some of their property? What sense would there be in that? He and Dorti were young and for them it would be nothing to risk all they possessed to keep the unity of the Tract. But for the middle-aged and the old, who had already seen years of great hardship, years of distraint on their lands in the old country, and who now felt they deserved better, the choice was a cruel one. John Eckley took a deep breath.

'Dorti Llwyd is right, Friends. I realise it is difficult for you to be asked to make more sacrifices when you have already done so much in the service of the Lord. But I am convinced we shall be serving the Lord's cause best by fighting to preserve the community of which he has seen fit to make us part. If we betray it now, we shall be betraying the very essence of our being. We shall become creatures without roots, unfit to serve either God or man.'

But he was not able to say all that was in his heart. How does one convey a love of one's heritage? Dorti and he looked at each other, bound by their common bond. Neither of them said another word.

In the end a compromise was reached. They decided to agree to pay quit rent from now on, but not retrospectively from 1682. John Eckley shook his head. Where was the victory in that? He was afraid that, like all compromises, it would satisfy no one in the end.

'Mam, may I go and tickle trout with Uncle Sion Ifan?'
　'No.'
　'But he's promised to show me how to do it.'
　'I've said no − and that's the end of it!'
　'But *why* not?'
Rhys's voice rose into a discontented wail. Lisa did not bother
to answer him, and after waiting a moment, he wandered slowly
and unhappily towards the door and stared in the direction of
Sion Ifan's cabin. Lisa turned to look at his straight, rebellious
little back. What harm was there in letting him go for once?
The boy was taking after her, happy as a wild creature when
he could wander over the fields and get his feet and clothes
wet scrambling over streams. They were all so busy in the
Tract. Time was too short and too valuable to waste on showing
a child the wonders of the forest; too short for everyone except
Sion Ifan of course.

After Lowri's death, Sion had stayed indoors for several
weeks, venturing out only when he had to, like someone who
had lost the habit of making decisions for himself. He did not
come to Meeting, and Lisa felt troubled every time she passed
his cabin and saw the condition of his land, the leaves left to
rot on the path outside and no smoke coming from the chimney.

But she did not dare call on him. On the contrary, she
deliberately kept away, out of sight. Had she not brought enough
grief and unhappiness to all around her, especially those whom
she loved most. She was convinced of this now. Her sister
Dorcas, Malan, Tomos . . . the righteous God was punishing
her for her desires, for daring to set the call of the flesh above
His Will. Her greatest anguish was to know that it was not she
herself who suffered, but her loved ones. She loved Sion Ifan,
the dearest of men. And it was her penance to have to avoid
him as much as she could. It was only this way she could earn
her own salvation and save her soul.

Until now it had been comparatively easy to stick to her
decision, but of late Rhys had been coming home saying he
had seen Uncle Sion Ifan chopping wood, or mending his fence,

or setting off shooting. Uncle Sion Ifan always had plenty of time to chat with Rhys, and tell him the strangest stories about his adventures; and Rhys would try to mimic people as he had heard Uncle Sion Ifan do . . .

So he was recovering. Lisa's heart sang at the thought of seeing the old Sion Ifan again stride purposefully over the fields, his laughter deafening everyone within hearing distance. At once she had to remind herself that it was not her business any more, that she must lock him out of her mind. And the only way to do that was by not speaking to him. And how could she do that if he and Rhys became too intimate.

'Come inside, lest 'ee catch a cold.'

Rhys hesitated a moment before obeying. Every gesture conveyed his unwillingness. He refused to speak to his mother for the rest of the day.

As she went about her housework, Lisa's doubts came flooding to the surface. Perhaps it was nonsense to worry. After all, Sion Ifan had not called on her, had not spoken more than a couple of words to her since Lowri died. Perhaps there was no need for her to keep away from him like this. Perhaps he did not really want to call anyway. If he really wanted Rhys to accompany him why did he not come and ask her permission?

Lisa held out her hand and stared at the swollen redness of her fingers, and the roughness of the skin. Slowly she raised her hand to her cheek and stroked it, thinking of that one occasion when Sion Ifan had put up his hand to touch this same cheek. Only for a second, but it was an impulse of his she could treasure in her thoughts for ever. It was what she would have to be content with from now on.

Rhys turned his face away when Lisa tried to kiss him when she had put him to bed that night. This was the first time he had really taken offence, but she could not find it in her heart to reprove him. She left him, hoping he would have cheered up by morning.

But by the morning there was no sign of Rhys anywhere. His bed was empty and his clothes and shoes were gone. Lisa thought he was playing a trick on her and began to look for him everywhere inside the cabin calling his name. Perhaps he had got up early and gone out for a walk; he had done that once before. But it was summertime then, and now the icy fangs of winter had started to grip the country.

Sion Ifan . . . he must have gone to Uncle Sion! All Lisa's good intentions disappeared, and without any more delay she started off towards Sion Ifan's cabin calling out Rhys's name as she went.

The door of the cabin was closed, which was only natural in this cold weather. She noticed with a sinking heart that no smoke came from the chimney either, and that the place looked empty.

Surely Sion would not have taken Rhys with him out into the forest so early in the morning, and without saying anything to her? As soon as the idea came into her head she became convinced that that was what had happened, and began to feel very angry with Sion Ifan for being so thoughtless. She banged with her fists on the door of his cabin, knowing she was doing no more than giving vent to her feelings. There was no sign of anyone. She looked towards the forest and a great fear came over her. This forest had caused the death of her husband. Would it be the death of her child too? Oh God, hadn't she been punished enough . . .'

She began to run, but could not decided in which direction to go. She had some idea of going to Ciltalgarth, thinking that was the best thing to do. Perhaps they had both gone to visit Dorti there. But this time of the morning? No, surely not. They must have gone into the forest after those silly trout.

But what if she were wrong, and Rhys had gone wandering into the forest on his own without Sion? Her footsteps became slower and once again she shouted into the all-enveloping darkness on her left. The mysterious forest stretched out endlessly.

'Rhys!'

How weak her voice sounded in the empty air. She started to pray. Oh God, only let Rhys be safe and I'll do anything thou asketh of me. She was running once again, this time straight into the darkness which opened up like a great mouth ready to swallow her up. She still called Rhys, and her call became more desperate each time. And now she was reproaching herself for being such an unkind mother and refusing her child's request; the next moment she felt furious with Sion Ifan for starting all the trouble by enticing the child away. Oh that it were yesterday again, with Rhys playing around her feet in the cabin.

She heard the sound of a waterfall, and in her imagination Lisa saw her child being hurled down the great foaming torrent to be thrown violently against the rocks in the river. She screamed out his name again, the roar of the waterfall increasing in volume as she drew nearer. Her clothes caught on the briars and were ripped, and her feet stumbled over the branches lying in her path. She felt her feet sinking into the marshy patches and mud splash up her legs, and all the time there was this terrible fear that she was going in the wrong direction and that Rhys was somewhere the other end of the forest facing a bear or an Indian. Lisa had never felt so lonely in all her life, never so helpless.

'Rhys!'

She felt as if she had been running and walking and struggling on for hours, and every moment seemed like a life-long nightmare. She was half-sliding down the bank towards the river when she suddenly saw something that terrified her. The body of a man lying there face downwards on the bank of the river, his right hand trailing in the water.

'Sion Ifan!'

She did not know whether it was a scream or a whisper that came from her. Then she almost fainted with relief. The head lifted, and the legs moved slightly. Sion pushed his hand deeper into the water, every sinew of his body tightening as he squeezed hard and then lifted the trout out triumphantly.

'Sion! Is Rhys here?'

'Lisa! What on earth are 'ee doing here?'

He had jumped to his feet and was staring at her in amazement.

'Lisa! . . . What's the matter?'

'Rhys is lost . . . isn't he with thee?'

Sion slowly shook his head.

'Well no, he isn't. Why should he be here?'

'He told me 'ee had asked him to come fishing,' said Lisa accusingly.

But Sion did not wait to argue with her now. Hastily he put the trout in a bag, took Lisa by the arm, and started to climb up to the path that led out of the forest.

'Come on, I have a pretty good idea where he is,' he said adding under his breath, 'the little rascal.'

Although she was still worried, Lisa did not feel lonely any more. She felt comforted at seeing this new Sion Ifan. The uncertainty and the hesitation had vanished. She knew she could leave everything to him now. Sion was in his element here, striding confidently over the leaves, his back straighter than it had been for a long time.

The forest opened out onto a rock-strewn area. The stones rose up from the grass like giants' houses. Sion pointed at one which seemed to tower over the others.

'Over there, look . . . there's a ledge between the rocks . . . Come on!' There was not a lot of climbing to be done, and after reaching the top, Lisa saw the mouth of a cave in the rock.

'Rhys!' called Sion into the darkness. 'If thou art there come out this minute!'

He stepped into the cave and dropped out of sight.

To still her beating heart Lisa started to count . . . one . . . two . . . three . . . four . . . But before she had reached ten Sion had reappeared leading by the hand a pale-faced tear-stained boy. Lisa rushed forward and embraced him tightly, half-crying, half-laughing.

'Rhys, my darling! Why on earth did 'ee come here?'

Sion had brought a bundle with him out of the cave and Lisa at once recognised her summer shawl, tied at each corner. Sion opened it out, exposing some half-eaten bread and cheese.

'Obviously he wasn't going to starve!' said Sion Ifan beginning to laugh — his old hearty mischievous laugh.

'It's my fault, Lisa,' he said apologetically. 'I've been telling Rhys the story of my arrival here in the Tract and how I lived for weeks in a cave. I'm afraid I showed this cave to the little devil, and . . .'

233

He put one finger under Rhys's chin and turned the tearful face upwards.

'Thou got more than thou bargained for, didn't 'ee, lad? What came over thee, little cuckoo, frightening thy mother like that?'

'She wouldn't let me come with thee.'

Since he was safe his fear had disappeared remarkably quickly. Feeling ashamed of having behaved like a baby in front of Uncle Sion he now felt obliged to put the blame on someone else. Sion looked at Lisa, and she flushed. For a moment the lost look came back into his eyes, but just as suddenly the mischief returned too and, oh, the wonder of it, the same tenderness she had known once before. Sion slowly reached out to touch her cheek.

'Perhaps, Rhys,' he began slowly, but it was not at Rhys he was looking, 'perhaps she wanted to come with us.'

No. She must not get caught in this net again. She turned her head away in confusion and began to tidy Rhys's hair.

'Lisa —.'

'No, Sion, don't touch me —' for he was trying to put his arms around her. 'I'm bad for 'ee.'

'What rubbish!'

'No, Sion Ifan.' She looked at him for the first time.

'Something awful always happens to everyone I love. And I might as well admit it — I do love 'ee, Sion Ifan. That is why I have to say this. There is bad in me. Thou hast no idea how bad . . . in Wales . . . and over here . . . and it's now I have to pay for it.'

Sion had one arm around Rhys and he was pulling Lisa towards him now with the other. She felt all her objections melt away in the warmth of his words.

'Listen my dear. I am not interested in the past. I was no saint myself in the old country. We are both rather wild creatures, different from the quiet Quakers. But you and I — we have the same nature.'

'But it's so soon after —.'

Lisa's voice was weak but her heart was singing out.

'After Lowri?' said Sion slowly. 'Look at me Lisa. I'm looking at thee now and our eyes are saying that too much time has been lost already.' Then he laughed out loud again:

'And look at Rhys here, for goodness sake. He certainly needs a father. Today has proved that!'

Rhys grew shy feeling their eyes on him. He jumped free of Sion Ifan's arms and started to run down over the hillock, whipping his buttocks as if he were on horseback. When he reached the bottom he turned to look back at his mother and Uncle Sion: they were both running after him hand in hand, and their laughter resounded around the rocks.

During the week that followed the Welsh reply to the Commissioners, Huw Roberts had been in a quandry. He could hear the words of Dorti and John Eckley in his head repeatedly. For the first time in his life he felt old and failing. Were the accusations made by some of the Friends back in Wales true, that the Fair Territory was now the territory of the rich? *Go and sell all thou hast . . .*

Before long he realised that others were feeling the same uneasiness. After the next Meeting for Worship he voiced what was in the minds of many of them: 'Friends,' he said, 'perhaps I shall be condemned for what may appear to be fickleness on my part. A troubled conscience can appear thus at times. I must admit now that having had time to consider what our young Friends said a week ago I have had no peace. I am afraid we have made a terrible mistake in trying to compromise with the Commissioners. I know what the feeling of the Meeting was at the time, and that Quakers accept that we are led by the Light towards the decisions we make. But that same Light is now trying to show some of us that we should reconsider the lead given by Dorti Llwyd and John Eckley. After a week of prayer I am led to believe that we should after all accept the conditions laid down by the Commissioners in full. It is our *duty* to sacrifice everything we have for the sake of our unity and independence.'

Huw Roberts had voiced all their feelings. The company felt a new relief. Not one voice was raised against this new decision to write to the Commissioners declaring their readiness to accept all the conditions in order to be able to keep the unity of the Welsh Tract.

But it was too late.

A few days later John Eckley and Doctor Gruffydd Owen stood once again before the Commissioners' long table waiting for their reply. George Keith's whole bearing betrayed his pleasure as he pronounced the verdict. This change of mind on their part only proved how fickle the Welsh were. The way they had delayed before presenting the second answer was a sign of their unsuitability to remain an independent entity. The Commissioners had better things to do with their time than to waste it rectifying the mistakes of a small minority among them. The matter had been decided the day the first answer had been received. Since the Commissioners had not been able to accept the conditions offered by the Welsh, it had been decided that the Welsh Tract should be divided up and become part of other more easily administered units.

Too late . . . the saddest words in any language.

John Eckley turned his back on the Council Hall and walked slowly in the direction of the quay. The river was busier than he had ever see it, ships in full sail, ships at anchor, loading and unloading their cargoes, and dozens of small boats weaving in and out between the big ships. It was a truly flourishing harbour. He stopped and looked back at the land. Not far from the landing stage one building rose arrogantly above all the rest, a narrow pyramid rising up to the sky. At the top of the pyramid he could see a cross shining in the sun.

A steeple-house − that had been George Fox's name for it. But George Fox was in his grave, and the steeple-house now reigned supreme in the land of the Holy Experiment. The anguish of one generation was a subject of wonder to the next. Is that how their anguish today would appear to the generations to come? Was it all no more than an insignificant grain of sand on a wide shore?

And then, as if the answer lay before him, he saw Dorti Llwyd standing at the landing stage waiting for the boat. She stood there looking across the river, her cloak clasped tightly around her against the keen wind.

As he watched her, he fancied that he was watching Heledd as he stood looking at the waste land of Pengwern, and he felt a constriction in his throat. He walked slowly down the landing stage towards her, as if this were all part of something that had happened long ago. He reached her side and stood there for quite a while before she noticed his presence, the dark water lapping against the stones beneath their feet.

The old lines came back to him.

Cynddylan's hearth is dark tonight . . .

Her head was held high, and he saw the warm tenderness in the look she turned on him. She was the only one who understood. Let us go back to Wales, Dorti. Let us escape from this land of disappointment . . .

Without fire, without a hearth . . .

Our coming here was all a mistake. Our dream of a new, purer Wales only an illusion. We turned our backs on our motherland. Tonight the castle is destroyed, our hopes in ruins. Let us go back now, back into the womb of the mountains . . .

Too late . . . too late . . . the native cannot return. He is a stranger now in the land of his fathers. We are here, without roots, without anchor, here in this land for ever . . .

I weep awhile, then am silent.

EPILOGUE

Part of the diary of Rowland Ellis found by his youngest daughter Elin after his death in the year 1731.

The 3rd day of the 6th month 1730.

Today my dear wife, Marged Ellis, departed this life. This is the last time I shall open these pages, for on this day Rowland Ellis's spirit also sleeps with his wife. Willingly now this body of his awaits the Lord to untie the last knots.

She was troubled during her last years by blindness, but the lives of all of those around her were lit by the bright flame of her soul. I can only be grateful for her quiet wisdom along the years and regret my frequence disregard of the guidance she tried to give me.

The Lord saw well to give us more than fifty years together. Having reached the age of eighty I look back now along the sorrows and joys of the years, and say with humility in my heart that they were good years.

From this window in the house of my daughter and her husband, John Evans of Gwynedd, I look out on the gentle tract, its fertile acres stretching out before me, the sun making golden ripples to play on the waters of the green river at the bottom of the meadow. The orchards are heavy with fruit, the barns overflowing with grain. This is truly the land of milk and honey. But a man's soul has need of more than milk and honey.

Of us all, Ellis Puw was the only one who did not need to be taught that one simple truth. He knew it in the deeper reaches of his pure soul. The memory of his last appearance

238

in the Meeting House, suffering severely, will remain with us for ever like a fragrance which lasts eternally. Weak of body, but fiery of spirit, he thanked the Lord for granting his request to be able to come and join us once more. He called upon us frequently to remain in unity and love, and to keep out of our midst as far as was possible every argument and disagreement, and when any situation seemed to be veering in that direction he implored us to stretch out our hands to put an end to discord saying that no one should trust his own hand nor his own eye nor his own judgement.

Ellis's book is being widely read, which would please its author very much. What Ellis did not forsee is that the translation which I made with the help of David Lloyd is also being widely read, especially by the young. Oh that the children of the Tract could read this simple, dignified work in the language in which it was originally written, but the Welsh tongue is disappearing from among the young, even in Meirion and its younger sister Gwynedd, where I am now.

All the brave attempts to keep us united failed, for the powers fighting us were too strong. The final dissolution came after the sudden death of Thomas Lloyd; and by the time I returned here from Wales — thirty five years ago now — the Meirion Meeting House was the only centre of Welsh life. In the Radnor and Haverford Meetings more and more interpreters were needed, the first indication of dissolution. It is true that some new life was breathed into the dying embers of our community by the arrival of new Friends from Wales in '98 following Huw Roberts's missionary visit, and they settled in this new township. But it was a temporary revival only. The new Deputy, Colonel Fletcher, did his best to complete the work of Captain Blackwell, and by now it is obvious that he succeeded only too well.

Did we do any good by coming here? Should we have stayed to see our cause flourish in our own country? I do not know the answer. Our hopes lay here. Had William Penn kept his powers . . . and yet, he was a good man. The powers working against him finally proved stronger than his vision. He died in the same year as Ellis Puw, twelve years ago. Where Ellis was straightforward and honest to the end, the Governor became possessed by a weakness not only of the body. He ended his days like an innocent child, quite happy, as far as I understand. This country remains an eternal memorial to his first vision, despite the many quarrels and disillusionments.

It is not in the highest councils that man finds what his soul seeks. I too was sent by the Welsh Friends to fill a place in the Assembly, but I had no liking for it. The basis of the administration had moved too far from the original principles of those of us who call ourselves Quakers. But there is an eternal fountain of sustenance. In the divine communion which I first tasted nearly sixty years ago, my soul finds its satisfaction.

Lisa came to see me today, having heard of my loss. She is the only one now remaining of the old Bryn Mawr family. Old age has given her sympathy and unusual understanding. She has had her share of pain in life, but through God's mercy, she had many happy years with Sion Ifan and was blessed with several children. She told me she had heard from my daughter, Ann Johnston. I told her that I too had received word from her yesterday. Reconciliation is the final happiness granted to me. I know that Satan lies in wait for me like a roaring lion to devour me but I find he is changed by a secret hand which limits his power so that he cannot harm me. That same hidden hand directed mine to write a letter of reconciliation to Ann and her husband, Richard, which brought Marged great happiness.

Marged. I write the name which is already written down in gold in the Book of Life. I can do no more.

This is my comfort in the days of my pain: for thy word has enlivened me . . . thy laws were my song . . . in the house of my pilgrimage . . .

THE END